Manifesto 2050

Humans First

A. K. Bhargava

Printed in India

IndiePress

ISBN: 978-93-6045-711-2

First Printing, 2024

Indie Press

A division of Nasadiya Technologies Private Ltd.

Koramangala, Bengaluru

Karnataka-560029

http://indiepress.in/

Edited by Ridham Bassi

Typeset by MAP Systems, Bengaluru

Book Cover designed by Sankhasubhro Nath

Publishing Consultant: Samyuktha Prasanan

Dedicated to Three Generations—

My Parents Vishnu Prasad and Satyawati;

My Daughters Richa and Archa;

My Grandchildren Hriday, Raghav, and Adya

I lovingly acknowledge the assistance rendered by Hriday in ideating some of the chapters

Chapter I

The morning in Kautukpur[1] on the first day of January did not conform to the idea of what Y2K had imagined the dawn of 2050 to be. As usual, it was cold, smoggy, and a little windy, with the air quality declared as 'severe.' The view from the large smart window, however, had shut out everything that was remotely unpleasant or not soothing to the eyes. It projected a clear, sunny view of the well-manicured garden with a fountain in the middle. Although the fountain had been non-functional for ages, the edited view showed it merrily gurgling in full flow, generating a pleasing musical sound in the background. The view at least made the morning bearable, if not special.

Y2K thanked technology for such small mercies. He had many more things to be thankful for. The previous night, taking advantage of the time difference, he had registered for a '*Ubiq*' presence at Sydney Opera for the New Year event. 'Ubiq' was a new technology that was much more than a 3D holographic presence. Sitting in his well-equipped study that was discretely fitted with sensors, cameras, projectors, and 8G devices, he could walk around the Sydney harbor, feeling and soaking the ambiance. The crowd was a mix of locals,

---

[1] *Wondercity*

tourists, and virtual tourists like him, who went ecstatic when fireworks exploded as the clock struck twelve. Witnessing the bright lights, loud sounds, and energy was exhilarating as reality and virtual imagery coalesced for Y2K.

An hour later, having witnessed the earliest debut of the second half of the twenty-first century in one part of the world, Y2K was ready to celebrate New Year's Eve in his part of the world. An air taxi took him to the iconic City Center, which by contrast, was noisy, chaotic, colorful, and filled with people, both of physical and virtual variety. The City Center was dotted with several bars and restaurants which were all packed to their capacity. Y2K went to his favorite restaurant, which played Bollywood music from 2000 to 2050. A combination of spicy but tasty food and a liberal amount of drinks had rendered him incapable of boarding the air taxi, which in any case, was delayed due to congestion in the air corridor. It was thus only in the wee hours of the morning that Y2K got back to Kautukpur.

When Y2K got up, he realized that excessive drinking and traffic congestion had disrupted further programs he had elaborately crafted for the new year. He had intended to catch an early glimpse of the sunrise over ice-clad Himalayan ranges from Darjeeling and the first rays shining over the Indian Ocean from Kanyakumari. Instead, he was now watching an edited version of the morning from the large smart window of his modest home. He felt disappointed because it was his fiftieth birthday, and he wanted the occasion to be more than a statistical ritual.

Y2K often fondly reminisced the stories about his birth. He was born at the dawn of the twenty-first century. To be more precise, he was one of the four babies in the world who were born exactly at zero hours on the first day of the twenty-first century. This unique coincidence made him an instant celebrity for a while. The local morning newspaper published a photo of his gangly face under the caption 'The Y2K Kid'. By afternoon, TV crews from various channels descended on his humble home. Without being overwhelmed by the cameras, his hundred-year-old great-grandmother effortlessly held him in her arms and proudly declared that her great-grandson would become a '*lat-saheb*[2]'. Pictures of the great-grandmother and great-grandson duo spanning four generations over a century were splashed many times on all the TV channels. Amidst the doomsday predictions of the Y2K bug causing widespread disruption in services the world over, these pictures epitomized the smooth ushering of the Year 2000 (Y2K).

All this hype about Y2K must have had some impact on the *Panditji*[3], who, after consulting the horoscope, declared that the name of the newborn child should start with the syllable 'Y.' *Panditji* further extended his ingenuity by naming him Yatindra Dwij Kumar. His father readily accepted the name as it abbreviated to Y2K, with '*Dwij*' in the middle name, meaning second-born. So it was that Yatindra Dwij Kumar came to be known as Y2K (Yatindra 2nd Kumar) for all practical purposes. A wry smile crossed over the face of Yatindra Dwij Kumar, *aka* Y2K, at the thought of being the firstborn in the twenty-first century.

---

[2] *Governor*

[3] *Priest*

Chapter II

'You look grumpy, grouchy, and a bit disgruntled. What has changed your mood?' commented *Popat* while serving breakfast. Y2K couldn't decide whether it was the correct assessment of his emotional state at that moment. 'It's just the hangover perhaps,' replied Y2K as he noticed a pill already placed on the table along with some orange juice. Y2K reminded himself that *Popat* was no ordinary attendant.

Popat was in fact an acronym for *P*ersonal, *O*bedient, and *P*owered by *A*rtificial Intelligence Robo*T*. The term was coined by an Indian software engineer who helped build the first prototype in 2034 that ran on 'Almost Human Artificial Intelligence', the 'Internet of People', and 8G, besides advanced Robotics. The prototype gathered dust till 2037, when Walnut Inc., founded by Jack Jhalani who was a young millionaire with dreams of becoming a trillionaire, acquired the IPR of Popat 1.0. Jack Jhalani had the exceptional talent for identifying the business potential of new technologies. He reckoned that the Popat 1.0 prototype could be transformed into a near-Humanoid by using advancements in Bionics, Biocomputing, and Bioelectronics. The commercial version of Popat 2.0, the first near-Humanoid, was launched in 2039. It became an instant hit as people queued up for miles to purchase Popats. By the time Popat 3.0 was launched in 2045, Walnut Inc. had become the most valued company in the world, having sold more than a billion Popats.

While Walnut Inc. was riding high on the strength of its technology, a company named Mitrasoft Inc. was scripting another success story mastering the art and science of Popats. Mitrasoft Inc. was founded by another tech maverick, Bill Bawa. Bill Bawa had patented an advanced Artificial Intelligence (AI) core operating system aptly called *Faith* or '*F*oundation of *AI* *T*hrough *H*umanoid-Languages' that powered all the Popats. Mitrasoft paved the way for *Popatware* that enabled the creation of any functionality in Popats by adding two more AI layers, namely *Gate* (*G*ateway to *A*I Applications and *T*opical *E*xtensions) and *Appu* (*A*I *App*lication *U*pdate) on top of the '*Faith*' core. The patented *Gate* layer that ran on the proprietary *Faith* core, enabled Popats to handle external world rules, regulations, norms, and values. The *Gate*, however, had open and secure interfaces that allowed a multitude of *Appus* to run on top. These Appus lent Popats their distinct personality and functionality. Thus an Indian Popat folded its hands in *Namaste*, the Japanese Popat bowed, while the British Popat maintained a stiff upper lip. All Popats could be customized to speak and understand the owner's mother tongue with all the dialects and pronunciation nuances, in addition to two more languages. Customize, localize, self-learn, adapt, and blend were the *mantras* that made every Popat a unique piece of art, science, and technology.

Popats were not the sole monopoly of the Jack and Bill duo of Walnut and Mitrasoft. In the early 2040s, a whole ecosystem developed around Popats by several start-ups run by clever millennials who helped make the Popats ubiquitous in all walks of life. While most Popats were developed for domestic purposes, many specialized versions of Popats were deployed for multiple purposes. For example, in the services sector, they were employed as sales and customer service agents who were promptly christened as Soopats (*S*ervice-*O*riented *O*bedient, and *P*owered by *A*I Robo*ts*). Clerks, inspectors, and engineers in civil departments were replaced by Chopats (*C*ivil *H*ierarchy *O*bedient, and *P*owered by *A*I Robo*T*s). Innovation in usage matched the ingenuity in naming convention. When Popats were ready to be inducted into the police department as Lampats (*L*aw *a*nd Order *M*aintenance Force *P*owered by *A*I Robo*T*s), a section of the labor union went to the court demanding their ban, claiming that such a move would denigrate their profession and reputation. The court opined that Popats were distinct entities in their own right who served individuals and society at large in various capacities and gave direction to keep in mind sensitivity in addition to accuracy, while naming the new entities of Popats and Appus. Accordingly, a new name was coined for Popats in the police department as Leopat (*L*aw *E*nforcement *O*bedient Force *P*owered by *A*I robo*T*) which found muted approval. By 2040, 'Popat' came to be known as a generic name for one of the greatest inventions of mankind that was set to change the way humans lived on this planet.

Controversies apart, each word in the acronym 'Popat' had a special significance. The word 'obedient' specifically defined the character, personality, and limits of a Popat. All the Popats had to interact and respond at four levels – with their owners, with the rest of the world, with other Popats, and with objects. A wider definition of 'obedience' also incorporated Asimov's three laws of robotics: that a robot shall not harm a human or, by inaction, allow a human to come to harm; that a robot shall obey any instruction given to it by a human; and that a robot shall avoid actions or situations that could cause it to come to harm itself. Being obedient, Popats had to be dutiful, submissive, and respectful. In addition, they had to be compliant with laws, rules, regulations, well-defined norms, and values. It ensured that even if a thief owned a Popat, the Popat did not learn to practice or abet thievery. If a Popat made a mistake, it quickly learned to self-rectify. So the people soon fell in love with them. Paradoxically, the more people loved their Popats, the equal number of people began to hate their or others' Popats. Humans, after all, are not designed to be Popats.

When Popats appeared in the market, they cost a bomb and were considered a luxury. The prices began falling sharply within a few years, and by 2045, they were being considered a necessity. Realizing that the increasing number of Popats correspondingly increased the GDP, governments went all out in promoting the use of Popats. In 2049, the UN declared the next decade to be the 'Decade of Popats' and set a goal of making a Popat available to every adult person in the world by 2057.

Y2K was not overly rich but wisely invested in buying a Popat in 2042. He replaced it with a new version in 2047 but continued to call him D2Y2, meaning 'Dost to Y2K'. D2Y2 was the only one who wished him a happy birthday in person, though it was exactly at noon. Y2K felt a little disappointed that D2Y2 had chosen to wish him after a full twelve hours. It was not the fault of D2Y2 who had understood zero hours of midnight as zero hours of noon. This small glitch was caused by some lazy programmer who would never know the consequences some sloppy software code could invite.

Out of irritation, Y2K was about to dismiss D2Y2 with a wave of hands when he realized that no one other than D2Y2 had so far wished him in person. There were, of course, dozens of 3D holographic messages that he had seen and disposed of while having breakfast. Almost all of them were system-generated. The only message of interest was a bouquet that his wife had managed to send from her space station with a promise to call later when she would find some privacy in the crowded space station where she worked.

Y2K fondly remembered the birthdays that his parents so lovingly used to organize. Those occasions were always full of people, and lots of gifts and laughter. Birthdays in college and the workplace were equally boisterous and lively, until Covid-19 intervened in everyone's social life. Post-Covid-19, more and more activities shifted online. That trend shifted to high-gear in the 2030s. The transition to 7G in 2038 and 8G in 2045, along with the popularity of Metaverse and all forms of Immersive Virtual Reality, changed the ways humans interact socially. The technology that almost tele-transported living images called '*Ubiqs*', brought the world closer to fiction and mythology. As the Popat density crossed the threshold, they took over almost all forms of interactions. By 2045, human-to-human contact became rarer and rarer. It occurred to Y2K that it had been more than six months before someone shook hands with him or had a meaningful conversation. Instinctively, Y2K knew why he felt 'grouchy, grumpy, and disgruntled'. He felt lonely. He wanted to meet real people and talk to real people. He needed interactive human contact.

Loneliness was the most common affliction of 2040s. On his fiftieth birthday, Y2K desperately wanted a solution to this malady. He couldn't possibly join his wife who was 3000 km away in space, orbiting the earth. He had lost his parents to Covid-19, and had no siblings. Relatives were nice till you kept aloof. There were few friends but he was out of touch with them. Any work-related engagements stopped the moment he retired, as a high-tech professional at the age of forty-eight. It was a desperately lonely situation for Y2K. So he turned to his Popat to arrange any meeting with any human. D2Y2 understood the problem but solemnly informed him that he had no appointment for the day.

'Maybe you could fix one,' suggested Y2K.

'Impossible,' replied D2Y2.

'Meeting with even a doctor or a lawyer would be fine,' insisted Y2K.

'Not possible. You will have to meet their p-Popat (professional-Popat) first. Why don't you go to a restaurant or a bar instead?' suggested D2Y2.

'I did exactly that yesterday and felt even more lonely. You can perhaps attribute my excessive drinking to that feeling.'

It was not the first time that Y2K had confided his feelings to D2Y2. Like all Popats, D2Y2 had interfaces to read or gauge the mood of his master, and was equipped with 'Behavioral

AI' that allowed it to understand and deal with such problems. D2Y2, therefore, came up with the most unlikely suggestion.

'Election is the only public activity that requires human gathering. So why don't you attend an election meeting that is scheduled today at 2 pm? As per my information, about a dozen people are likely to attend this meeting,' suggested D2Y2 rather helpfully. 'Why not, even if it is a little weird?' thought Y2K. He had never attended an election meeting but had nothing better to do. So he picked up his *Concon* (*Con*verged *Con*traption) and confirmed his participation in the meeting.

Concon, a successor of the smartphones of 2020s, assimilated almost all the personal electronic gadgets that could be found in a home in the 2030s. Powered by AI, Concons took over the role of a personal secretary, handled half of the conversations, and carried out half of the tasks a man was required to do. Besides AI, the power of Concon lay in convergence, standardization, and open interfaces which were missing in the earlier gadgets. It could, therefore, perform any conceivable task that required some communication, computing, or control. As a result, PCs, laptops, modems, routers, gaming consoles, accessories, and all such sundry devices almost vanished by 2032. This led to a mini-economic crisis in 2034 as big companies tumbled and stock markets crashed. However, the world economy staged a recovery by 2036 with a spurt in demand for Concons. The emergence of Popats in 2035-45 did not diminish the utility of Concons as they complimented each other. Concons were the identity, resource center, experience center, and gateway to the world, all rolled into one. Popats were the intelligent but obedient slaves of the humans. Concons and Popats became a constant fixture in everyone's life by 2050.

Chapter III

The venue for the election meeting was only a block away, and the autonomous taxi arrived exactly as scheduled by Concon at 1.48 pm. D2Y2 had mildly suggested that all election meetings start late and Y2K could safely leave half an hour later, but decided not to press his wisdom. Instead, he accompanied Y2K to the porch, as was the protocol. The taxi was driverless and the doors opened as soon as the identity and presence of the passenger were established automatically. D2Y2 pretended to open the door, held it respectfully, and shut it when Y2K was seated. Acting out this protocol was not a part of Popat's core function. This feature was enabled by an AI Appu (*App*lication *U*pdate) supplied by a company called 'Jeeves'. Y2K had considered such protocols unnecessary and frivolous but realized that a Popat without an Appu like 'Jeeves' was considered a rung lower. Appu like 'Jeeves' lent a distinct personality to Popats. Though they replicated human biases that some attributed to snobbery and some to good manners, they proliferated and became an important part of the AI ecosystem.

When Y2K reached the venue at 2.10 p.m., the convener greeted him warmly and profusely thanked him for reaching well in time. The chief guest hadn't arrived so the gathering had leisurely rounds of *chai-samosa.* For some unknown culinary reason, *chai-samosa* always generated an atmosphere of bonhomie. Therefore it was on a cheerful note that the meeting started an hour late, even though the chief guest had still not arrived.

The convener of the meeting introduced himself as Mungeri Lal, whom everyone knew as *Netaji*[4]. Even Y2K, who had never met Mungeri Lal earlier, could identify him as *Netaji,* merely by looking at his dress and observing his mannerisms. Almost all *Netas* in India wore a *kurta, pajama,* and *topi,* following some unwritten dress code that had survived for more than a century. Of course, not everyone who wore a *pajama-kurta* was a *Neta,* and not all the *Netas* wore a *topi* all the time. While any Indian could spot a *Neta* from a hundred meters away, it was almost impossible for an AI algorithm to solve this conundrum. It meant that *Netas* went unrecognized quite frequently. This infuriated many of them so much that they even got a privilege motion tabled in Parliament. The tricky problem was finally solved by the famous political scientist, Chanakya Shastri. He realized that all *Netas* had certain characteristics like attitude, ego, humility, obeisance, belligerence, etc., which varied depending upon the context. Similarly, a *Neta* would subtly change the characteristics of the dress, like the color or style of a *kurta-pajama* or *topi,* depending upon his allegiance and interest. Based on the correlation between such attributes, Chankya Shastri developed a mathematical model that was ninety-nine percent accurate in spotting a *Neta.* This seminal work not only helped avert future privilege motions in the parliament, but also laid the foundation for a new branch of

---

[4] *Politician*

technology, namely 'Perceptive AI', and was extensively used in the algorithms designed for Popats.

Mungeri Lal, aka *Netaji*, fitted into the level of a lower-rung local leader, who aspired to be a middle-rung leader by owing allegiance to a higher-rung leader. The color and angle of the *topi* he wore betrayed his allegiance to Appuswamy, who was an established highest-rung leader. Even higher-rung leaders had to contest elections, and Appuswamy had chosen to contest elections from Kautukpur.

Elections had to be conducted as per the Election Act 2037. In the 2030s, elections around the world had been vitiated so much by digital fakery and digital hijacking that the public revolted and demanded overhaul of the electoral process. The much celebrated Election Amendment Act 2037 came into existence in response to this huge public disaffection. It basically attempted to control the technology invasion in the election battles.

Amongst other things, the Act required that every candidate be endorsed by a majority in a local election meeting, physically attended by not less than a dozen voters, before he could file his nomination. Mungeri Lal had convened this election meeting to secure the endorsement for Appuswamy. After endorsement, Appuswamy was to proceed to the election office in a boisterous procession to file his nomination. So far, everything had gone as orchestrated, except that Appuswamy had not yet made his grand entry.

No *Neta* worth his salt ever turned up on time, and Appuswami was no exception. Though Mungeri Lal had tried frantically to contact Appuswamy, he was unable to do so. He had automatically attributed it to the busy schedule and higher status of Appuswamy. The audience finally started getting restless, despite *Netaji's* valiant attempt to keep them engaged with his meager oratorical skills. *Netaji* was desperately hoping that Appuswamy would make a grand entry at any moment when a short beep from the Concon interrupted him. He jumped at seeing who the caller was and excused himself.

When *Netaji* returned, his face was troubled, and all the verve in his voice and mannerism was gone as he announced, 'I have just been informed that in keeping with his national stature, Appuswamiji has decided to field himself from another bigger and safer constituency. To represent this constituency, he has selected his cousin, Shri Kappuswamiji, who will file his nomination directly. Appuswamiji has assured me of his continued support for the people of Kautukpur and hopes that we all will be able to join Kappuswamiji and work for his victory.'

The dozen-odd audience was jolted out of stupor at this sudden announcement. Y2K, for whom it was the first election meeting of any kind, found the situation outrageous and even farcical. He was the first to react.

'I think we have been taken for a ride by an arrogant politician who thinks of himself as too big. I find it ludicrous to think that we gathered here to endorse such a person. The need of the hour is to choose a candidate who will be sincere, competent, and committed to Kautukpur. It will, therefore, be appropriate if we search for a local candidate, preferably from amongst us.'

Y2K's outburst met with instant rebuttal.

'It is easy to preach but difficult to practice. Elections are within the domain of politicians, and we are not politicians. Let fighting elections be left to the professional politicians,' responded someone from the audience.

'I agree that fighting for the seat of power is a full-time occupation and needs professionals. Unfortunately, politicians, as we know, are not professionals trained in statecraft, governance, or public service. Most of them are opportunists, rent-seekers, and power-hungry profit hunters with giant egos and overbearing attitudes. Therefore, we need to ensure that we nominate a good leader,' said Y2K who was suddenly discovering his voice.

'You perhaps consider yourself to be a good leader. So will you offer yourself as a candidate?' retorted another from the audience.

'Yes, why not?' replied Y2K. It was just an argument after all, so there was no question of backing down. At this point, out of the blue, someone sitting in the middle stood up and said solemnly,

'In that case, I propose your name as our candidate.'

Equally unexpectedly, the person sitting next to Y2K said, 'I second it.'

All of this could have passed as well-meaning banter, but for Netaji Mungeri Lal's decisive intervention. He was feeling peeved at not being nominated as a replacement for Appuswami, and had been considering his options since that moment. He could nominate himself but that would be considered rebellious, irking Appuswami. He needed

Appuswami in his political scheme of things and was not bold enough to risk Appuswami's displeasure. At the same time, he had to register his dissent somehow. *Netaji* realized that the ongoing discussion presented him with a way out of his predicament. If Y2K was made the candidate in this meeting, it would be a show of protest as well as a demonstration of his strength. He could easily explain and wriggle out of this situation, if needed, at a later stage.

Netaji made up his mind and announced,

'In deference to the wishes of this august gathering, I declare Mr. Y2K as our candidate. If anyone has an objection, they can raise their hand.'

No one raised any objection.

'In that case, may I request Y2K to come up on the stage?' announced *Netaji*.

Y2K had not anticipated this turn of events and instinctively moved to the stage, where *Netaji* waited with a huge garland in his hands to felicitate him.

Garlands, mostly made of marigolds, have a huge symbolic value in the Indian political system. You are not anointed as a *Neta*[5] till you are garlanded by another *Neta*. The more the number of people garlanding you, the bigger the *Neta* you are. The bigger the stature of the person garlanding you, the bigger the *Neta* you become. Besides being a welcome protocol, the act of garlanding also serves to show obeisance, loyalty, respect, or hierarchy. On rare occasions, it shows an act of benevolence. On this occasion, *Netaji* was

---

[5] *Leader*

intent on showcasing his act of benevolence as he put the huge marigold garland, originally procured for Appuswami, around Y2K's neck.

After having garlanded Y2K, *Netaji* announced, 'All of you are well aware that today is the last day of filing nominations, which has to be done in person at the election commission's office. I, therefore, request all of you to proceed to the election office right away. I had arranged a cavalcade for this purpose which I am now putting at Y2Kji's disposal as a goodwill gesture.'

The generous offer and subtle use of the suffix '*ji*' did not go unnoticed by Y2K. As everyone came forward to shake hands with him, Y2K realized that he had got himself into an unenviable situation without giving much thought to it. He had no escape route. Y2K made up his mind to play along, and profusely thanked the convener and everyone else for showing faith in him as the meeting ended.

Even though *Netaji* had excused himself, Y2K was happy to see six people, including the proposer and seconder, accompanying him to the cavalcade. Y2K was still trying to find an answer to the question 'Why me?' as he moved out of the meeting venue. He turned to the guy who had proposed his name and asked,

'May I ask, sir, why did you propose my name?'

'Because I recognized you from your name as the Y2K kid. You are after all the first millennial on the earth,' replied the proposer.

'How can that be considered as a qualification?' questioned Y2K.

'If the mere fact of being born in a family of leaders can make you a big leader, a unique statistical coincidence of birth can certainly qualify you as a unique leader,' explained the proposer.

Y2K now turned to the guy who had seconded his name and asked,

'Could you please tell me why you chose to second my name?'

'Because you were sitting on my right side and I always endorse people who are on my right side,' answered the seconder rather metaphorically. Y2K was not convinced but assumed that they were being honest. Unwittingly, they had propelled Y2K, who had never undertaken any political activity of any kind in his entire fifty years' life, into the league of a middle-rung leader ready to fight an important election.

As the cavalcade moved slowly on its arduous journey, Y2K wondered where this journey would lead him. What did destiny have in store for him? All he could think of was his great-grandmother's prophecy that '*Mera beta laat sahib banega*'[6].

[6] *My son will become a Lt. Governor*

Chapter IV

The scene outside the election office was noisy and electrifying. As Y2K entered the election office with his rather large entourage, he found himself waiting in the queue at number ten, while more than a hundred had already registered. It appeared that public service had become a rage by 2050.

Y2K was given a six-page form to be filled in ink and signed at eight places. He had last filled out a form in ink in 2035, but he went about the task without complaint. Nostalgia sometimes makes even a painful task not only bearable but even pleasurable. Y2K was also asked to put his thumb and finger impressions in ink on another piece of paper. This was something that he had last undertaken in 2015, when he got his *Aadhar Card*. His extensively used *Aadhar* became obsolete in 2036 when the 'One Man, One Concon Bill' was passed, and Concon became the identity as well as the manager of the identity. Y2K also dug up money in his savings account and reluctantly paid a not-so-inconsiderable amount as the security deposit.

After completing these formalities, he was seated before the election officer. The officer glanced at the papers duly hand-filled by Y2K, endorsed by a proposer and seconder, pre-checked by p-Popat on duty, and proceeded to count the number of pages and number of signatures put in the form. Having thus satisfied himself, he picked up a palm-sized stamp and brought it down in a flourish, marking a neat rectangular impression on the last page with 'Approved' embossed in blue. He then signed the little blue artwork that his stamp had created and busily announced, 'Done. Next'. It had been a hectic day for the officer with six more candidates still waiting to be served. Y2K, however, remained seated with a puzzled look on his face.

Realizing that Y2K was a first-time candidate, the officer decided to take a minute out of his busy schedule and explained, 'We do a thorough job here, though it may not be apparent to you. When you were busy completing the formalities, our system read your face and your iris impression, noted your mannerisms, scanned your thumb and fingerprint impressions, and verified your signatures. All this information enabled us to access the third level of your unique and secure identity which allowed us to authenticate all the details you supplied to us. Our AI system can read the hand-written prescription of even a medical practitioner, so reading your hand-filled form was a breeze. The innocuous-looking stamp is our proprietary IoT device which has triggered many necessary processes as soon as your nomination was approved. You will now find your election identity, security deposit receipt, election schedule, code of conduct, and election guidelines in your Concon. You have also been assigned a p-Popat which will answer your queries, if any, and also keep a tab on you in accordance with the election guidelines. If you follow the guidelines and prescribed code of conduct rigorously, you will not need to visit us again.' Having got the terse and crisp briefing and having secured the coveted nomination, Y2K moved out of the election office with his entourage.

Outside, there were still a lot of people responding to the call of elections in their own ways. Only a few days ago, he would have dismissed such frenzy as absurd and foolhardy. However, this whole frenzy suddenly made him realize the complex need that motivates people to engage in the arduous journey called elections. Despite being an accidental candidate, he could feel the heat of competition and excitement. Though there were more than a hundred registered candidates who had a better chance than him, Y2K reminded himself that he was there to win.

Right now, he needed to consolidate the support of six of his supporters who were about to leave. He first asked his proposer,

'Every candidate needs to have a team to run his campaign. Since you have been kind enough to propose my name, would you be able to join my campaign team?'

'That is too much to ask,' responded the proposer. 'The best I can do further is to assure you of my vote. For the rest, you are on your own.'

Response from others was similar. Y2K was disappointed at his bunch of supporters who shook his hands, assured him of their votes, and left. The last one, however, stayed and said,

'My name is Manavendra Nath Mattu. If you want, I can join your election campaign team.'

Y2K was startled and looked with disbelief at his first committed supporter.

'I am grateful, Mr. Mattu. But I have to ask you this question. Why have you agreed to join my election campaign team?'

'Because you happen to be my neighbor, and one always helps his neighbor. At least that is what my grandfather taught me,' replied Mattu.

Y2K was dumbfounded. The face seemed vaguely familiar but he had failed to place him. Feeling embarrassed, he stammered, 'I am sorry; I could not recognize you earlier. I am blessed to have a wonderful neighbor like you. Welcome to the team Y2K.'

'No problem and no hard feelings, Y2K. You can call me Mattu and call upon me without fixing an appointment,' replied Mattu graciously. They both shook hands and rode home together.

'You look elated, excited, and exhilarated,' commented D2Y2 as Y2K reached home. 'How quickly the time changes,' thought Y2K. Only a few hours ago he looked 'grouchy, grumpy, and disgruntled' to D2Y2. Only a few hours ago he had felt lonely, desolate, and desperate for human interaction. Since then he had been overwhelmed with a surfeit of activity, plenty of drama, and a busy schedule to look forward to.

Y2K finally had enough reason to feel upbeat and cheerful on his fiftieth birthday. He had an election to fight, half a dozen votes in the kitty, and a committed supporter to assist in the campaign. Y2K smiled to himself and went to sleep. He could now dream big.

Chapter V

When Y2K woke up after the tumultuous and hectic first day of 2050, he was in an ebullient mood. D2Y2 had noted it and set the lighting through the window glass to give the impression of a bright and sunny morning, despite the weather outside being dull and hazy. Y2K smiled approvingly when D2Y2 served a breakfast of *aloo-parantha* with dollops of white butter, curd, pickles, and a cup of piping hot *kadak chai*. Y2K recalled that the earlier version of D2Y2, which was equipped with 'Jeeves', always served toast, boiled eggs, and watery English tea, when not instructed specifically about the menu. No amount of direction could change this behavior. It was a group against racism and bias that discovered that the AI learning software of 'Jeeves' had been infected with the bias of its coder. A startup solved the problem by coming up with a new 'Jeeves-Jeevan' Appu, which served toast and English tea when the owner was grumpy and *Aloo-Parantha* and *Kadak Chai* when he was ebullient. It was a fine example of how to nullify bias and synthesize two cultures. Y2K was happy to have D2Y2 upgraded with 'Jeeves-Jeevan' Appu.

D2Y2 reminded Y2K that he was to read the guidelines and instructions sent by the election commission. Y2K had already planned to spend the day gathering election-related information. He quickly retired to his *Adda* (*A*bode of *D*igital *D*evices *A*rray), which was quite in stark contrast with the old-world study room. By 2033, books had disappeared from the study room even as adornments. Heavy wooden furniture gave way to the sleek, self-propelling, and remote-controlled furniture, crafted from the new-age composite material that could be dynamically arranged as per numerous functions. *Adda* also had a *Vunic* (*V*irtual *Un*iverse *C*ontroller), which took care of all kinds of virtual world experiences like the Metaverse, Holographic Presence, 3D meetings, 3D theater, and Immersive Reality of any kind. Y2K decided that his *Adda* was going to be the election headquarters for the next month and a half.

Y2K, who became eligible to vote in 2018, had been mostly indifferent to politics, until 2035 when he joined the protests demanding changes in electoral and governance system. Protests led to setting up of a commission headed by Professor Chanakya Shastri. The core finding of the Chanakya Commission was that the Indian version of the British parliamentary system was highly inefficient and ineffectual. It recommended that the three-tier system be replaced with an 'Optimized Decentralized-Centralized' system which many people thought was akin to the US presidential system. This model provided for one thousand '*Mandals*' to be governed by elected Lt. Governors called '*Mandal Governors*'. Kautukpur happened to be one such '*Mandal.*'

The changes introduced in the election process were equally radical. Recognizing that elections in India were no less than reality shows, the process of election was designed on an 'elimination rounds' basis. The public got to rate the candidates on a daily basis and eliminate them in a number of rounds spread over a month and a half. This made the use of money and alcohol to garner votes a really expensive and impractical affair. The high drama created by the elimination rounds guaranteed assured eyeballs and recurring revenues for the news channels. While many had predicted the demise of conventional TV news channels by 2040, the reinvented great Indian festival called elections not only rescued them but ensured that they continued to flourish. They were after all the fourth pillar of democracy.

When the demand was raised that a voter should have a right to not only elect but reject a candidate as well, it struck a chord even in an indifferent voter like Y2K. The Constitution Amendment Bill 2037 gave every voter three choices - a positive vote, a negative vote, and a 'none of the above' option. This novel provision caused huge upsets, mostly for the *Bahubali*[7] candidates with criminal records. Brain Power quickly overtook muscle power in elections. Many observers, however, were still wary of the dangers posed by the new breed of DDWs (*D*evious *D*igital *W*arriors), who were quickly displacing the old-time *Bahubalis.*

The new electoral system generated lots of discussions and debates. Experts differed on its efficacy and efficiency, consultants held forth eloquently in international seminars, and researchers came up with theories and conclusions that were most often contradictory. Numerous PILs were filed before the Supreme Court, and a great legal battle ensued. The Apex Court finally put to rest all controversies by declaring that the amendments were akin to replacing an 85-year-old

---

[7] *Strongman*

dilapidated building with a new one and that this makeover did not alter the basic structure of the Constitution. Elections were held under the amended act on January 1, 2038, which was promptly declared as Constitution 2.0 Day and added to the list of ever-growing holidays.

With drastic changes brought about in the electoral process, a new shiny building was supposed to replace the old dilapidated one, as the Apex Court had put it, and a new set of centennials and neo-centennials were supposed to take charge. However, those who inhabited the corridors of the new building still resembled the old *Netas* and their shenanigans were reminiscent of the same old world of *Netagiri* and *Rajniti*. Y2K did not fit into this scheme of things. Despite knowing that he had many handicaps, Y2K wanted to give his election bid a decent chance. His professionally trained mind told him that the best way to begin was to familiarize himself with the process and gather as much information as possible.

Y2K had been engrossed in the study of election rules, regulations, and acts for more than two hours when D2Y2 announced that he had an unexpected visitor.

Chapter VI

Y2K had not had a visitor over the last six months. Visiting someone's home had gone out of fashion since the 2030s, though people still met over lunch or dinner on special occasions. Visiting someone unannounced, however, was unheard of. Y2K was not expecting anyone and was startled when he saw that the visitor was a police inspector. D2Y2 noted the look of surprise on Y2K's face but busied himself with serving tea and biscuits to Inspector Godbole, who had seated himself comfortably by then. Serving tea was an Indian hospitality trait that D2Y2 had acquired quickly. Inspector Godbole dutifully explained the purpose of his visit to Y2K.

'You have filed a nomination for the elections, and I am here to verify the information you gave in your nomination form.'

The p-Popat in the election commission had already done the verification but it was customary to ask the local police inspector to 'verify' the antecedents.

'I shall be happy to answer your questions,' answered Y2K agreeably.

'I have done a thorough examination and everything appears to be in order,' paused Godbole before adding, 'except the small matter of a traffic ticket which you seem to have overlooked to pay.'

Y2K almost jumped out of his seat and exclaimed, 'How could that be? For the last ten years, I have not even driven a car.'

By 2037, autonomous cars had become commonplace, and people had stopped driving cars. Those who wanted to, could not get a driving license since the driving criteria were set on par with those of autonomous drivers. A human driver had to pass a driving test in one hundred and thirty-six randomly simulated situations that autonomous vehicles easily navigated. Conditioned to flout traffic rules even under normal conditions, Indian drivers found it almost impossible to react precisely and correctly under the provocative stimulus.

'I am aware that you have not driven a car over the last ten years, Mr. Y2K. The traffic ticket I am referring to pertains to 2019. Though the original amount was insignificant, the compounded interest and penalty has made it substantial,' said Inspector Godbole with a smug smile. He then handed over an almost faded paper that was a traffic ticket for straddling the yellow line in 2019. Y2K was now confused. In 2019 he had made numerous visits to the hospital where his parents were admitted for Covid-19 treatment. Straddling the yellow line could be a distinct possibility, given his state of mind.

'I do not recall having been handed over or delivered this challan,' protested Y2K. 'You may be right but once we write it down, technically we consider it as delivered,' countered Godbole.

Y2K found it grossly unfair but he was a rule-abiding citizen. So he offered,

'It is a huge amount for me but I shall settle it if you could tell me how to pay this paper challan.'

'Oh, dealing with a paper challan is a big problem in 2050. I'll have to check and get back to you,' replied Inspector Godbole. Suddenly changing his track he further added,

'I can see that you are a *sharif*[8] person. Take my advice and withdraw your nomination. I shall do my best to help you in the matter of this old traffic ticket.' With this cryptic remark, Inspector Godbole left quietly, leaving Y2K confused. Why dig up such an old traffic ticket now? How could such an innocuous challan become so hefty? Does it have any connection with fighting the election?

Feeling perturbed, Y2K asked for lunch, which D2Y2 dutifully served. D2Y2 was not only an expert cook, he had an automated, intelligent, and integrated kitchen at his disposal. There was nothing that could not be cooked with a chef-like precision and with a variety so vast that no meal needed to be repeated in three years. Y2K, however, preferred humble *dal-roti* most of the time.

Y2K had barely finished his lunch when he had another visitor. The visitor introduced himself as a Property Tax Inspector and presented a challan showing a dreadful figure that again included a compounded interest and penalty. The inspector alleged that Y2K had understated the covered area of his dwelling, resulting in lower property tax. Y2K was incensed but checked himself and calmly asked the Inspector

---

[8] *honourable*

to prove it. The inspector had a portable p-Popat with him who expertly did the measurements and calculations within a few minutes. Unfortunately for the inspector, the area turned out to be one square foot less than what was declared. Unfazed, the inspector told Y2K that the slab that was applicable happened to be higher than what Y2K had used for calculation. Y2K was perplexed. Such routine filing was taken care of by D2Y2, who took extra care of verifying the return from a consulting-Popat. He, however, could find no argument to counter the Inspector and said defensively that he would pay up after taking an explanation from his consulting-Popat. Satisfied, the Inspector got up, shook his hands, and said,

'I can see that you are a *sharif*[9] person. Take my advice and withdraw your nomination. I shall do my best to help you in this matter.'

The Inspector left quietly, leaving Y2K confused for the second time. Why this double whammy? Why this unsolicited advice? Why the vague offer of help? Does it have any connection with fighting the election? Y2K had no answers to these questions. His thoughts were interrupted when D2Y2 remarked,

'You look worried and confused. I think you should take advice from a well-wisher.'

It was not a very profound remark, but it made Y2K think. He suddenly remembered the offer of help from his neighbor, Mattu.

---

[9] *decent*

Chapter VII

Mattu was surprised to see Y2K, who had barged in unannounced, but he did not show it. He quietly welcomed Y2K and offered him *Kahwa*[10]. As Y2K sipped the sweet and flavored concoction, he blurted out the whole story of two inspectors and numerous questions. Mattu contemplated over the whole incident and replied gravely,

'It is obvious that the whole episode is connected with your nomination. All the manual inquiry and verification is a routine bureaucratic exercise, despite the checks that p-Popats have already done. No harm there. But there is a selective and clever twist. For example, the traffic ticket in the first place was never valid. Even if it was, its realization is time-barred after thirty years. As for the property tax, you were correctly shown the slabs that were changed last year, but those slabs are not applicable for properties older than ten years like yours. Both of them will therefore cancel their challans and not bother you again.'

'Why did they go to all this trouble then?' asked Y2K incredulously.

[10] *Kashmiri tea*

'Oh! You can only guess. There must be more than one hundred and thirty candidates in the fray. No one likes so many candidates in the race, making the election complex, unmanageable, and unpredictable. Hence, many influential people will be happy to see large numbers withdraw their nominations. So if you withdraw your nomination, the inspectors score some brownie points for their gentle persuasion. If you don't, they score points with you for their help. Whichever way you look at it, it is not a futile exercise.'

'So what happens next?' enquired Y2K.

'Expect a few more friendly visits, say from the income-tax, health department, or some even more sinister-sounding departments. You can enjoy their attention and march on with your election journey or give in to the mild intimidation and withdraw. The choice is yours,' replied Mattu.

Y2K sat thoughtfully for a few minutes and finally said, 'I have made my choice. I would not succumb to intimidation easily.'

'In that case, you have passed the first test,' said Mattu approvingly.

'How do I prepare for the further tests?' asked Y2K.

'Election is a month-and-a-half long test match. Build your team before the match starts. You are the captain and currently you have only one member in the team,' counseled Mattu.

Y2K was impressed by the perceptive analysis and encouraging advice given by Mattu which no Popat could have done. He thanked Mattu for his advice and took leave. He had a lot of work to do.

Chapter VIII

Y2K could not afford to hire people for his campaign team. He had to have volunteers he could rely upon. It was obvious to Y2K that only some friends could fill that gap. His Concon gave him a list of friends which was not pretty long. Nonetheless, he worked on the list and was able to short-list three names who fitted the bill and did not refuse.

First on the list was his college mate, Lalit Tuteja, known to all as *Lattu.* Besides the obvious abbreviation derived from the name, there were many other explanations for his rather delightful nickname. *'Lattu'* in Hindi means a spinning top, and Lalit was capable of giving a spin to any argument in a manner that would resemble the trajectory of a spinning top. Another explanation was related to *'Lattu'*, meaning a light bulb. On occasions, Lalit would be the first to comprehend a point, and someone would jokingly whisper, *'Lattu jal gaya'*[11]. When used as a verb, 'to be *lattu'* meant 'take a fancy to'. Lalit literally took a fancy to any girl who was able-bodied and was above the age of sixteen. Regardless of the explanations, Lalit Tuteja sportingly accepted being addressed as *'Lattu'*. Y2K had full faith in Lattu and his sterling qualities.

---

[11] *Bulb has lit up*

Next to volunteer for Y2K was Sattvik Uppal, who happened to be a schoolmate. Since calling someone by his full name, first name, or surname sounds almost formal, it is common amongst friends to abbreviate or distort the name. Hence, the name Sattvik Uppal was abbreviated by his schoolmates to *Sattu*, which so appropriately described his simplicity and earthiness. *Sattu* is a healthy dish that used to be a staple of poor people in the North. Sattvik, aka *Sattu*, was healthy in a very rounded proportion and never tired of reminding everyone that he came up from a poor background against all the odds. Y2K hoped that *Sattu* would be able to bring his much-acclaimed enterprise and solidity to the election campaign as well.

Kattappa Upreti was the third person to accept Y2K's request to be part of his election campaign team. They both had worked for the same company in their early career where they had two sets of people, 'Jeeves' types and 'Jeevan' types. 'Jeeves' types were those who would open an umbrella in Delhi when it rained in London, and 'Jeevan' types were those who would ask for *'Makki di roti and Sarson da sag'* when dining in London. Amongst the 'Jeeves' set, Kattappa Upreti was known as 'Cool Ku', and amongst the 'Jeevan' types, he was popularly called *'Kattu'*. Kattappa Upreti found no difficulty in straddling the 'Jeeves' and 'Jeevan' divide, but it was the nickname *'Kattu'* that finally got stuck. What also justified his name 'Kattu' was his ability and propensity to find a counter-argument more often than necessary. With the addition of managerial and argumentative talent that Kattu brought with him, Y2K was satisfied that he had the team he wanted.

The Y2K team of five met in the evening, ostensibly to discuss the election strategy, in the bar that Y2K usually frequented. Although the booze and the bar had both undergone a huge transformation by 2050, men's attraction to both remained the same as ever. As expected, bar-tenders had given way to Popats, who conjured up drinks and cocktails of humongous variety with ease and precision. New wines in the old bottles literally proliferated in the form of synthetic and hybrid drinks. A case in point was the hybrid wine labeled *'Narangi'* that was produced in *Jhumri Tallaiya* in India. It became very popular in the late 2030s across the world since it looked, felt, and tasted like Champagne. Some wine tasters claimed it to be even better. It incensed French to no end, not only because the impersonator drink was cheaper by half and selling by double, but also because *'Narangi'* meant orange. France successfully argued in the WTO that a bottle of sparkling wine cannot be labeled by a misleading term like *'Narangi'*. Following the WTO's order, the manufacturer in *'Jhumri Tallaiya'* promptly re-labeled it as *'Angoori'* which doubled its sales. French also did not lose as they doubled the price which made Champagne even more exclusive, which in turn helped in doubling the sales and quadrupling the profits. Y2K team had no biased view on this international controversy which had almost strained the diplomatic relations between the two countries. They simply opted for *'Angoori'* because it reminded them of the struggling days in the 2020s when they would imbibe a local concoction called *'Angoori'* on occasions when they were not able to afford foreign-made whisky or beer. They all reminisced about their school days, college days, and struggling days, and had a good time. It was like a reunion meeting till it was time to pay up.

The bill-paying moment is that brief period when the most inebriated person also thinks clearly and makes sense. It was in such a moment of clarity that Y2K reminded everyone of the purpose of their meeting. He asked,

'*Bhai Logon*[12], may I remind you that I am fighting an election and I need your help?'

'Yes, we remember and be rest assured that we'll all vote for you,' said everyone in unison.

'I was not talking about your votes, but about the votes that you will go and get for me. I need around half a million at least,' explained Y2K.

'Half a million! We don't have that kind of money,' exclaimed everyone.

Y2K was about to raise his hands in exasperation when the light bulb lit up and Lattu intervened,

'Guys, you are right. Y2K needs money to kickstart his election campaign and we need to help him raise some funds. I suggest we pledge one month's salary on our part and Y2K will put four months' salary on his part.' Everyone concurred. Y2K was grateful for the selfless gesture and suggested that Mattu look after the finances. Mattu agreed and immediately took charge on the condition that payment for booze would be strictly from the personal account and Y2K would personally foot the bill for drinks till the elections last. Y2K was alert enough to deflect the googly from Mattu by declaring that henceforth all election meetings will be held daily over breakfast. They will meet for drinks only once a fortnight

---

[12] *Dear brothers*

and the mode of payment will be on the Dutch system. All such weighty resolutions were then agreed upon and passed unanimously over the last drink for the road.

When Y2K managed to reach home, he was in high spirits. Things had gone well for the day. Far from being alone, he now had a team of four selfless, though a bit eccentric, friends. It was a reason enough to feel cheerful and confident.

Chapter IX

The next day morning, D2Y2 was busier than usual. He had coordinated with Popats of the Y2K team and found the common preference for breakfast to be *idli*, *sambhar*, and filter coffee. The hot coffee that D2Y2 served, cleared the previous night's remaining hangover, and the team was ready to discuss elections with full gusto.

Y2K began the meeting by thanking all for their support and narrating the entire story of his quirky nomination and unexpected visitors. He then added on a serious note,

'Friends, today is the last day for withdrawing the nomination. Now that you all are on board, it would be appropriate to discuss whether to continue or withdraw. It is obvious that even saving the security deposit is going to be a herculean task, and winning the elections appears to be almost impossible. In such a situation, will it be worthwhile to invest our time, money, and energy in fighting the election?'

'Don't worry and go ahead. *Hum honge kamyab,*[13]' said the ever-optimist Lattu.

---

[13] *We shall succeed*

'*Karmanye vadhikaraste, ma phaleshu kadachana,*[14]' quoted Sattu, straight from *Bhagavad Geeta.*

'We need to be objective and rational. We can do a SWOT analysis first and then decide,' intervened Kattu, and all nodded in agreement.

'Let us look at our strength. We have a candidate who is fresh, well-qualified, and non-controversial. He is balanced in his views, honest in his dealings, and can take a non-partisan stand. More importantly, he is one of us and voters can easily identify with him. Our candidate is our strength,' began Lattu.

'A candidate is as strong as his team and I have a team that is talented, competent, and selfless. The team is our strength,' corrected Y2K.

'Then let us examine our weaknesses,' said Kattu.

Sattu, who had known Y2K for the longest time, was thc first to react rather undiplomatically.

'Just like the strength, our candidate is also our biggest weakness. He has never dabbled in politics. Politics is not for a *Ghotu*[15] or a *Ghissu*[16]. A simpleton like him cannot survive in politics.'

Sattu was giving vent to the general belief that the studious became professionals, enterprising ones entered the business, and the rowdies joined politics. Y2K was beginning to feel a

---

[14] *Your right is to perform your work, but never to the results*

[15] *crammer*

[16] *studious*

little uncomfortable, and it was Lattu who did the balancing act.

'Do not get personal, Sattu. There are as many well-meaning, selfless, and brilliant people in politics as the lotus, ruffians, and thugs. In any case, the politics of 2050 is a lot different than the politics of yesteryears.'

Lattu was referring to the massive political changes that swept the world in the mid-2030s as a reaction to the ever-falling standards and values in politics. Political reforms and technology eliminated the unwanted, changed the way people voted, and ushered in the golden decade for democracy. It was widely believed that politics in the 2050s would be dominated by professionals, professors, and geeks.

Kattu picked up from where Lattu had left and said,

'I agree that the nature of politics is changing. But, the fact remains that none of us knows how to garner the votes. We all know how to sell a product but the election is all about selling a promise. That needs experience and expertise that we all lack. However, we can think of ways to surmount our weakness later,' everyone agreed.

As the discussion moved on, Lattu asked,

'Okay. What about the opportunity?'

'In my opinion, the biggest opportunity is to bridge the gap between a voter and the politician. We all have come to believe that only a typical politician can occupy the office of the Mandal Governor. The opportunity is to show that a quintessential voter, that Y2K is, can also do so,' replied Sattu.

'Like opportunity, we ought to be aware of the threats in these times. Threats may be from fake news, misrepresentation, falsehood, deceit, intimidation, inducement, and incitement abounding in politics that may set us off the track. The threat may be from the very system that we wish to change. The threat may be from the establishment that we wish to challenge. The threat would be from the competitors who are ruthless and crafty. But the biggest threat right now is that the hopelessness of our situation may force us to lose hope,' added Kattu who was in full flow by now.

Before Kattu could make it look even more daunting, wisdom dawned on Lattu and he summed up,

'We should not lose hope. The conclusion from the SWOT analysis is that if we can plug our weaknesses, we can give a good fight. We can do nothing about our collective inexperience in fighting an election, but we can overcome this handicap by hiring a professional election strategist.'

'That is a brilliant idea. In fact, I happen to know a person who will fit the bill. Her name is Vartika Chawla. She is a Ph.D. in electoral science,' said Kattu.

By mid-2040, all countries in the world had adopted a democratic form of government. As a result, 'Electoral AI' was firmly established as an independent academic discipline. Many election strategists, managers, and consulting firms had mushroomed, but a Ph.D. in 'Electoral AI' was still rare. Everyone wanted to know more about Vartika.

'She has worked in the election campaign team of one senator and one governor. She works for a multinational and is currently on sabbatical. More importantly, she is in

Kautukpur and wants to study the local election mechanism closely,' Kattu said helpfully.

'She seems to be overqualified and her salary may be unaffordable,' said Mattu who had unofficially assumed the role of CFO (chief finance officer) within the group. It was becoming apparent to Y2K that a corporate structure was emerging in the team with Lattu chipping in as CTO (chief technical officer), Sattu as COO (chief operating officer), and Kattu as CMO (chief marketing officer). 'We perhaps need to get a Ph.D. in electoral science as Chief Strategy Officer to get the right mix,' thought Y2K. Kattu read his mind and proposed,

'I shall fix up a meeting with her this afternoon. It is up to Y2K to convince her. If she is onboard, we go ahead and fight. Else, we recommend that Y2K withdraw.'

Everyone agreed that it was the right decision. With that decision the meeting concluded, leaving Y2K a little anxious. He had never met an election strategist, let alone hire one. And so much was riding on hiring this particular one.

Chapter X

D2Y2 had set up a meeting with Vartika the same day. When she appeared at the appointed time, Y2K greeted her with a tinge of admiration and nervousness. If someone could be stern-looking and beautiful at the same time, it was Vartika. Y2K tried to hide his nervousness and fumbled.

'I thank you for agreeing to meet me at such short notice. I hope you have the brief and the background for the meeting.'

'I do have the brief and the background, and I am impressed by your audacity to think of hiring me for your campaign,' said Vartika mildly. It was her sweet and captivating voice that took the sting out of her statement.

'Nothing short of audacity can save my campaign. I have a team of four good guys, half a dozen assured votes, and meager funds. If I don't get the benefit of your experience and expertise, I may as well withdraw my nomination today.'

'A good candidate never owns up to his weaknesses, and a good politician never lays all his cards on the table,' teased Vartika.

'I am not electioneering here. Since I am only trying to enlist you in my team, a little transparency upfront is in order,' replied Y2K.

'But why should I join your team?' asked Vartika. It was clear to Y2K that Vartika was conducting the interview and not the other way around. Y2K acknowledged it and replied,

'I need you more than you need me. You can easily join a more winnable candidate and claim credit for an easy victory. I am a nice guy but nice guys don't win elections. The real challenge for you lies in making a nice guy win. Helping me fight, therefore, will be much more worthwhile than one extra bullet point in your CV.'

'I see that you can argue like a politician after all. In case I decide to join you, what will be the terms?' inquired Vartika. There was not much to offer but Y2K had thought of it.

'I don't expect you to work *pro bono.* As for the salary, the maximum I can offer is equal to one month's salary that I last drew. After all, I am the boss and you can't expect a salary more than mine!'

'You do sound reasonable, even magnanimous while offering very little. That is a prerequisite in any politician worth his salt,' observed Vartika, and continued with questioning.

'You know that my experience and expertise are outside of Kautukpur. Why do you want to engage me?'

'Experience and expertise in politics may be specific but the application is universal,' answered Y2K diplomatically.

'Any other reason why you want me to be on your team?' persisted Vartika.

'Well, if you join, it will correct the gender imbalance in my team,' replied Y2K who could not think of anything else.

'How politically correct! You do have some attributes of a politician,' smiled Vartika for the first time. Emboldened, Y2K asked,

'And what political attributes do I not possess?'

'You do not have a politician's attitude and you are better off without it. You also underestimate yourself, which a politician never does. That is something we can work on if the offer of a job is still open,' said Vartika, and the tension between them suddenly eased. Y2K was prompt to reply,

'The job is yours for the asking. Send the contract and I shall sign it right away.'

'In that case, I shall join you for the team meeting tomorrow morning. However, feel free to contact me on any election-related matter any time,' concluded Vartika, as she waved and disappeared.

Y2K felt hugely relieved at passing the interview.

Chapter XI

It was exactly a minute after six o'clock when Y2K received a barrage of messages from the office of EC (Election Commission). EC informed that after the withdrawal of thirteen candidates, there were one hundred and nine candidates left in the fray including Y2K. There was a long list of Dos and Don'ts along with notices on restrictions that would come into force. A code of conduct was enclosed that every candidate was advised to follow, besides an advisory on fake news and the use of Popats and Concons. There was a detailed note on the election process and a schedule that would last for forty five days. At the end was the intimation about the election symbol of candidate Y2K, which was randomly allotted. It was a neatly drawn 'Pigeon' in black and gray.

Y2K's immediate reaction was that of disappointment. A tiger, a lion, or an elephant would have been great as a symbol. A horse, a cow, or a peacock too would have been nice. But, the gray pigeon was not a symbol that could catch the voter's imagination. Even a white pigeon would have been acceptable. After all, there is racism in the animal kingdom as well. A white pigeon is identified as a symbol of peace but a gray Indian pigeon counts for nothing. It is at best ignored, shooed away, or dismissed as a harmless creature. Y2K felt that he had lost half the battle with such an ordinary symbol to bank upon.

Maybe, there is a provision to change the symbol! It was this hope that prompted Y2K to call up Vartika who didn't seem to be too happy to be disturbed. Y2K insisted it was an emergency and blurted out,

'I just received my election symbol and it is a disaster.'

'What is the symbol that you are so upset with?' asked Vartika calmly.

'The symbol allotted is a gray Indian Pigeon,' said Y2K in despair.

'Well, thank God that it is not a crow,' replied Vartika and hung up.

Y2K could not decide what Vartika said was humor, sarcasm, or simply the height of optimism. D2Y2 perhaps read his mind and said philosophically, 'You look confused right now. When you don't understand what is said, just reflect upon what is not said.'

D2Y2 occasionally came up with such gems of wisdom that had a calming effect on Y2K. Reflecting upon the whole situation, he realized that his symbol was exactly like him - harmless, unobtrusive, and nondescript. He could not probably win without accepting who he really was. Y2K smiled as the clouds of confusion suddenly cleared and he was at peace with his election symbol, himself, and his journey.

With nothing else to do, Y2K decided to take it easy before the great game, called the Indian Elections, began.

Chapter XII

The addition of Vartika Chawla to the Y2K team brought some seriousness that was hitherto missing. She was warmly welcomed and unanimously voted as their VC or 'Vice-Chief'. In keeping with the newly found tag of 'Vice-Chief', Vartika immediately assumed the charge of election campaigning. She reminded them that by the end of the first elimination round tomorrow, all but one hundred candidates would get eliminated. With Y2K currently lying at the bottom, the campaign was in danger of vanishing before it even began in earnest.

'How do we then negotiate this elimination round?' enquired Mattu.

'Get at least one hundred votes in the preliminary round tomorrow,' replied Vartika with a straight face.

'Only a hundred!' exclaimed everyone.

'Let me explain the mathematics of early rounds of voting. The voting percentage in the initial rounds tends to remain very low but picks up gradually. There are one million eligible voters in Kautukpur, out of which only five percent are likely to vote in the preliminary round. Ninety percent of these votes will go to ten percent of the candidates, leaving around five thousand votes to be shared between a hundred candidates. Now, remember that these votes are not evenly spread. The bottom five may not even cross the count of five, as even their children may not vote for them. Theoretically, therefore, fifty votes will let you slip past this round, but our goal should be to avoid being in the bottom ten of the surviving candidates. Calculation from my statistical model shows that one hundred votes will do the trick,' explained Vartika patiently.

Everyone, including Y2K, was impressed with her insight.

'Getting one hundred votes should be easy. All of us can talk to five of our friends, who in turn can talk to five of their friends. Thus we can reach the figure of a hundred in no time,' enthused Lattu.

'I would encourage you to do it for the long haul. However, getting a hundred votes in two days this way is easier said than done. Please remember that only five percent will vote, so none of the friends you contact may vote in this round. Even if they do, they tend to vote as per their individual preference and rarely on friendly reference. Even if they do, they may not be enthusiastic enough to call others and the chain will most likely break at the second stage. In any case, the average number of friends a person in 2050 has is two. Y2K is lucky to have five,' explained Vartika again very patiently.

Y2K noted that Vartika had included herself in the list of his friends and smiled happily. Sattu, however, was not much amused by the mathematical analysis of Vartika and offered,

'I have an alternate and quicker method, VC. We can launch a campaign through Concons or hire an agency to canvas and get votes.'

'That is an outdated mode of campaigning. The right to privacy is strictly implemented and a sophisticated AI-controlled algorithm ensures that no unwanted message ever slips through. Till the 2030s, most resourceful candidates outsourced to agencies who would launch digital dogfights to win elections by any means. Such digital dogfights and digital skulduggery got plugged in 2040 when the EC hired a piece of 'virtual network slice' for the entire *Mandals* where elections were being held and implemented an Appu, aptly named *Seshan 2.0.* This ensured that unwanted activities were proactively detected, stopped, and punished. The fear of *Seshan 2.0* made subsequent elections the fairest elections in the world. Currently, the EC earns ten percent of its revenue through royalties from *Seshan 2.0* Appu that is used across the world as a standard tool,' explained Vartika. She was in a mood to launch into further intricacies but was interrupted by Mattu.

'Does it mean that we have no right to freely campaign?' asked Mattu.

'Of course, you have the right but that right is subject to the protection of other rights like the right to privacy and also subject to restrictions under the election code of conduct. Within such constraints, you can use Popats and Concons but it may only garner an additional dozen or half a dozen votes,' replied Vartika.

'Why don't you then suggest a plan?' demanded an exasperated Kattu.

'I have no suggestion to make,' replied supremely patient Vartika.

'Who will make the suggestion, if not the chief strategist?' retorted Kattu.

At this point, Lattu, who never liked a discussion turning acrimonious, intervened and said randomly,

'Forget this fight for the moment and let us go and paint the town red.'

Before Lattu could explain what he meant, Vartika jumped in and said,

'I have a suggestion to make after all.'

'And what is that?' asked everyone eagerly.

'Let us go and paint the town red or white for that matter,' replied Vartika with a straight face.

'What do you mean by that?' asked Kattu, who was as confused as the rest.

'I mean let us close the meeting and plan how we paint the town red or white. I need you guys for that. We have lots of work to do. And by the way, we shall assemble for the breakfast meeting tomorrow a little late,' said Vartika whose stern face suddenly had acquired a hint of mischief. She busily got up, and all the four of them followed suit.

Y2K felt left out and inquired,

'You haven't told me what to do till tomorrow's meeting.'

'Since other candidates in your position are frantically running around, you should just relax and chill. Tomorrow we shall discuss how to keep you engaged for the day,' said Vartika smilingly.

Y2K again could not decide whether it was sarcasm, humor, or simply the height of confidence. He looked at Vartika who was seven years younger than him, was his deputy, and answerable to him. Realizing that he was the boss around here, Y2K pulled himself up and said to Vartika with as much authority as he could muster,

'I can see that you are up to some mischief. But I want the whole gang to know that, though we are desperate for the votes, we'll always play by the rules.'

'Yes, Boss,' replied Vartika, and the whole gang trooped out.

Chapter XIII

Kautukpur was one of the thousand PUR (*P*lanned *U*rban *R*esettlement) that came up between 2032 to 2045. These were massive greenfield cities that used all conceivable cutting-edge technology and rose vertically. The roads in every 'Pur' were designed for autonomous vehicles, water was conserved and recycled, electricity was generated from every conceivable method, everything was connected with 7G, bullet trains sped past, and airports vied to be the best in the world.

In contrast, the old city of Kautuknagar was a mixture of old and new, incorporating the good, bad, and ugly of both worlds. While Kautukpur inhabited only the rich, not-so-rich, and the middle class, Kautuknagar encompassed the not-so-rich, middle, and poor class as well. It was a city of change, though certain things never changed. Here the newly laid roads somehow developed the potholes, the fool-proof electric system managed to generate outages, and the water supply occasionally ran dry purportedly due to water conservation overdrive. Monsoon made its presence felt by flooding the streets, police made its presence felt by reaching hours after an incident, and the administration made its presence felt by not being there when needed. Yet, the city made impressive strides from being a sleepy town to a bustling city. To highlight the development that had ostensibly taken place, the city council had long ago declared it a smart city, proving that ignorance is bliss.

Nonetheless, all tell-tale signs of development could surely be found in Kautuknagar. The city boasted of Popat-density higher than the world average. It was dotted with glittering malls manned by Popats. Autonomous vehicles roamed the city, though they frequently went into a 'loop' and created traffic jams. Undeterred by the jams that the narrow lanes of Kautuknagar created, locals upgraded their vehicles with *Jugad-Appu* that miraculously enabled them to navigate both the man-made and the algorithm-generated glitches smoothly. No wonder, the city was aptly called the city of bewilderment. The road connecting the twin cities of Kautukpur and Kautuknagar passed via the Pigeon Square which was a large semi-circular platform where pigeons flittered, creating the impression of serenity in chaos. Some residents derisively called it the Trafalgar square of Kautuknagar while a few others dismissed it as the '*kabooterchowk*'.

It was here at Pigeon Square that the Y2K gang of five assembled early in the morning and started frantically painting the 'Vote for Y2K' and 'Vote for Pigeon' slogans. Two lanes around Pigeon Square were closed to traffic until nine in the morning, and they had no difficulty doing the painting job. After finishing their task, they stationed themselves around the square. Every one of the gang members was carrying an electronic placard displaying the same slogans with a 3D image of a pigeon waiting to fly out of the placard. There were only a few people in the street early in the morning since the morning walk had gone out of fashion. A Topat (Traffic-Popat), however, promptly appeared at eight in the morning and immediately detected the painted slogans. A painted slogan did not match with any sign or pattern used on the road, and his database provided no further clue. Topat, therefore, decided that it was a matter fit enough to be referred to his human supervisor, who happened to be Inspector Godbole.

Inspector Godbole was in a foul mood, having been disturbed early in the morning. On reaching the site, he immediately proceeded to hurl the choicest expletives on his Topat. The Topat, however, remained equanimous as it was programmed not to react or use any of the expletives. Having vented his anger, Inspector Godbole then turned and noticed the Y2K gang, who readily admitted to painting the road red, err white. A furious Inspector Godbole declared that Y2K and his gang would have to pay a heavy penalty for the offense. It was just when Inspector Godbole was about to ask his Concon to issue an e-challan that the paint on the slogans started vanishing. Inspector Godbole instinctively moved to catch the vanishing paint. The paint vanished within a few seconds, leaving Inspector Godbole dumbfounded. This ludicrous moment—Inspector Godbole trying to catch the vanishing paint—was vividly captured on camera for posterity.

It was this image being telecast repeatedly in full 3D glory that Team Y2K was relishing more than the hearty breakfast served by D2Y2. Vartika had come up with the idea of using vanishing paint to avoid any problems with the law. The vanishing paint was invented by Vichitra Gupta, a local paint manufacturer, who was conferred with the ignominious 'Golden Owl' award for his efforts. After all, who would use paint whose distinguishing feature was to vanish? Everyone complimented Vartika for the ingenious use of Golden Owl Paint. They were also impressed with the way Vartika had planned the whole show and how she had managed to position a *Jholu* (*J*ournalist *h*olding *o*n to *l*ittle *u*tterances) on the spot to precisely capture this moment.

Jholus were a special breed of Popats who were specifically designed and manufactured for media. Thanks to the clever use of Artificial Intelligence, Jholus always asked obvious questions, were skilled in quoting selectively, and had a penchant for repetitive monologues. News channels loved them because they worked twenty-four by seven, doubled up both as cameraman and correspondent, had a three-sixty-degree vision, and most importantly, took no pay. As a result, by the mid-40s, Jholus had replaced all the poor crew members and correspondents on the beat. Vartika had persuaded Jholu4 of Kautukpur News4 (KN4) to troop to Pigeon Square just in time.

Jholu4 had done a magnificent job of capturing the whole sequence. The story that ran under the caption: 'Inspector Stupefied With The Vanishing Act', immediately started trending. Within an hour, all the Jholus of all the local news channels had descended on the Pigeon Square and had a field day shooting the fluttering pigeons and asking any passersby their silly questions.

In the meantime, Inspector Godbole had reached his office and was in a rather pensive mood. A few Jholus were hounding him for a comment, but he was too sharp to fall further into their trap. He had deftly passed on the case to Inspector Pahad Singh of Kautuknagar, stating that the

Pigeon Square, where the incident took place, falls under the jurisdiction of Kautuknagar. Inspector Pahad Singh dutifully passed the case back to Inspector Godbole, countering that the incident was first covered by his Topat, and Inspector Godbole himself was a witness to the incident. While this ping-pong between the two seasoned inspectors was going on, the story caught the attention of a Jhallu (*J*ournalist *ha*nging on to *all l*ittle *u*tterances).

Jhallus were the senior and expensive version of Jholus, who operated from the calm and cool environs of their studios but were experts in generating heat and turbulence all the time. They wore their designer attitude up their sleeve, asked weighty questions, but listened to no one. They had a penchant for raising their pitch, and were trained to be dismissive of everything they were dealing with. News channels not only loved them but actively promoted and branded them. Jhallu5 of KN10 (*K*autukpur *N*ews10) in this case decided to host a small discussion on the topic 'Graffiti in election times', linking it to the morning's incident. Discussions on KN10 hosted by Jhallu5 were always a serious affair which were attended by the usual set of *Lappu* known as Learned-Popats.

Learned Popats differed from both personal and professional Popats. They were the Popats on which advanced and privileged Appu of a particular field was applied. Thus a Popat when applied with Taxation Appu was called *Tappu*, applied with *Ch*ef Appu was called *Chappu*, applied with Learned Appu was called *Lappu* and so on. Lappu were the Popats who were master of all but expert in none. Being the exalted variety of Popats, Lappu were in great demand in the News Channels.

Jhallu5 on this occasion had chosen two Lappus from two different camps for the discussion. To the question of whether the slogan painted on the road qualified as graffiti, Lappu1 nodded in affirmative while Lappu2 maintained that it was not 'writing on the wall' and hence did not qualify as graffiti. Jhallu5 pointed out that under law, graffiti was to be removed by the originator, and in addition, a fine could be imposed. When he asked whether painting the slogan on Pigeon Square Road was punishable, Lappu1 nodded in affirmative. Lappu2 argued that since the slogan itself had vanished, there was no cause left for punishment. To the question whether the slogans on the road were an obstruction to the traffic, Lappu1 nodded in affirmative while Lappu2 maintained that since the slogans were removed before the traffic was resumed, there was no obstruction to traffic and hence no penalty could be imposed. At this stage, Jallu5 displayed a few clips of graffiti immortalizing messages from some leaders on the walls of Kautuknagar, and asked why those have not been removed and offenders punished. This started a free-for-all argument. With both the Lappus vociferously defending their masters, they almost came to blows. At this point, having achieved the desired effect, Jhallu5 closed the show.

Inspectors, who were playing the 'passing the buck' game, in the meantime, realized that the situation was getting out of their hands. So they decided that it was a fit case to be reported to their *Clown* (*Cl*oud-*O*perated-*W*izard-*N*etwork).

By 2040, each department, ministry, company, or organization had its own *Clown.* Clowns were endowed with computing power more than the supercomputers of the 2020s, were powered with customized AI algorithms, and were repositories of all the rules, regulations, policies, data, decisions, experience, and everything else connected with their 'working'. Soon, they became ubiquitous, replacing all varieties of clerks, executives, managers, or sundry middling having any pretension of making decisions. They gave orders to Popats and sometimes to common humans, but took orders only from a *Gappu* (*G*od's *A*pproved *Appu*).

Gappu were the privileged humans who thought that God alone had given them the power to lord over the Clowns, Popats, and humans lower down in hierarchy. They were in effect the converged version of the species, earlier known as VIPs, ministers, bureaucrats, and CEOs, etc. Though Gappus and Clowns were meant to bring a little order and serve the public, they mostly ended up creating chaos and lording over the public through that chaos.

The Clown who received the request from Inspector Godbole was prompt to act. The AI of any public department Clowns had many tools and strategies like 'refer, defer, deter, jump, or dump' the matter. The Clown, in this case, determined that this case pertained to an election matter, and promptly referred it to the EC Clown. The EC Clown referred it back to Inspector Godbole for sending a report before the end of the day. Inspector Godbole referred it back to his Topat, knowing that being AI-powered, all Popats were proficient in writing copious reports. His Topat obliged with a detailed report concluding that he found nothing untoward or unlawful in his jurisdiction during the course of his duty and hence no further action was required on his part. Inspector Godbole concurred and submitted the report to his Clown. The Clown got it approved from his Gappu and passed it on to the EC Clown who filled it with the remark 'Action taken'. It was a testimony to the efficiency achieved in 2050 that such a laborious task, that would have taken a few days normally, could be finished in less than half an hour.

With all the twists and turns of the morning having been cleared, Vartika decided to bring her candidate before the media. Friendly Jhallu Number One of Channel Number One interviewed Y2K in his evening show. The show went along predictable lines. Y2K took a statesmanlike position and thanked Inspector Godbole for his scrupulous handling of the case, reposed his faith in the fair and just functioning of the EC, and praised the media for its vigilant and detailed coverage. He also said that he believed in clean and calm electioneering, and this morning's event was an attempt in that direction. He exhorted fellow candidates to follow the same path and make the Kautukpur elections exemplary amongst all the Mandals.

At this point, Jhallu1 asked the punch question: 'Don't you think the whole incident was much ado about nothing?' Y2K had not anticipated the question but answered promptly, 'It may literally seem so, but our exercise in the morning was much more than just a mere attempt to ask for the votes. The idea was to bring Pigeon Square into focus. Only a few people know that this square is more than two thousand years old, and the carvings around the platform are a testimony to its past glory. It was here that singers sang, magicians performed, and craftsmen displayed their work, creating a sense of wonder that gave the city its name, Kautuknagar. Unfortunately, there is a pending bill seeking to demolish this square to build wider roads for autonomous vehicles. While traffic can be managed with simple measures, precious heritage once lost can't be re-created. If I get elected, I shall scuttle this bill forthwith, and further restore Pigeon Square to its glorious past.'

Besides the story of vanishing paint, it was this call to preserve Pigeon Square that played on all the local channels during prime time and resonated with everyone. By the time voting lines closed at 9 pm, Y2K had garnered more than enough votes to pass through the first qualifying round.

Chapter XIV

The next day when team Y2K met for the breakfast meeting, everyone was excited. Each member had a sense of participation and achievement. Once they finished congratulating each other, Vartika reminded them that mathematically their task was still challenging. She pointed out that by tomorrow, only six dozen candidates will remain in the field. Y2K had not only survived the treacherous first round but had galloped to the seventy-seventh position from nowhere. However, a drama cannot be recreated every day, and climbing a few positions in a day was still a formidable task. As earlier, everyone looked up to Vartika for a way out.

'The platforms an aspiring politician can use are Hyde Park, Jantar Mantar, and Ram Lila Maidan,' said Vartika. Acknowledging the quizzical looks from the rest of the team, she continued, 'Hyde Park is about sharing your ideas and thoughts, Jantar Mantar is about registering your protest or dissent, and Ramlila Maidan is all about showing your strength and support. Every politician traverses his journey from Hyde Park to Jantar Mantar to Ram Lila Maidan, except for a few privileged ones who directly leapfrog to Ram Lila Maidan. What it essentially means is that a *Neta* has to be good at delivering *Bhashan*[17], sitting on *Anshan*[18], and appealing to *Janman.*[19]'

As usual, Kattu raised a serious concern. 'Our candidate is not even remotely connected with these exalted tasks. He has never given a *bhashan*, let alone participated in a protest march or a rally.'

Kattu's point-blank remark made Y2K a little uncomfortable. Vartika, however, came to his rescue and quickly added, 'We all know that our candidate starts with zero experience. That is a handicap but not a disqualification. In politics, the job is open to everyone. And unlike your career jobs, it is never too late to begin. I think it is time that our candidate debuts at Hyde Park.'

'But where is the Hyde Park in Kautukpur?' asked Sattu innocently.

Vartika answered with a smile. 'In old times, every *Gali*, *Mohalla*[20], and the municipal park was a Hyde Park. In the age of the Metaverse, there is a proper and exact replica of Hyde Park in every Mandal which is owned and operated by EC. It is one of their initiatives to promote democracy through the use of technology.'

'So, what am I supposed to do there?' asked Y2K with some concern.

'Nothing. Just go out there and tell the whole world why you want to be the Mandal Governor,' replied Vartika.

---

[17] *speech*

[18] *hunger-strike*

[19] *people's heart*

[20] *street corner, locality*

'You can be a little more helpful than that,' persisted Y2K.

'Well, the Hyde Park appearance is a registered event during election season and I have managed to book you for a ten-minute slot in the evening. I shall pass on all the necessary details so that you may join from your *Adda.* I shall also try to ensure that some friendly *Jholus* cover your event.' On the last count, Vartika was telling only half the truth, since no *Jholu* worth his salt could be friendly while covering an event.

Y2K joined the event smoothly, and to his surprise, he found a reasonable crowd present. Some were the election regulars who kept the minutest details of the happenings while others were mere onlookers who had nothing better to do. Vartika had delivered on her promise as three *Jholus* were also present with their trademark mics ready in their hands.

Y2K was introduced as a first-time candidate, with Pigeon as his election symbol. Y2K looked at the disinterested faces of the audience, examined the inscrutable expression of the *Jholus,* and suddenly felt a lump in his mouth. He had labored on his speech for an hour using inputs from a professional speech-writer Popat, hired by D2Y2. Y2K then practiced delivering the speech several times till D2Y2 was satisfied. However, just when he was face to face with his audience, the futility of the whole practiced exercise dawned upon him. Speechwriter Popat had done a professional job, but it must have done so for so many candidates. No wonder, all election speeches sounded similar. On an impulse, Y2K switched off the Concon that was prompting him on what to say and began speaking from his heart.

'My dear fellow citizens, I stand before you in all humility and honesty. But for a quirk of fate, I would perhaps be listening rather than addressing you. That is only a small change of role, and rather than giving a lecture, I intend to listen to you more. Frankly, I do not qualify to be a politician. I am neither a career politician nor a political legatee who considers being elected as a natural progression. I am neither a lawyer nor a big businessman who conveniently jumps into the role of governing. I am not even a bureaucrat or a diplomat. I do not flaunt or exploit my surname, and I do not represent an interest group either.'

Jholu4 of Channel Eight with the tagline 'KN8 carries Weight' was getting impatient. His Channel ran an 'Ideological Algorithm' which assigned an ideological color index to every person, event, or issue. The Algorithm would then give a tilt to the coverage according to the index. Jholu8 was given the task of marking every candidate on the left, right, or center of the political color index. Jholu8 wanted to finish his task quickly, so he asked directly, 'We are not interested in knowing who you are and where you come from. Just tell us where you stand – left, right, or center?'

Y2K had not given a thought to such a weighty question but answered nonchalantly. 'I do not believe in such single-dimensional coloration of everything. I think political positioning should be on the three-dimensional axis of People, Potential, and Progress. When applied to this three-dimensional function, none of the prevalent ideologies work out singularly well. In that sense, you can say that I do not have any particular conventional ideology'. Jholu8 immediately seized upon his headline, 'A candidate with no ideology', and retreated quietly to report his story.

By now, an old man from the audience had got interested in the discussion and asked, 'If you have no ideology, then on what basis do we elect you and if elected, on what basis will you govern?'

Y2K had asked the same question to himself over the last few days and some random thoughts had crossed his mind. He simply shared his thoughts,

'I think we should distinguish between ideology, politics, and governance and put them in proper perspective. Most people misunderstand the interplay of ideology, politics, and governance and mess it up all. The result is that the blind followers of 'The Wealth of Nations' have caused the concentration of wealth in a few, and *'Das Kapital'* zealots have ended up embracing *'Das Maluka'* philosophy.' The old man was aware of the *Das Maluka* philosophy which proclaims *'Azgar kare na chakari, panchi kare na kam; Das Maluka kah gaye, sab ke data Ram*[21]*'*, and nodded approvingly. Encouraged, Y2K continued,

'To my understanding, ideology is about direction, politics is about power to propel, and governance is about the execution in a manner that the public welfare is maximized.'

The mention of the word 'welfare' alerted Jholu1 of Channel1 whose job of the day was to collect a summary of all the welfare schemes, especially the freebies offered by the candidates. He thrust his mike before Y2K. 'Talking about public welfare, what are the freebies you are offering to the public?'

---

[21] *Snake does no job, birds do no work; Das Maluka says that Ram provides for all.*

Y2K had a clear stand on this and stated unhesitatingly,

'I offer no freebies at all for many reasons. Firstly, no one has a right to offer what he does not own. Secondly, pre-election promises of freebies turn into uncontrolled competitive bidding, leading to serious economic consequences. Thirdly, they are discriminatory and are used to create a captive vote bank. Lastly, there is no evidence that freebies maximize the public good. Freebies are justified in the name of redistribution of wealth but in practice, they achieve only the redistribution of electoral dividends. I am not against the merit-based redistribution of state resources but that is best achieved by good governance and not by irresponsible offers of freebies. I offer good and responsible governance and not the freebies promised by my competing candidates.'

There was a round of applause as Y2K finished, but Jholu1 of KN1 was nonplussed. He decided on his headline, 'Candidate who offers no Freebies', and left quietly.

Jholu5 of Kautukpur Channel, KN10, had refrained so far from asking any questions. He had been assigned the task of reporting on the manifesto of the candidates. All candidates except Y2K had released their manifesto. Jholu5 had not found anything newsworthy in their manifesto since each manifesto looked similar to at least ten other manifestos. Jholu5 knew that they all originated from the same speechwriter Popat. Y2K's was the only unknown manifesto, and Jholu5 found it an opportune moment to ask about it. 'From what you have said so far, you seem to be an unknown element. So where is your manifesto?'

Y2K had half anticipated this question but had left it hanging. He had not had a chance to discuss it with his Gang of Five which was focused so far only on mustering past the initial round. The manifesto was too serious a document to be left to the speechwriter Popat. Y2K needed to think deeply, look around, and discuss before finalizing his manifesto. He wanted it to be different and something that would address the problems unique to 2050. He wanted it to be comprehensive, covering even the smallest issue that nobody would pay attention to. And he needed time. He hit upon an idea instantly.

'I do not come with a preconceived manifesto. I'll consult, discuss, look around, talk to the people, and then build my manifesto brick by brick, alphabet by alphabet. From tomorrow, I'll pick one issue as per the English alphabet every day and unfold the A to Z of my manifesto by the time the next round of election finishes,' announced Y2K.

Jholu5 summed up this rather unusual way of announcing the manifesto in his headline, 'Candidate Y2K to learn ABCD of manifesto from tomorrow', and quietly left as the audience applauded. A few other channels carried similar headlines 'Candidate with no manifesto', 'Candidate who will teach us ABCD of manifesto', 'Watch out for the ABCD of manifesto-2050', 'Y2K to build his manifesto alphabet by alphabet', etc.

Y2K felt buoyed as he reflected upon his performance. However, the feeling of exuberance gave way to wariness as slanted headlines trickled in. All local channels carried his maiden public appearance, but the twisted headlines and slanted coverage left Y2K wondering whether he was a hit or a miss.

As Y2K became tense and apprehensive, he decided to call Vartika.

'Can you meet me for dinner?'

'Are you asking me for a date or a business meeting?' asked Vartika pleasantly.

'It is no time for a date, silly. Meet me by eight at *Mahan 2050.'* Mahan 2050 was an Indian restaurant that specialized in serving Indian dishes without chilies. 'There are already enough chilies in the news headlines,' thought Y2K wryly.

When they met for dinner, Vartika was ebullient and cheerful, unlike Y2K. As soon as they were seated, Y2K asked,

'How was my performance today?'

'You did brilliantly. You are a natural,' replied Vartika with a smile.

'The news channels do not seem to think so,' said Y2K dourly.

'Don't worry about that. The fact that every news channel mentioned you, augurs well,' consoled Vartika.

'The way they covered me was all slanted and negative,' blurted Y2K.

'Oh, that's routine. If the channels report verbatim, they will be mere photocopiers. Putting a little slant and a twist makes a news channel newsworthy. Viewers are discerning enough to glean the right message.'

'How?'

'Take for example the headline, 'Candidate without ideology'. People have seen enough *Netas* who make an about-turn on ideology every six months, with every turn resulting in a worse outcome for the polity. In contrast, you came out as honest, sincere, and pragmatic with your refreshing views on ideology. Similarly, the headline, 'Candidate who offers no Freebies', will fetch you more votes than you would have got by offering a few freebies since voters are now getting tired of the freebie culture.'

'What about the manifesto fiasco? You should have prepared me better on this.' Y2K was still cut up with Vartika that she had not thought of as basic a thing as a manifesto. Vartika, however, explained patiently.

'No amount of tutoring can make a leader out of an aspirant. Left to yourself, you came out with a strategic gem in the form of manifesto-building, day by day, and alphabet by alphabet. Today, Jhallus across the channels debated manifestoes of leading candidates and took them to the cleaners, but none forgot to mention that they look forward to the unfolding of A to Z of your manifesto. One Jhallu went to the extent of saying that yours is a new way of doing politics. And I readily believe him.'

Y2K was suitably placated and felt relieved. He noticed for the first time that Vartika looked gorgeous in the pink dress. A bright smile had replaced that distantly stern look, and she was exuding grace and beauty that were enticing. By the time he could think of an appropriate compliment, food arrived. Breaking news that Y2K had cleared this elimination round and stood at the sixty-second position, made the desserts of '*Rum Gulabjamun*' and '*Jaggery Jalebi*' even sweeter.

Chapter XV

A week had elapsed since the fateful first day of 2050 when Y2K got sucked into the election storm. In this short span, he had transited from a lonely, virtual-world life into real-world life dealing with real people. Sitting in his *Adda*, he was now ready to discuss real issues with a real team. His teammates were impressed by his performance the day before and were primed for more action.

Vartika took the lead as usual and spoke, 'Yesterday was a milestone in our election campaign. We have now moved from a hopeless position to a promising sixty-sixth rank. From today onwards, we are in for a long haul of campaigning lasting a whole month. Every day there will be polling and ratings will be announced for each candidate. At the end of this round, out of six dozen candidates, only a dozen top-ranked will qualify. This is the most exhausting and tedious round in which front-runners may suddenly falter, and laggards may surge ahead. In this game of 'ratings', skill and strategy will see us through while a mistake or misadventure will derail our mission. Yesterday our leader spoke not only about who we are and where we stand, but also announced the building of our manifesto alphabet by alphabet, day by day. By doing so, he has charted the whole course of our election strategy.'

Y2K noted the use of the word 'leader' instead of 'candidate' or just 'Y2K' as everyone nodded. Managing the second round on his own could not have qualified him as a leader. After all, he had depended on his team to clear the first round. 'Charting your own course of action makes you a leader,' Y2K concluded to himself, and resolved to internalize this learning.

Y2K's reverie was broken by Sattu's response.

'In keeping with Y2K's announcement, today we need to identify an issue beginning with 'A' for our manifesto. I think 'A for Agriculture' is the obvious choice. Agriculture has been the mainstay of our country for centuries, but nowadays nobody seems to care about farming or farmers.'

Kattu, however, had a contrary view and argued,

'Agriculture has never been in a better condition than it is in 2050, thanks to science and technology. After the green revolution of the last century, we have witnessed a green revolution 2.0 since the late 2030s, when Kappus first appeared on the scene. Now ninety percent of the agriculture production comes from Kappus and not farmers.'

Kattu was referring to the '*K*isan *App*lication *U*pdated Popats' or Kappus who specialize in farming, capable of performing any task needed to be carried out on the farm. 'Kappus collect soil conditions from the IoT sensors embedded in the farms, check weather conditions, decide upon the best-suited crop, and use the right kind of seeds. Using AI, they constantly calculate and ensure the optimal use of water so that not a single drop is wasted, and spray just the right amount of pesticides. They plow, thrash, and operate all kinds of implements. As if that was not enough, they connect to the logistics and Agro-marketing Clowns to dispose of the produce at the best possible price at the right time. Since the Agro-marketing Clowns are connected to Industry 5.0, every single ton of produce can be stored, processed, and sold to the consumer with zero waste and at optimum cost. Agriculture now is fully integrated with the global production and supply chain like any other industry. As a result, global production in agriculture has doubled over the last decade, while consumption of resources like water and fertilizers has halved. Technology has taken good care of the problems in agriculture, leaving only politicians to lament and protest,' said Kattu.

Sattu was nonplussed at Kattu's explanation and retorted,

'Just get out of the comfort zone of Kautukpur and visit the Kautukgram. Then you will see for yourself what the real issues are.'

Sattu was alluding to the vast rural area of Kautuk Mandal called Kautukgram, which accommodated one-third of the Mandal's population but accounted for only one-eighth of its economic value. Kautukgram's vast green fields hid the dilapidated houses and crumbling infrastructure. Despite the country becoming the leading economy in 2050, the average per capita income of Kautukgram was below the world average and less than half that of Kautukpur. Y2K was vaguely aware of the poor condition of Kautukgram, which seemed to be in a perpetual state of disrepair.

Y2K cautiously asked if the idyllic picture that Kattu presented had holes in it. Mattu replied in affirmative and explained,

'Only around fifteen percent of farmers own Kappus and the connected technology infrastructure, but they account for thirty percent of the revenue. Sixty percent are medium and small farmers who rent out such facilities fully or partially and account for sixty percent of the revenue. The remaining twenty-five percent of very small farmers have no or very little access to the technology and manage to eke out only ten percent of the revenue share. They simply cannot compete with those who have access to technology. These small and very small farmers are the residents of Kautukgram, which explains its state of disrepair and the glaring disparity. The disparity is a natural byproduct of technology.'

'What can we do in this case?' asked Y2K.

'Every candidate is asking the same question and responding in two ways, in an attempt to woo the vote bank. Half of the candidates are offering Kappus as freebies to very small farmers if they get elected. In return, they will get twenty-five percent extra votes but will empty the Mandal coffers. The other half wants to ban all the Kappus so that everyone goes back to the good old ways. They will get the votes of small and very small farmers but spoil the Mandal economy that is growing on the back of technology,' elaborated Vartika.

'There must be some other alternative as well,' asked Y2K.

'Agriculture is a sacred cow. You can placate but not reform. The best thing is to keep quiet, maintain the status quo, and get the undecided votes from all the sections,' suggested Vartika.

'That is no way to solve a problem,' protested Sattu.

Lattu was keeping quiet so far and it fell upon him to close the debate as he remarked,

'I can see the intractable situation. Yesterday, Y2K expressed his views against the freebies, so the option of giving away Kappus is ruled out. Banning Kappus is also against his promise of responsible governance. Keeping quiet means we need to find another topic for today's manifesto agenda. It will only be appropriate if we leave it to our leader Y2K to decide.' Everybody concurred with the suggestion.

Y2K was pleased to be treated as a leader, but at the same time was wary at having to make a decision. He turned to Vartika for help.

'What do I do now? Any suggestions?'

'Well, you can begin by doing what every candidate does,' replied Vartika casually.

'And what is that?' asked Y2K.

'Visit an astrologer. Most candidates begin their campaign after consulting an astrologer. I am making this claim based on a pretty authentic survey,' replied Vartika with a straight face.

Y2K was shocked at this ridiculous suggestion and replied promptly,

'I do not believe in astrology, and I do not wish to waste my time meeting an astrologer.'

'You don't have to always believe in it. As a politician, you need to meet people from all walks of life. So why not an astrologer? Think of him as a wise person and meet him.

If not, meet him as a voter. Maybe use 'A for Astrology' as today's agenda point.'

It occurred to Y2K that he had not met a single real voter since his fateful nomination. So he fell in line.

'You must have already fixed an appointment,' asked Y2K peevishly.

'Yes, of course! I have fixed a meeting today at eleven thirty with Professor Ashwini Acharya. Non-believers call him Professor A-square or simply as Professor. Believers address him as Guruji. He is quite popular and a bit eccentric. He knows the politician's penchant for reaching late and has warned that you better not be late since the *Rahu-Kal* will start from twelve ten onward,' briefed Vartika. Y2K was uncertain as she wished him good luck and departed.

Every third person Y2K had met socially had the pretension of being an astrologer but he had never met a professional astrologer. Professor Acharya was no ordinary astrologer. He had a Ph.D. in astronomy as well as political science with a large number of research papers to his credit, especially in 'Predictive modeling in Political Science'. After a promising career abroad, he had returned to teach at Mandal University. While teaching was his profession, astrology was his passion.

Professor's Popat received Y2K with a *namaste,* seated him in the office which was spartan and yet comfortable, served herbal tea, and left Y2K immersed in his thoughts. Y2K was startled when he heard the Professor saying,

'You are wondering why the hell am I here when I could be doing more important things?'

Y2K was thinking exactly that at precisely that moment. Is this man reading my mind, thought Y2K to himself?

'I am not reading your mind. I use that technology sparingly. What you were thinking was written large on your face, and you can say that I am a good face reader,' said the Professor affably.

Mind-reading was no big deal in 2050. A bio-chip was implanted in the body, which detected the very faint electric signals from the brain and transmitted them using 8G. It was predicted that by Y3K (year 3000), no one would speak, and the communication between humans to humans and between humans to machines would be directly through the mind. 'That would be a different time and different world,' thought Y2K.

'Y3K will certainly be an interesting period and you would live to see Y3K as per your *Kundali*,' said Guruji to Y2K as if he was keeping up with his thought process.

'In that case, everyone who has the same *Kundali* as mine should survive till the hundred years, and you know that is not true. How do you explain this paradox?' asked Y2K, determined not to be influenced by the Professor.

'There is no paradox here. It is only a matter of understanding. Consider life as a complex equation having innumerable variables that can be assigned infinite time-dependent values. Your time, place, date of birth, and planetary positions assign values to only limited variables. Rest is determined by your karma, dharma, destiny, and that invisible hand of god. So everyone having a *Kundali* matching Sachin will not become a master cricketer, and everyone having a *Kundali* like Ambani will not become a billionaire.'

'By stating the obvious, you are trying to show the pseudoscience of astrology as a science,' said Y2K, rather impertinently.

'Not at all. I readily agree that astrology is not a science, not even a pseudoscience. But that is no reason to dismiss it altogether. Let me explain. When you go to buy an insurance policy, they determine your coverage based on a scientific method called actuarial science. Even when all the people paying a similar premium end up having different life spans, you call the system scientific because it calculates the probability of survival based on the correlation of facts and data. Astrology, on the other hand, not only calculates probability, it attempts to do a more difficult thing, that is to predict and give a definite answer in an indefinite world. The correlation function here is a matter of belief and not a matter of fact. So call astrology a belief system if you like.'

'But why do we need this belief system at all?' persisted Y2K.

'Because we don't like uncertainty. Because we seek answers when in doubt. Because we need an excuse for our failures and a hope for our success.'

'You may be right. Ever since I joined the election fray, I have been troubled by the question of whether I shall win or not. Though I do not believe in astrology, I have been tempted to consult an astrologer,' confessed Y2K.

'I know that you have already consulted a Jappu, and you are troubled because it predicted that you will get eliminated from the race in this round.'

Y2K was stunned by the Professor's answer. The Jappu meant a *J*yotish *App*lication *U*pdated Popat which specialized in the *Jyotish-Shastra* and trained under a *Jyotishacharya*. Y2K had consulted one such trained Jappu before coming here, but there was no way that such consultation could have been known to the Professor. As if on a cue, Professor continued,

'I again assure you that I don't do mind-reading, but I am good at making deductions. A methodical person like you would have consulted a Jappu before meeting me, and based on your *Kundali*, almost every Jappu would have told you that the planetary alignment is not in your favor. All I can say is that the prediction made by your Jappu is wrong. My prediction is that you will sail through to the final round of the elections.'

The prediction that Professor made was music to his ears, but Y2K had a doubt.

'Why is your prediction so different from that of a Jappu?'

Professor smiled as he was anticipating this question and said,

'Instead of explaining it in jargons like Jupiter in the eighth house, Mars in retrograde, or Saturn in ascendance, let me explain it in terms of life being a complex equation. A Jappu will reduce this equation to variables denoting planets and assign standard values, but an Acharya will consider many variables and many values. This consideration comes from intuition, *Dhyan*, *Sadhna*, experience, and deep reflection, which can't be learned or acquired through Artificial Intelligence. Hence the difference.'

Y2K was not convinced but was thoroughly enjoying the discussion, notwithstanding his impiety.

'What is the most significant prediction you have made that no Jappu ever would have made?' he asked out of curiosity.

'Well, last year I predicted that the serving MG (Mandal Governor) would lose his job within six months. Soon thereafter, a whistleblower filed an FIR implicating him in a scam. The MG saw my prediction as a conspiracy and brought a bill to ban the practice of astrology. However, before this bill could be signed, he was found guilty and removed from the job, making my prediction come true,' replied Professor.

'I knew about the removal of MG but was unaware of the bill banning astrology. Bringing such a bill was not only spiteful but a misuse of power and public trust. If I get elected, I shall immediately drop this bill,' pledged Y2K.

'I am sure you will,' smiled the Professor.

'One last question. You predicted that I would be in the top two, but you didn't tell whether I would win or not,' asked Y2K.

'Well, the final round is more than a month away and like a good politician, a good astrologer does not open all his cards,' replied the Professor, still smiling.

'If not the final prediction, then give me some final advice instead,' urged Y2K.

'Well, while exercising power, always follow the *Rajdharma*. Power only tells you what you can do, but *Rajdharma* also tells you what you should not do. Also remember that to be able to follow the path of dharma, you need to do due diligence before you act,' said the Professor as he raised his hands in blessing. This time Y2K addressed Professor as Guruji. Y2K bowed to Guruji and left.

Meeting with Guruji had a deep impression on Y2K. Remembering Professor's advice about diligence, he settled down to study all the half a dozen pending bills, including the bills banning astrology and the Kappus. He realized that all of them had ulterior motives and all needed to be withdrawn. Y2K had his agenda ready for the day.

When the Hyde Park meeting began, Y2K noticed that there was one additional Jholu present and the crowd was a little larger than yesterday. His 'A to Z manifesto' idea had apparently created some buzz. Y2K began earnestly,

'My dear citizens of Kautuk Mandal, yesterday from the same podium I announced that I shall build my manifesto alphabet by alphabet, meeting real people, and taking up real issues, howsoever big or small they are.

It is our custom to visit and seek the blessings of a wise man before undertaking an arduous task. Today, I visited Professor Ashwini Acharya, a prominent scientist whose profession is astronomy and whose passion is astrology. Though I do not believe in astrology, we had a good discussion on it. As suggested by him, my today's manifesto agenda is 'A for Astrology', under which I propose to set up a Department of Astrology in the Kautuk Mandal University. The professor also told me about the pending bill that proposes to ban the practice of Astrology. I find such a bill revengeful and excessive. Making legislation is the prime duty of a Governor, and this bill is the prime example of what legislation should not be. This bill fails the test of good governance miserably. Therefore, if elected, the first item on my agenda will be to officially withdraw this bill. Not only this bill, but the five other pending bills also fail the test of good governance and hence they all will be withdrawn. One such bill that needs special mention is about banning the Kappus from agriculture,. In my opinion, instead of banning technologies, services, or practices, governance should be about taking constructive steps. Accordingly, I shall not only withdraw the bill banning the Kappus, but I shall also take steps to develop a low-cost Kappu model suiting the needs of our small and very small farmers. The technology that widens the disparity can also be deployed to bridge that gap as well. The locally developed Kappus will supplement and not substitute the farmers. That will be my way forward for the future of agriculture. Although I do not practice astrology, I can safely predict that our farmers in Kautukpur will have a bright future.'

There was a round of applause as Y2K concluded, and the Jholus scribbled their headlines.

Y2K was not sure whether he had handled the agriculture issue well or whether the astrology touch was necessary. As usual, he called up Vartika for a meeting over dinner, and she asked the usual question, 'Business or a date?'

When Vartika turned up for dinner, she was looking as cheerful as ever. Vartika put to rest Y2K's apprehensions as she said, 'You are a natural and today you proved that again.'

'How?' asked Y2K.

'Diversion is an effective tool in politics and you used it well by bringing in the Astrology Bill, while axing the Agriculture

Bill was the real target. You also did well by making some constructive promises. A politician who makes no promises can't go far. That way you have adroitly managed to keep the frontline warriors on the agriculture front at bay from generating negative votes against you.'

'Does it mean that I'll get sufficient support to improve my rating?'

'Surely, because the bonus will come in the form of support from Professor Acharya's followers. He is better known as Guruji on popular channels and has a decent fan following.'

Vartika was vindicated when Guruji appeared on one of the channels. He was telling his unusually respectful Jhallu,

'Keeping up with the election time, I met a bright candidate named Y2K today. I was impressed with him, not because his Kundali has Rajyog, but because he seems to understand the Rajdharma. His pitch of 'A for Astrology' is going to be lucky for him. Though the odds against him are said to be one in eighty, I predict that he will be the main challenger in this election.' As Guruji went on to explain the nuances of the planetary positions further, Y2K felt hugely relieved and grateful.

Even the Chef seemed to be caught on the alphabetic pitch as he served '*Aloo Tikki Chat*' and '*Akhrot Ke Kabab*', followed by '*Aloo Dam*', '*Achari Paneer*', and '*Aloo Stuffed Nan*'. Noticing the menu selection, Y2K suggested that they meet for dinner regularly and try out different dishes alphabetically every day, while discussing the election manifesto and strategy.

'Here goes my chance of a date for the next twenty-five days,' commented Vartika, and they both laughed. As the dessert of

'*Ananas ki kheer*' and '*Ande ka halwa*' was served, the election ratings were announced. Y2K unexpectedly moved up the rankings by eight positions, riding on Guruji's endorsement. It was a good start to the month-long qualifying round.

Chapter XVI

Vartika had suggested a dress code to Y2K till the elections last. He was to don a white *Kurta* and *Churidar* or a plain-looking and loosely fitting shirt and trousers while appearing in public. Turning up smartly was taboo. When Y2K protested, Vartika asked, 'When you dress up smartly, people say you look like a hero. Do they ever say you look like *Neta*, if you dress well?'

'No. But that is stereotyping people and professions,' argued Y2K.

'Exactly, because stereotyping paradoxically differentiates you from the others as a class, affords you an easy identity, and a ready-made image. In Politics, you just exploit and benefit from stereotyping. In any case, haven't you heard of the wise saying *Yatha Desh Tatha Vesh*?' Having no answer, Y2K had acquiesced and ordered a few dresses as suggested by Vartika.

The white *Kurta* and *Churidar* fitted him well as Y2K admired his attire in the mirror. The gray and golden pigeon embroidered on the front pocket gave it a designer look. Y2K decided to test it out with D2Y2 and asked,

'Do I look like a *hero?*'

'No.'

Do I look like a *Neta?*' asked Y2K again.

'Yes, of course,' replied D2Y2.

'Do you accept me as your *Neta?*

'I do not accept anyone as my *Neta,*' said D2Y2 nonchalantly. 'Blessed is the world of Popats,' thought Y2K. His further conversation with D2Y2 was interrupted as the whole gang trooped in and greeted him with a 'Wow, you look like a *Neta*' remark. 'Maybe it's time to discuss about a bit of *Netagiri* as well,' commented Vartika as they all laughed and settled for discussion over breakfast.

Vartika had asked D2Y2 for a specially heavy breakfast which was dutifully laid out. Therefore, it took a while before anyone broached the subject of a manifesto issue beginning with 'B'. Nobody had given much thought to it.

'The world is full of problems but choosing them alphabetically is a hell of a task,' complained Mattu.

'I cannot think of anything big beginning with 'B' either, especially after yesterday's mix-up of Astrology and Agriculture,' commented Sattu who was still miffed at agriculture being dealt with by some subterfuge.

'Yesterday's take on Astrology was a big success. Why don't we do something along the same lines?' suggested Kattu. His remark lit the bulb as Lattu exclaimed, 'Hang on there. Why do you think our digression on Astrology clicked?'

Everyone was now alert as Lattu continued,

'According to a survey, the three top things that occupy the average Indian's mind-space are Astrology, Bollywood, and Cricket. That can be our ABC of catching the voter's attention as well. Talking about Astrology got us the votes yesterday. There is no reason why B for Bollywood should not get us a few more votes today.'

'I agree with Lattu. Bollywood movies, and for that matter all the regional movies have been the most powerful tool for social change and awareness. In terms of impact, Bollywood has always punched above its weight,' said Sattu.

'Bollywood has actually become heavyweight since 2040. After the decline through the 2020s, Bollywood not only has revived but has left even Hollywood behind, riding on the back of technology. Bollywood was always producing the largest number of films at the lowest possible cost but was criticized for its cliched approach and lack of technical finesse. That changed from the mid-30s.'

Kattu was referring to the transformation that Bollywood had undergone in recent times, exploiting cutting-edge technologies to the hilt. Bollywood was the first to cast a Popat in a movie, and also the first to produce a movie with only Popats. All-Popat cast allowed Bollywood to innovate with new formats. In the early 40s, Bollywood came up with technology that allowed the viewer to choose and play a role within the movie. Another format allowed the viewers to act, direct, and manipulate the sequence and the course of a live movie. The viewers were now the masters of drama and surveyors of their dreams, aspirations, and biases. The new formats enabled Bollywood to demolish Hollywood's two most distinguishing features, technical excellence and white supremacy bias. Smart Cinema, pioneered by Bollywood, had truly become global as well as local by 2050.

'We are all enamored of technology used by Bollywood. But have we ever thought of how it shapes us and our society?' questioned Sattu.

'That question is food for thought which we are going to answer by eschewing food for the day,' interjected Vartika, who was listening quietly so far.

'Why talk in riddles, Vartika?' asked Kattu.

'Well, if you want to know about the riddles of Bollywood, then the best person to go to is K-cube and it so happens that K-cube is sitting on *Anshan* at *Jantar-Mantar* in support of his movement. That is a big opportunity for us. We can all go to Jantar-Mantar, support his movement, and hope that he will reciprocate by supporting us,' explained Vartika.

K-cube needed no introduction since everyone knew him as the lone Bollywood star of Kautukpur. His real name was Kautuk Kumar but he always introduced himself as Kalakar Kautuk Kumar, earning the moniker K-cube. During his college days in Kautukpur, he had spent more time at Pigeon Square doing pranks and street theater, than in the classroom. Driven by his dreams and passion for acting, he migrated to Mumbai. After the usual struggle, he had just begun to make his mark when the technological upsurge in Bollywood interrupted his journey and he slowly faded away. Disillusioned, he returned to Kautukpur where the disenchantment continued.

'Why is no one talking about K-cube sitting on *Anshan* or his movement? There is no coverage in the media at all.' asked Sattu.

'Because no one understands his mission. They think that the *Anshan* by a jobless movie star is merely a ruse for dieting or grabbing attention. And the Jholus will prefer to report some Bollywood gossip rather than a non-political *Anshan*,' guessed Kattu with some degree of accuracy.

'Yes, people do react in a stereotypical manner. But I have read that K-cube is a man of substance and a person who is deeply devoted to promoting the performing art. I think we should all go to *Jantar Mantar* to support him,' proposed Y2K who had been silent so far. The idea was immediately seconded since they all were keen to meet K-cube in person.

Everyone knew the way to Jantar Mantar. Originally, Jantar Mantar was known as an observatory consisting of stone-built instruments which came up in the eighteenth century. Over a period of time, it came to be known as a place for demonstration or *dharna* instead of a place for astronomy. *Dharna-pradarshan* being an integral part of the Indian polity, every Mandal came to boast of a place designated as Jantar Mantar. Kautukpur had a patch of land near *Ghantaghar*, the eternally dysfunctional clock tower, which gradually came to be known as the Jantar Mantar of Kautukpur. Here, groups of all kinds regularly assembled to shout slogans or to sit on *dharna* in the best tradition of democracy. K-cube was currently lodged there in a smart tent on his mission, *Anshan.*

The smart tent was made of temperature-regulated weatherproof fabric, fitted with all modern amenities. In keeping with the *Dharna* tradition, a few mattresses covered with white sheets were lying on the floor along with a few long and round white cushions to give support. In the name of furniture, there was a single low-height writing desk, also known as a *Gandhi Desk.* The *Gandhi Desk* had gone out of fashion long ago and was put on display only during an *Adhiveshan* or *Anshan.* Since nobody ever wrote by hand during such momentous occasions, its only purpose was to indicate that the person sitting behind the desk was the leader. Symbolism is as powerful a tool in politics as in Art and Literature.

The tired-looking K-cube was sitting behind one such Gandhi desk as the lonely leader when Y2K and his gang trooped in. They were the first group of visitors since K-cube had ceremoniously embarked upon his *Anshan* twenty-four hours ago. K-cube was elated and received them warmly. Y2K was pleasantly surprised when K-cube recognized him and referred to him as the man in search of his manifesto. Y2K surveyed around the tent, which was dominated by a huge screen that prominently displayed the photo of K-cube in his heyday. In the background was a replica of a painting whose story Y2K knew well.

The painting titled 'Human First' was the first one ever drawn by a Pappu (a Popat upgraded with a Painting Appu), which was auctioned for over a million dollars. The Pappu was owned by an art dealer, and learned the nuances of painting from a popular painter known as '*Dadhi Wale Picasso*' or 'Bearded Picasso'. After learning the art from the master, Pappu churned out many paintings that were just ordinary, but the 'Human First' turned out to be particularly striking. Critics hailed this painting as a fine example of futurism, while a few others found in it a new fusion trend of surrealism and cubism. However, before the painting could be transferred to the highest bidder, a dispute arose between Pappu's owner and 'Bearded Picasso', both claiming a part of the proceeds from the auction, while the creator of the painting happened to be Pappu. To resolve the issue, a committee was appointed. The committee deconstructed the painting and uncovered some new facts. The Pappu had actually copied from a child's painting depicting a giant human hanging from a rainbow and given it a spin in the futurism style. Pappu had then painted its own distorted image to complete the background in the true surreal style of a *Dali.* New findings complicated the dispute as the number of claimants expanded. At this point, a PIL was filed by K-cube requesting the Court to declare the painting public property and donate the proceeds to the Artist Relief Fund. The Court promptly obliged, and K-cube's name got associated with the painting 'Humans First'. Y2K realized that K-cube was a man of substance after all, and not just a mere actor. Noticing Y2K's deep examination of the painting, K-cube casually commented,

'I find this painting as an appropriate logo for the movement that I have launched to save Bollywood and indeed every art form,' and pointed to the line emblazoned across the painting. It read, '*I am Human. Human First.*'

The concept seemed a little abstract to Y2K as he could not fathom the context. K-cube smiled and explained,

'Like you, most people do not understand what this movement is all about. They think that I am a cranky artist or an old-fashioned loser who resists change. Far from it. Change is good, but it is even better when it is in the right direction.

The best for us is that we control the change before we lose direction.'

K-cube now had the attention of everyone as he continued,

'When the first Popat was cast as a double for the difficult stunts, I welcomed the change. It was the right use of technology, enhancing safety and performance. Then Popats were used in the extras' roles, and no one complained. Production houses loved Popats because they worked in three shifts, never complained, were never late, and never made a mistake. But Popats could not be given the meatier roles because they could not emote, could not deliver the dialogues in style, and could not act.'

'Yes, I know the problems with early Popats. I worked for an Appu development company that specialized in dealing with speech, feelings, and emotions,' interjected Kattu and continued,

'Initial Popat prototypes were just advanced robots fitted with the power of supercomputers and AI. They understood the text and speech and reacted to them according to the algorithm and AI. Then they were imbued with the five senses of touch, hearing, sight, smell, and taste although they had no physical needs like humans. It opened up a vast area of development in Popat science. A stimulus to these five senses produces a vast range of feelings depending on the situation, context, and environment. A human internalizes these feelings and expresses them in the form of emotions. If Popats were to serve as obedient servants of humans, it was essential to understand the feelings and emotions, codify, and convert them to algorithms. In order to codify them, we needed standards. They were readily available in the ancient text of *Natyashastra of Bharat Muni*, which propounded eight *Rasa*. They are *Sringar* (attractiveness), *Hasya* (laughter, comedy), *Raudra* (fury), *Karunya* (compassion, mercy), *Vibhats* (disgust, aversion), *Bhayanak* (horror, terror), *Veer* (heroism), *Adbhut* (wonder, amazement). A ninth *Rasa* of *Shantam* (peace, tranquility) was added later to make it Navarasa. An actor displays his feelings or emotions through any one *Rasa* or a combination of them. So we managed to digitize them, label them, and process them with the help of huge databases, complex functions, self-updating matrices, and algorithms. The Popats could now decipher and understand feelings and emotions,' explained Kattu to his audience which was listening with rapt attention.

K-cube knew all about it and responded,

'Understanding human emotions and feelings was only one part of the development. The other part was how to react to the stimuli from the five senses and to other people's feelings and emotions. This was difficult and uncharted territory. It was, however, realized by the developers that Popats themselves need not have any feelings or emotions and that they only need to respond. The response standard that was wisely incorporated in the Core of Popats approximated the *Shantam* (peace, tranquility) *Rasa* to make the transactions between humans and Popats two-way. This worked wonderfully well in every field that Popats were put to use, except in the movie industry. After all, you cannot put a saintly creature in every role that a movie has. Popats could raise the pitch, modulate the dialogue delivery, or modify their expressions within the limits of '*Shant Rasa*' but that was the maximum range of their acting, or rather reacting, which did not click. The big boys of Bollywood took note and wanted Popats who could act and not just react.

It was a subject that Kattu knew intimately and so he expounded,

'Our company developed the first Popat for Bollywood that could act well. We again relied on the standards for acting set out in the *Natyasastra* which lists eight *bhava* corresponding with eight corresponding *Rasas.* They are *Rati* (love), *Hasya* (mirth), *Shoka* (sorrow), *Krodh* (anger), *Utsah* (energy), *Bhaya* (disgust), and *Vismaya* (astonishment). We developed an Acting Appu for each *bhava* and algorithms that would connect them with the other interfaces. Now Bollywood had the *Atpat* or '*Actor T*heatrical Popat' who could fit into the roles of a comedian, a villain, or a good Samaritan. Producing Heroes out of Atpats was still difficult since they needed charisma to make the cut for a hero. It took years of hard work to decode the charisma conundrum. Proprietary technology now could produce Atpats who had the personality, presence, and panache of a Sylvester Stallone, Johnny Depp, Tom Hanks, Amitabh Bachchan, Shahrukh Khan or Rajnikant. This gave Bollywood a tremendous head-start as they churned out hit after hit.'

K-cube patiently waited for Kattu to conclude and then chipped in,

'You have beautifully described the evolution of Popat technology in filmdom in an 'all is well' manner. However, all tales do not fit into the 'lived happily thereafter' category. Bollywood has created larger-than-life Popat heroes and, in the process, started a dangerous trend. Now everyone wants their Popats to be heroes molded in the image of these Bollywood heroes, and therein lies the problem. In order to create the charismatic Atpats, the Core and Gate layers were modified, enabling them to obviate the constraints put by the rule of obedience and *Shant Rasa.* If such modifications are allowed in all the Popats, we would be putting the safety and well-being of human life at risk. It is obvious that we need to put humans first. And the danger lurks not only at a physical level but at a subconscious level as well. The purpose of performing art is to raise the level of consciousness, but the use of unregulated technology in art can produce the opposite result. Bollywood has put the machine called *Atpat,* the demonic but charismatic Popat on a pedestal, and the man now looks up to a Popat, learns from a Popat, and worse, acts like a Popat. This has to stop.'

Lattu at this stage protested and said, 'You are taking the line of doomsayers and scaremongers who predict that the machines will one day rule the world. Or, are you influenced by old movies like Matrix? The reality is that these machines, called Popats, and their numerous versions are governed by the rule of obedience which says, 'I am Popat. Obedience first'. As a corollary, Popats will never be able to rule the man.'

K-cube replied with equanimity,

'It is true that Popats will never rule us. But it will be a pity if efficiency, style, and technique that characterizes Popats take precedence over feelings, emotions, and compassion which characterize us. It will be a pity if the acting becomes the substance, the algorithm becomes creativity, and the virtual becomes reality. It will be a pity if in the process, humans become Popats. And I am not talking out of my imagination. We are slowly getting enamored of the persona that is digitized and programmed. We want to act out the script instead of living life. And in our eagerness to create machines that are larger than life, we are putting the safety and security of humans at risk. We, therefore, need to remember that we are humans and should put humans first. Always.'

Y2K, who was silently engrossed in the discussions so far, understood the importance of what K-cube expounded and said respectfully,

'I appreciate the deep insight that you have given us. I am here with my team to support your movement. If I include your concerns in my manifesto, will you kindly break your *Anshan* and support my campaign?' K-cube looked at Y2K, who was dressed like a *Neta*, but sounded like a genuine person, and nodded.

Y2K's gang thanked Vartika for ordering an extra-heavy breakfast as lunchtime passed without any food being served. Slowly, a small crowd started to assemble. Vartika had formulated a 'law of crowds' which stated that: if X number of people assemble at a place in protest, the crowd will automatically swell over a period of time in a bell curve. She estimated that the crowd would peak at around five in the evening which would be the right time to break the *Anshan* and had arranged the presence of Jholus accordingly.

Four Jholus appeared in the spacious smart tent just before Y2K offered a glass of orange juice to K-cube and requested that he break his *Anshan*. As K-cube drank the juice, there was a round of applause. K-cube thanked Y2K for extending his support and for his pledge to carry the movement forward. Y2K then took to the podium that Vartika had so thoughtfully arranged. He spoke with an intensity that perhaps *Anshan* brought on.

'My dear fellow citizens, It is a privilege and an honor to stand here today in support of Kalakar Kautuk Kumar, who is an icon and the pride of the whole Kautuk Mandal. We fondly remember the roles he played in Bollywood movies. But in times to come, we shall remember him for his great insight, wisdom, and the movement that he has initiated. The world of 2050 is vastly different from what most of us have known, and in the last two decades, it has changed at a pace so rapid that we are in danger of losing our balance. The invasion of Popats in Bollywood is a prime example of the perils that we shall face if we do not regulate the pace of technology, especially the one involving Popats. Uncontrolled use of technology is distorting our art, affecting our creativity, our behavior, and our ability to connect. Allowing Popats to play with emotions and feelings is like playing with fire. By centering our entire lives around Popats, we are in danger of losing our identity, our soul, and our sensibilities. We, therefore, need to wake up and remind ourselves that we are humans, and humans should always come first, whatever our endeavor or enterprise.

It is a task that needs global action, but we need to start locally. Accordingly, I have decided to extend full support to the movement initiated by K-cube by making 'B for Bollywood' as part of my manifesto. If I get elected, all movies that use *Atpats*, that is, Popats with a modified Core and Gate, will be banned. I shall also establish a 'Humans First Commission' that will implement the 'Human First' policy in all forms of human enterprise or endeavor. I do not believe in banning any form of art or expression. However, if the value added by humans in any form of art is found to be less than fifty percent by the Commission, it will attract double taxation in order to create a level playing field. I am sure this 'Human First' policy will not only put Bollywood back on track but will also guide Kautuk Mandal to greater glory.

I pledge to put 'Humans First' as the guiding principle of my manifesto. To raise awareness about this movement, I adopt 'I am Human. Humans First' as my campaign slogan. I exhort all of you to support me in this endeavor. As a mark of your support, please repeat the slogan after me.'

Y2K then shouted, 'I am Human', and as if on cue, the crowd shouted, 'Humans First'. Y2K repeated the exercise three times with the crowd raising the decibel level each time. As Y2K felt the mesmerizing power of sloganeering firsthand, he felt exhilarated.

Jholus, though Popats themselves, did not detect a conflict of interest or a class bias against them in the whole proceeding since they were not programmed to have any interest of their own. They dutifully filed the reports of the event at Jantar-Mantar. Their captions varied from 'Bollywood inspires Kautukpur manifesto', 'Y2K raises slogan, K-cube breaks *Anshan*', to 'B for Bollywood leads to Humans First Commission', and 'Y2K and K-cube join hands'.

In the evening, Y2K and Vartika met for dinner in the same restaurant at the same time, and Vartika didn't ask whether they were meeting for business or a date. The restaurant owner, Mahesh Mahan, appeared and told Y2K how impressed he was with Y2K's 'Humans First' policy and informed him that his was the only restaurant in Kautukpur where human employees were more than eighty percent. Mr. Mahan was also rightly clued into the alphabetic menu, be it food or manifesto. He suggested *'Bajare ki Roti'* with *'Besan ke Gatte'* and *'Baghare Baingan'* for dinner. Vartika thanked Mahan for curating a wonderful manifesto of food beginning with the alphabet 'B' and returned to her analysis of the day.

'Today we have accomplished many things. Your political journey shifted from virtual to real when you marched to *Jantar Mantar* and participated in your first *Anshan.* We also got our first election slogan which is already making an impact. And that painting titled 'Human First' is perfect to be our election motif. I have already ordered a few prints with our name and slogan emblazoned and a Pigeon added to the design. But best of all, we got a celebrity supporter in K-cube. What more could one ask for in a day's campaign?' said Vartika animatedly.

'Maybe a few more votes,' answered Y2K smilingly as he finished his dessert of *'Besan ke Laddoo in Caramel Custard'*.

The votes did come in for Y2K, as he jumped seven places to occupy the fifty-second rank in the day's polling.

Chapter XVII

Breakfast meetings were by now turning into a predictable pattern. Everyone concentrated on food and small talk till Vartika intervened to initiate the discussion. So it was Vartika who opened up the discussion by saying,

'Guys, Lattu's assessment regarding ABC of the Indian mind-space, which is Astrology, Bollywood, and Cricket, was spot on.'

Everyone clapped for Lattu, who beamed. Vartika continued,

'Talking about astrology and Bollywood has given us a great start. So let us now talk about 'C' for cricket.'

'While we discuss cricket, why don't we switch on the BHPL match between 'Wonder Thunder' and 'Whirlwind Warriors'?' requested Mattu. Y2K, being a gracious host, obliged as the live match, in its full 3D-holographic glory, brought on by the 2050 version of *Vunic* flooded the *Adda.*

BHPL was the '*B*reakfast-time *H*ybrid-Cricket *P*remier *L*eague' that started in 2040 and featured ten hybrid teams of men and Popats, with each team representing a hundred *Mandals.* While the use of Popats in sports was only a decade-old phenomenon, leveraging computers and AI in sports began more than half a century ago. The most famous early demo of AI power was when IBM's supercomputer, Deep Blue, beat Gary Kasparov in chess in the 1990s. Outdoor games, though, remained unaffected for quite some time. The advent of Popats, however, changed the ball game altogether.

Popats intruded the cricket world with a back-door entry as ground staff, support staff, coaching staff, etc. Next, Popats replaced the field umpires which ruffled many white feathers. Being equipped with the best sensors, super three-sixty-degree vision, and exhaustive software, Popat umpires always produced unbiased and accurate results. This made the job of the third umpire redundant but they were still retained since interruptions on appeal generated significant advertising revenues.

Gradually, Popats began to be inducted as players as they learned their strokes and mastered bowling of all varieties. They were first inducted as a twelfth man in the hybrid teams, which generally helped in averting the bruised ego of the left-out player. Eventually, Popats emerged on the big stage, and all hybrid teams got to incorporate five Popats as a rule. The inception of BHPL made Hybrid-Cricket very popular. By 2044, the role of Popats in cricket had fully evolved.

In 2045, an *A*ll-Popat *C*ricket *P*remier *L*eague called ACPL was launched, which featured teams comprising only Popat players. ACPL team owners spared no money in acquiring and training the best possible Popat talent from anywhere in the world. These Popats were unaffected by pressure, impervious to how the crowd behaved, did not tire, did not slacken, and their concentration never wavered. As a result, the matches in ACPL always produced consistent shots, precise bowling, a nail-biting finish, and bumper records, which made the league popular enough to occupy prime time.

It was the BHPL and ACPL rivalry that immediately became the point of discussion.

'I prefer to watch ACPL rather than BHPL. BHPL sucks. Half of the human players give a below-par performance with the same excuse of playing under pressure. They get without scoring in double digits, miss three catches out of six offered, or leak runs like a torrent. There is no consistency at all,' complained Kattu.

'Don't you know that the game of cricket is full of uncertainties, and it sparkles with individual brilliance? Instead of appreciating the nature and spirit of the game, you are enamored of ACPL which is the epitome of mediocrity. Your All-Popat teams may be efficient but not brilliant. To my mind, watching the ACPL is awful,' retorted Mattu.

Mattu was referring to the fact that even in 2050, though the processing power of Popats exceeded that of a human mind, the physical ability of Popats could not surpass the best that humans could produce. Humans are not only the most intelligent species but the most optimized ones in physical activities as well. A Popat in 2050 performed all the physical activities with the same ease as a human. But different physical activities in Popats required a trade-off between their limited resources, which gave just above-average results when optimized. Therefore, a Popat could not run like Usain Bolt, dribble like Pele, swim like Phelps, or bat like Sachin. In other words, they were not designed to be brilliant. Kattu, however, was not convinced and retorted,

'You should know that cricket is a team game and not an individual sport. A team in which every player produces just about an average performance will win nine out of ten times as compared to another team that relies on the brilliant performance of one or two. That is why an all-Popat team will always defeat an all-human team nine out of ten times. I can bet on it.'

'What I can bet on is that soon there will be no human players left to play cricket if the current trend continues,' butted in Sattu.

'You are being cynical as usual,' retorted Kattu.

'Not at all. All-human teams are already extinct and the hybrid-teams are barely surviving. They are plagued by the 'rotating quota system' engineered by the likes of Kappuswamy, who control the Mandal Cricket Associations. More often than not, the players nominated through '*sifarish*' turn out to be poor performers compared to Popats. This further justifies Kappuswamy's demand to remove the cap on the number of Popats in a team. Ultimately, only Popats will play cricket. The humans will become mere spectators, busying themselves with the immense statistics that the artificial game will churn out. I think we should put a stop to such nonsense if we get elected,' said Sattu.

'I don't think it will be appropriate for the *Mandal* government to interfere in the matters of sport,' objected Kattu.

'When, where, and how the state should intervene is a delicate matter. Let us leave that to Y2K to decide,' said Lattu in an obvious attempt to extricate himself from the heated debate.

Cricket was Y2K's passion as well, and he was quick to answer.

'The issue is not about the state versus cricket but is more about technology versus cricket. I am not against the use of technology in sports, but I am against technology overtaking and overwhelming the sport. We need to preserve the game of cricket the way we know it. So for a change, why don't we play cricket today the old-fashioned way?'

Y2K's suggestion was enthusiastically endorsed. Vartika and Mattu were chosen as captains, and they agreed to play a match at the *Lal Maidan* in the evening. *Lal Maidan* was an unfenced, dusty patch of land, opposite the Kautuk Mandal Cricket Association (KMCA), which was neither a park nor a proper playground. Yet, once upon a time, one could find many teams playing cricket from morning to evening, accompanied by shouts, laughter, and occasional fights. However, the cricket players gradually disappeared, and now only an eerie silence pervaded as no one trod the ground.

It was almost after a decade that *Lal Maidan* saw the stumps being installed as Vartika and Mattu mustered their teams for a game of good old cricket. Lattu inveigled himself into Vartika's team, and so did Kattu. Sattu and Y2K opted to play under Mattu's captaincy, who seemed to be supremely confident of winning as he introduced Jyotsna Javeri along with her gang of four players. Jyotsna was the only Kautuk Mandal player to ever play for nationals and would have been a big celebrity if women's cricket did not suffer from gender bias. Vartika, on the other hand, had roped in five out of the six supporters who had originally endorsed Y2K. Y2K was pleased to meet them, as he wondered how cricket was able to bring people out of their closets. The ace up Vartika's sleeve was, however, twelve-year-old Hritik Sharma, who was already being touted as a cricket prodigy. Her team was complete when Inspector Godbole rambled in whites instead of his familiar khaki.

Mattu won the toss and elected to bat. As the wickets tumbled, Jyotsna and her gang stemmed the rot to put up a decent total. Vartika's team had an equally perilous start but Hritik dug in heels and took the game to the last over with six runs needed on the last ball. As Jyotsna bowled a vicious delivery, Hritik audaciously lofted the ball that soared and soared to cross the ground and shattered the glass windows of the KMCA. Unmindful of the damage, Jyotsna and her gang lifted Hritik, celebrating victory in defeat. It was as if the beauty and purity of the game had uplifted the spirit all around.

Vartika had managed to rope in a record number of Jholus for the match, though *Lal Maidan* was not on their usual beat. Many spectators had gathered by the time the match ended, allowing Y2K to make his manifesto speech after the game. Y2K spoke spiritedly.

'Dear Citizens of Kautuk Mandal,

The agenda of the day is 'C' for cricket. But before I begin, let me apologize to KMCA for the damage done to their premises. I promise to get the repairs done expeditiously at my cost. But let me remind you that about three decades ago, the shattering of these windows was a regular phenomenon since this was a ground where the atmosphere reverberated with cricket chants. That atmosphere gradually changed as technology intruded on sports and people got closeted indoors. It should, therefore, come as no surprise that a cricket match was played here after almost a decade. And what a remarkable game it was, with Jyotsna giving a glimpse of her glorious past and Hritik showing what the future beckons for him. More importantly, it brought back the joy, the spirit, and the camaraderie that we seem to have lost touch with.

To preserve and promote the purity, simplicity, and essence of the game, I propose to introduce a scheme called '*Gali Gali Mein Cricket*', if elected. This is to counter the complete Popatization of the game of cricket that people like Kappusawmy are seeking in their pursuit of money and power. While my manifesto will detail the scheme, I also propose to introduce some safeguards for the game. Any team that includes a Popat will be levied a Popat-Tax of twenty percent per Popat. Such a step will provide a level playing field between the new formats of cricket and old-fashioned cricket. My proposals may annoy powerful office-bearers like Kappuswamy, but they will save the game of cricket for the future generation. I fervently hope that in the years to come, it will be the likes of Hritik and not the p-Popats who will come out victorious.'

As Y2K concluded his speech, he brought Hritik to the forefront for a long round of applause. Jholus, in the meantime, had their headlines ready, which varied from fair, to neutral, to downright critical but attracted good TRPs. The headlines read 'Y2K offers *Gali Gali Mein cricket*', 'Y2K to introduce Popat-tax in cricket', 'Windows broke off the broke KMCA', 'Y2K bats for stone-age in cricket', and 'A match, a message, and lots of nostalgia'.

When they met for dinner, Y2K was exuberant, but Vartika seemed to be pensive. Y2K was eager to discuss the match, but Vartika was thinking of its aftereffects.

'The positive from today's match is that we have been able to bring out your supporters in good numbers. Your original proposer, seconder, and others will form the second tier of our campaign management team along with the gang of Jyotsna. The negative part is that by strongly criticizing Kappuswamy, you have taken him on a little too soon. He is leading the race so far and is not going to take any criticism lying down,' said Vartika.

True to her prediction, Kappuswamy appeared on Channel Three. To an innocuous question from the Jhallu of Channel Three, he answered pompously, 'I condemn the vandalism that took place in the KMCA premises today. It was instigated by a desperate candidate, Y2K, who seems to be Lost.'

'What do you mean by 'Lost'?' asked the Jhallu rather deferentially.

'By 'Lost', I mean '*L*eader *O*f *S*mall *T*hings'. Look at what he has talked about so far - Astrology, Bollywood, and now Cricket. Kautuk Mandal does not need a Leader Of Small Things,' replied Kappuswamy as he gave his trademark look with a scornful laugh.

Y2K was stung. Before he could protest about the unfairness of it all, Vartika reminded him that everything was fair in love, war, and realpolitik.

'The good thing is that you are getting noticed. Unfair criticism is the price you pay for getting noticed,' remarked Vartika like a teacher, and Y2K promptly asked like a student,

'What should we do now? You certainly would have thought through some strategy.' Vartika nodded as she spoke, 'You can do nothing about it. Just ignore it and change your track. The impact of the barb will hopefully wear off quickly. In the meantime, concentrate on the food.'

The food consisted of '*Chaat*', '*Chapli Kabab*', and '*Chicken Vindaloo*'. By the time '*Carrot Halwa*' was served, the voting results were announced. Vartika declared that despite Kappuswamy's stinging barb, improvement in the rankings by five positions was a decent achievement.

Y2K that day was not unduly worried about the votes and the rating. He slept well and dreamed of a cricket match where fours and sixes rained, unplayable deliveries were bowled, impossible catches were taken, and he marched to victory amidst cheering crowds.

Chapter XVIII

The gang of Y2K had seen Kappuswamy hurling the barb 'Leader Of Small Things' and wanted to rebut and retaliate. It was *Amritsari Lassi's* breakfast and not Vartika's counsel that dulled their sense of revenge. As usual, they veered around to the view that Vartika was best placed to suggest the right strategy in this matter. Vartika was quick to open the discussion on strategy.

'When on the backfoot, a good politician follows the well-trodden political path. When in doubt, a wise politician reinvents the old issues. Over the last seven to eight decades, there have been four broad issues that politicians have successfully exploited. The first one was *Garibi Hatao*, the second related to *Roti, Kapada Aur Makan*, and the third was about *Bijli, Pani Aur Sadak*. But the evergreen path that politicians love to tread is that of *Vikas*, or Development. You can take your pick,' elaborated Vartika.

'The issue of *Garibi Hatao* is dead since poverty was officially declared eradicated in 2037. It led to unexpected situations when assured vote banks disappeared, *langars* went unattended, and many NGOs shut down for lack of poor clientele. Funnily, with the number of poor people dwindling, many politicians and officials turned poorer as well since their source of 'cut' income from subsidies and freebies for the poor dried up,' answered Mattu, who liked to dish out figures and analysis in his unique manner.

'That is a piquant analysis, but not a very accurate one. The fact is that poverty has disappeared, but not the poor. Every decade, the rich are getting richer and the poor are getting poorer,' protested Sattu, who always saw himself as the champion of the poor and underdogs.

'That is the consequence of the natural structure of society being a pyramid. The large population of the poor forms the base, tapering off with different layers of the middle class as you reach the steep top. The best a politician can do is to offer subsidies and freebies, hoping that it will reduce the base of the pyramid,' commented Kattu.

'The best we should be doing is to change the structure itself from a pyramid to that of a *Kalash* or a round pot that has a bulge in the middle, enough room at the top, and a bottom that is small but well-rounded. Such a structural change can only be brought about through development, development, and more development. In that sense, removing poverty and development are the two sides of the same coin,' espoused Sattu.

'That settles it. D for development is going to be our manifesto theme for today,' said Lattu emphatically.

'We have been beating the drum of development for well over half a century, so much so that this slogan has now become a bit trite and tiresome. In any case, as we enter 2050, we have seen enough development. Last year, we became the largest economy in the world. We have the highest number of Popats, Concons, and 7G subscriptions. We have the largest number of smart cities, and our Industry 5.0 churns out smart products, topping both in terms of revenue and quantity. And to manage all this, we have the largest, youngest, and smartest talent pool. Development is now in auto-pilot mode. Politicians do not matter much,' interjected Kattu.

'Seasoned politicians are hardly ever daunted by the prospect of irrelevance. Making promises is their business, and exaggeration is the virtue they employ while making those promises. Look at the promises made by your fellow contestants regarding the development. All of them have promised the moon,' said Lattu.

'Then let us promise our voters the moon,' replied Y2K, who had kept quiet so far.

The whole gang was taken aback by Y2K's remark. Y2K was not given to making light comments, but what he said was very uncharacteristic of him. Y2K saw the quizzical look on his colleagues' faces and smiled as he explained.

'I am saying it in all seriousness. I want to promise my voters a piece of the moon. You are all aware that space exploration and colonization are going to be the next big thing in the latter half of this century. Big space stations are already as common as the skyscrapers in this city, and space travel is more frequent than an expedition to Mount Everest. The Popat technology, however, is going to be a game changer. Already, several spaceships are carrying specialized p-Popats to the moon along with tools and equipment. They will set up a self-sustained colony for themselves and start exploring the moon. Ten years from now, they will perhaps send the first lot of processed rare minerals back to the earth. By the end of thirty years, there will be many Popat-colonies on the moon as well as on Mars. They will then construct small colonies that are habitable for humans. By the end of this century, humans would start inhabiting them. The next century will see humans colonizing the moon and Mars, and maybe a few other terrestrial bodies. The next big discovery, the next big opportunity, the next big competition, and the next big battleground will be space. Those who do not act now will be literally left behind,' elaborated Y2K with a passion that did not surprise his friends.

It was Y2K's passion for space that had shaped his adult life. As a child, he dreamed of becoming an astronaut but ended up being a consultant for a space agency dedicated to building space stations. It was here that he met his wife, Vyoma, who was training to be an astronaut. Three years after their marriage, Vyoma made her maiden space flight. Thereafter, she literally lived up to her name, which meant 'the one who lives in the sky'. She gradually spent more and more time in space and was currently among the top twenty astronauts who had spent more than a hundred thousand hours in space. Though Y2K resented the long duration of separation, he was mighty proud of his wife and believed in what she did.

Kattu voiced the question that was on everyone's mind when he asked, 'Your vision is inspiring, but how does it fit into the election manifesto of development?'

'Well, I propose to develop a Kautukpur Colony on the Moon and Mars in the next twenty-five years, for which the work must start now. To that end, I intend to commit one percent of Mandal revenue for space-related activities, make space start-ups tax-exempt for ten years, nurture a space ecosystem in Kautukpur, and develop space-related skills amongst the young. I hope the voters realize that development in space enhances the development on earth,' answered Y2K, hoping for approving nods.

Sattu, however, was not convinced. He asked the pertinent question.

'Many voters may not relate to your lofty ideas, and 'we owe it to our future generation' argument. Despite all that we have achieved, we are still dubbed a 'just about developed' country. There are still a hundred million people who don't own Popats, twenty percent of habitation is not accessible by autonomous vehicles, and a million and a half people do not even possess Concon, which has been declared a basic necessity. I think there is a serious issue of 'Development Deficit' which needs to be addressed first. Otherwise you will still be called '*Lost*', meaning a '*L*eader of *S*mall *T*hings'.'

'You have a valid point, Sattu, and I certainly do not want to be labeled as '*Lost*'. I agree that being sensitive to the reality on the ground is more urgent than promoting a fancy program for space. Accordingly, I propose to set up a 'Humans First Fund' by levying a small surcharge on all transactions done by Popats. The fund will then be used to develop common infrastructure that will help in diminishing the development deficit,' answered Y2K. His balancing act satisfied Sattu.

Y2K repeated the same thoughts in the evening in his regular briefing at Hyde Park, and the audience seemed to approve them as well. Jholus promptly came up with simple headlines like 'D for Development' and 'Y2K proposes Humans First

Fund' to tedious ones like 'Y2K espouses dual development path' and 'Development model that straddles both the moon and earth'. The standout headline, however, was 'Y2K promises the moon'.

Y2K was not sure how people would receive his development pitch. However, any doubts that Y2K had were laid to rest when he met Vartika for dinner at their favorite restaurant. The restaurant owner, Mahan, appeared as soon as they were seated. He was accompanied by his twelve-year-old daughter. The cute little girl introduced herself to Y2K and said, 'I am Mishti, which means sweet. I liked your idea of developing a colony on the moon and Mars. I will open up a café chain in those colonies when I grow up.'

Y2K laughed affectionately and said,

'That is an excellent idea, Mishti, but are you aware of the challenges of running a café on the moon? There would be no fresh ingredients for your signature dish; cooking would take ages and yet not give the desired texture and aroma; carrying dishes to the table would require a juggler's skill; and saucers and cutlery would fly around at the slightest push.'

Mishti, however, was dead serious, as she said,

'I am aware of these challenges and I have been working on solving these problems in my spare time. I have recently published a paper on growing vegetables and their cooking techniques on the moon, and will be ready with a prototype in a year once I get the funding.'

Y2K looked at Mishti Mahan, aged twelve, with amazement and respect as he said, 'I am sure you will work it all out.

Maybe I'll be lucky enough to visit one of your cafés on the moon someday. In the meantime, could you please suggest some Indian food here on earth, starting with alphabet D?'

Mishti gave him a sweet smile as she said,

'Try our *Dahi Kebab*, *Dal Bukhara*, and *Daab Chingri*. Follow it up with *Dal Halwa*. I have instructed the chef to use some of my new cooking techniques to enhance the texture, aroma, and taste of these dishes. Enjoy your meal.'

As Mishti left, she rubbed off her optimism on both Y2K and Vartika. Y2K instinctively knew that the voter of 2050 was confidently optimistic when he received more than expected votes and improved his ranking by four positions.

Both Y2K and Vartika were in high spirits when they came out of the restaurant after a superb meal and a favorable result. Their spirits, however, dampened as the electricity across Kautukpur went out just after boarding the autonomous taxi. Despite being a full-moon day, it was pitch dark due to clouds. The autonomous taxi algorithm detected that its navigational cameras were unable to function safely and decided to halt. It also asked the passengers to dismount for their safety. As they did so, their Concon informed them that the blackout's cause was unknown and the restoration would take some time. Concon further suggested that the fastest way to reach their destination would be to walk. Both complied.

It was the first time in their lives that they were taking a long walk in the middle of the night. The clouds hid the awkwardness that they both felt initially. As they walked silently, Vartika clung to Y2K's arm, and they felt warmth despite the chilly breeze that was blowing lightly. As the full moon suddenly came out of the clouds, they realized that their arms were wrapped around each other. Instinctively, Y2K did what he had not done in the last twenty years. He softly let out a very old Hindi song that was aptly filmed in almost a similar setting. Surprisingly, Vartika remembered the song and responded to the duet in her melodious voice. It was beautiful and almost surreal. Just as Vartika kissed Y2K goodnight, the power returned. The moonlight that had created the surreal effect faded. As Y2K's eyes adjusted to the bright lights, he had a sudden nagging feeling of being followed. He looked for the moon, but it had again vanished behind the clouds.

Chapter XIX

The electricity outage last night was the natural topic of discussion over breakfast. While Y2K and Vartika remained awkwardly silent, the conversation turned nostalgic for the rest of the gang.

'When I was a kid, electricity availability in our village was an exception rather than a rule. But playing hide-and-seek with electricity was such a fun. When electricity would make its rare appearance during summers, we kids used to gather under the solitary fan and play Ludo. As soon as the electricity would vanish, we all used to go flying kites. We never had to study during the night time, and '*bijli nahi thi*' was a more acceptable excuse than the '*pet mein dard tha*' for not doing the homework,' reminisced Sattu. Mattu shared his experience, saying,

'If I recall correctly, while we children could cope, adults were frustrated. My grandmother was an avid watcher of those *saas-bahu* TV serials, and the electricity would somehow fail exactly at the moment when their quarrel reached the climax, making her grumble a lot. My mother was exasperated, waiting for electricity to operate the mixer or the oven. And my father was always annoyed because he could never fully charge his precious 2G phone, which would conveniently get discharged during a call from his boss.'

Lattu joined the banter and added,

'Power outages agitated people to no end, but they were powerless except for their voting power. Those in power, didn't care about the power and were occasionally voted out of power. Those eying for power, promised cheaper power but forgot to improve the power situation once they were voted into power. While power played hide and seek with the voters, politicians too played hide and seek with the voters. Such power games continue even today.'

Kattu had a different perspective as he intervened,

'We always overestimate the power of politicians. They only know how to beat the drum, hurl the blame, and take credit for anything positive. Things don't change on the back of politicians as they claim but change on the back of technology, investment, and enterprise of the people. We are in 2050 and a lot has changed on that front since the year 2000.'

Lattu, the CTO, was quick to acknowledge, as he added,

'Indeed, a lot has changed, especially on the technology front. Due to technology breakthroughs since 2030s, non-conventional sources have become mainstream, and numerous new sources of energy have been added. More importantly, technologies like AI, IoT, and 7G have made everything smart, helping save electricity. Every watt saved is an extra watt generated. Smart grids, smart devices, and smart meters are doing exactly that. So, as the generation capacity has increased and become green, the consumption is controlled and smartly managed.'

'Why is it that despite all those advancements, we are still having an erratic power supply, exemplified by yesterday's blackout?' asked Sattu.

Kattu answered,

'That is because the Mandal Electricity Supply System, or the MESS as they call it, is incompetent, inefficient, and indifferent. The system is not as smart as it should be, investments are abysmal, and their policies have led to profligacy. The result is that the MESS is in such a mess.'

'In that case, why don't we take up the issue of 'E' for electricity or energy? It will fit well with the strategy of re-engineering old issues like '*bijli, pani, and sadak*'. Y2K can present this as a manifesto item for the day in his speech at Hyde Park,' suggested Lattu. Vartika smiled and said,

'Making speeches can move the public a little bit. But if you want to move the system, you have to come out into the street and stage a '*pradarshan*' or demonstration.'

Mattu said, 'It is easier said than done. In 2050, nobody likes to venture out into the street. You can of course try and organize a virtual demonstration with *Ubiq* participants.' Vartika smiled again and said,

'A virtual demonstration will not have even one percent of the intensity that a real demonstration can generate. Politics is not a virtual cup of tea. You need real people and real drama to make the real impact in politics.'

Sattu immediately questioned, 'Why bring in *Dharna* politics in something that is a common concern?'

'Because politics is all about dealing with everybody's concerns. *Bhashan*, *Dharna*, and *Pradarshan* are legitimate tools to address such concerns. Y2K has done enough of *Bhashan*. We also joined one *Anshan*. It is now time that we graduate to holding a *Dharna-Pradarshan* of our own,' replied Vartika.

None in the Y2K gang had ever participated in a *Dharna-Pradarshan* or a protest of any kind. Kattu had his usual doubts and asked,

'For a meaningful political protest, you need at least one and a half dozen people. We are only half a dozen. Getting another dozen people is a herculean task in 2050. These days, with marriages going virtual, it is difficult to gather a dozen people even for a *Barat*.'

Vartika smiled again and said,

'Isn't election a paradox as well as a blessing in disguise? While an election creates dispute, division, and discord, it also draws people out of their comfort zone to express their opinions, articulate their aspirations, or merely rub shoulders with fellow citizens. For that reason, gathering more than a dozen people is eminently possible.'

To which Kattu said,

'You need a committed cadre, hiring power, or charisma to mobilize. We are not in that league as yet.'

Vartika replied calmly,

'You have a valid point. We need to break into the big league step by step. That is why you need an election strategist like me. Let me remind you of more than three dozen candidates who have withdrawn or have been eliminated so far. I have been in touch with them, and a dozen will come on board.' Y2K smiled appreciatively and enquired, 'I take it that you have worked out all the modalities. Is there anything else that we need to work out?' 'Yes, we need to finalize the slogans,' replied Vartika. Sattu responded, 'Why worry about that? There are standard slogans like '*inquilab zindabd, jo ham se takraega, choor choor ho jaega, gali gali mein shor hai - xyz chor hai*', which can be used in any demonstration on any issue.' 'I agree that these are universal slogans and will form the bulk of our repertoire. However, we need a few catchy and earthy slogans of our own to capture the essence. Right slogans are the most valuable soft assets of any campaign,' replied Vartika.

Kattu was a marketing genius. With a little help from Sattu, he came up with these gems of slogans: '*Chalti gadi udati titli - hamein chahiye poori Bijli; Yeh kaisi man mani hai – Bijli ani jani hai; Nakara aur namakul – unki hogi batti gul, Y2K ko lao - Mandal sahi chalao*'. Every slogan met with a roar of approval, and Y2K gang was ready for their first protest.

The Y2K gang had the first-mover advantage as they moved to the MESS headquarters immediately after the breakfast meeting. Vartika took the lead and raised the mix of slogans that had been discussed and agreed upon. Even for the uninitiated, the slogans, when shouted in unison, worked as adrenaline boosters.

Protests were not uncommon even in 2050, and the security Popats had been programmed with a standard operating procedure, which kicked in when the Y2K party assembled and raised slogans. As soon as the decibel level of slogans crossed the threshold limit, the security Popat informed his Clown, who in turn alerted the Gappu-in-charge of MESS. The Gappu decided on a two-pronged strategy to deal with the situation. He issued a press statement attributing the blackout to excessive demand and the 'dice of destiny'. Simultaneously, he requested the police disperse the protestors and put them in jail. The press statement was promptly picked up by the waiting Jholus, but Inspector Godbole took his usual fifty minutes to appear on the scene.

Y2K had asked everyone to be peaceful, but Vartika insisted that a little sound and fury would do no harm. So it was that as soon as Inspector Godbole appeared on the site, the sloganeering reached its crescendo. When Inspector Godbole warned them to disperse or face arrest, he was greeted with even louder shouts and raised fists. Inspector Godbole was a professional and moved with alacrity. He called enforcement and encircled Y2K and Vartika. Anticipating this, Vartika put up a mock resistance, diverting attention from Y2K. It allowed Jholu Number One from Channel Number One, who had positioned himself well, to thrust his microphone in front of the encircled Y2K. As he did so, Jholu1 asked, 'The MESS has given a statement on the blackout. Do you believe that?' Y2K replied, 'No, I don't.' 'Why?' persisted Jholu. 'Because I smell a rat there,' shouted Y2K over the ensuing din. Inspector Godbole noticed the little interaction with Jholu and quickly moved in. He grabbed Y2K and led him away. As he did so, he whispered in Y2K's ears, 'I am sorry to put you under arrest but I have orders from the top.' Y2K nodded in understanding and complied.

Ensconced comfortably in the prison, Y2K watched the full story unfold. Jholus had done their investigation and were gleefully recounting their findings. It transpired that well before the power load crossed the threshold, the Popat on duty went into sleep mode due to fatigue. 'Fatigue' in Popats was a classic case of poor maintenance, when their charging system, batteries, and self-healing systems degenerated and were not refurbished or replaced. Since the Popat failed to respond, the Mandal Load Dispatch Center informed the controlling Clown, which issued an instruction to the dispatch Center to send all the data. It was precisely at this moment that the Center lost its connectivity as the rats ate for dinner the critical electronic components of the Center's 7G communication system. The backup optical fiber route was already down courtesy of another colony of rats eating the underground optical fiber cable. Cut off from the outside world at peak load, the AI-enabled smart software interpreted it as an emergency and ordered the Center to shut itself down. When the Center tried to auto-restart in the degraded mode, it attempted to send data to the Clown as instructed but couldn't and consequently went into an endless loop.

The Jholus ran headlines screaming that it was not the 'dice of destiny' as declared by MESS but the shenanigans of the rats that had caused the havoc last night. As the channels beamed their conclusion, they juxtaposed the frame of Y2K shouting, 'Don't believe them. I smell a rat there.'

Y2K was released deliberately after the scheduled time for his Hyde Park meeting was over. He was, however, not unduly worried as the channels kept hammering the 'I smell a rat' theme. By the time Y2K finished his dinner with Vartika and the results of the day's poll came in, he had improved his position by three ranks. All thanks to the rats.

As Y2K and Vartika stepped outside the restaurant, they noticed the full moon hovering above the glittering smart street lights. They nodded and decided to walk. The lights today were shining bright and so was the spirit.

Chapter XX

The few hours spent in prison evoked a different reaction from each member of the Y2K gang. Y2K was apologetic for the inconvenience caused to the gang. Vartika termed it a professional hazard. Mattu felt it was an excessive use of power by the state. Kattu found it a sobering experience. Lattu thought it was a picnic, and Sattu was charged up for more of such action. However, all of them had one complaint, which was the denial of food while in detention. They had been detained just after lunchtime and released just before dinnertime. Consequently, they had gone without food for the whole day. Skipping a meal was no big deal, but the prospect of being denied food by design or circumstances was annoying. When Lattu suggested that 'F for Food' be their agenda for the day, they all nodded in approval except Kattu.

Kattu, as usual, countered and said, 'Food is a cliched and forgotten issue. Why dig it up now?'

'It is not a forgotten issue. It has been around for centuries. Remember the revolution triggered by the shortage of bread? Old-timers always considered *Roti, Kapada, Aur Makan* as the defining issues, with *Roti* being the number one priority since the poor had to constantly worry about '*Do Joon Ki Roti*'. We may perhaps re-engineer those worries and fears about food to garner some votes,' replied Lattu.

'I do not like exploiting the 'food for vote' strategy. In any case, *Do Joon Ki Roti* became a non-issue long ago. By 2035, it was not the lack of food but the issue of malnutrition that needed a fix. Power-hungry politicians tried a mix of tricks but failed to fix the problem of malnutrition. In 2040, the *Rodalino* technology solved even this conundrum,' responded Kattu.

Rodalino was a food technology pioneered in 2037 by Roti Research and Innovation, Inc. It was founded by an Indian AI technologist who abhorred cooking and was experimenting with 'smart-hybrid foods' dubbed 'sHmart' foods. Her research suggested that *Dal-Roti* was the healthiest and most sustainable diet for humankind, so she decided to invent a sHmart version of *Dal-Roti*. In 2037, all kinds of nutritional components needed by the human body were easily available in chemical form, but mixing them could at best produce a plastic *roti*. By then, the taste, texture, and flavor had also been coded and digitized. So she integrated those techniques to produce a sHmart *dal-roti* that was essentially a small candy-like cube. When she ate this cube for the first time, she exclaimed with joy '*Ro*ti-*Dal Inno*vated!' Her Eureka moment gave the new technology its name, *Rodalino*, and the cube was christened *Rodino*.

Initially, *Rodino* was cleverly marketed to the rich as an exclusive and expensive product with twin benefits. First, it saved time since you could eat it faster than fast food. Second, it guaranteed smart slimming. Smart slimming was a rage that essentially meant taking in an optimal amount of calories and nutrition prescribed by an AI-assisted nutritionist without eating anything unpalatable. Rodino fitted the bill, and the rich lapped it up.

Noticing the success of *Rodino,* the Chinese copied and produced *Noodlino.* Not to be left behind, the Japanese came up with *Sushino* and the Italians with their own *Pastino.* Americans, however, had the last laugh with their aggressive branding and marketing of *Burgino.* Faced with increased competition, *Rodalino* was transformed into an open platform that was integrated with Industry 5.0. Now, any food could be mass-produced anytime, anywhere, and in any quantity in the form of cheap and appealing cubes. This new industrialization of everyday food, known by the generic name, *Rodino* triggered an unprecedented socio-political revolution.

Politicians and governments of every color, leaning, and ideology rushed to put the *Rodino* cubes on the common man's plate, giving rise to the @Cube Movement. The UN declared war on malnutrition and advised poor countries on strategies to strengthen the @Cube Movement. NGOs of all hues chipped in to distribute cubes of all varieties all over the world. As the cubes became ubiquitous, the media ran stories showing malnourished children transforming into budding athletes, and experts produced voluminous reports documenting the impact of the @Cube Movement on world hunger. In 2042, the UN declared the world free of hunger and malnutrition.

In parallel to the @Cube Movement, another movement known as the @UnCook Movement was brewing. It had its origins in an obscure book titled 'Don't Cook'. The book argued that cooking was a human invention that had outlived its utility, cooking chores were the biggest hurdle in the true liberation of women and a few men, and cooking was the biggest contributor to pollution on earth. The book, therefore, exhorted all women and a few enlightened men to stop cooking. This clarion call found no followers until *Rodinos* appeared on the scene. The sHmart foods became cheaper and cooking food at home became dearer. As the economics turned in favor of the @UnCook Movement, people gradually gave up cooking. By 2047, within a decade of the invention of *Rodino*, people had forgotten how to cook.

None was better informed of the food scenario in 2050 than Sattu, and he was not the one to be easily persuaded. He continued the discussion by saying,

'Ahead of every successful technology, there lies a problem. *Rodalino*, no doubt, is one of the most successful technologies of this century. *Rodinos* are the healthiest, tastiest, and cheapest foods with the longest shelf life. They can be easily stored, transported, and consumed without the hassle of cooking. Yet, despite being a dream product, *Rodinos* have triggered a new wave of problems.'

Everyone knew about the 'new wave of problems'. The *Rodalino* tech smartly replicated nutrition, taste, and flavor but it could not replicate 'satisfaction'. When people ate *Rodino*, they got the calories and taste but not the satisfaction. Not satisfied, they ate more. They ate as per routine, they ate for change, they ate for taste, and they ate out of boredom. They ate for a variety of reasons, and unwittingly became victims of obesity that silently crept in. By 2045, ninety percent of the world had become obese. WHO as usual woke up late and issued a warning in 2047 about the spreading obesity pandemic which they named as '*Rodino Syndrome*'. The politicians and governments reacted to the '*Rodino Syndrome*' disparately. Those in power tried to shrug it off as not their problem, but the opposition of all hues united to demand a ban on *Rodinos*. When the pressure mounted, a few governments panicked and banned *Rodino*. Soon, they faced food shortages and riots, and the pressure mounted again to lift the ban.

The *Rodino* controversy attracted Jhallus all over the channels across the world, who took it upon themselves to further muddle the mess with the help of an assortment of Lappus. The *Left Lappus* saw it as a class division engineered by self-indulgent corporate powers. In their analysis, the world had been segmented in an unfair manner in which the decadent elites enjoyed the food prepared by humans, the bourgeois relied on the food made by Popats, and the proletariats had to make do with *Rodinos*. The *Leftout Lappus* pointed fingers at the exploitation of human cooks by the decadent elites. Terming it a capitalist conspiracy, they vowed to wage a war against it with violent protests and agitations. The *Right Lappus*, on the other hand, touted it as another success story of the free markets that helped banish hunger from the world. The *Righteous Right Lappus* were sure that there was a deep-rooted devious design to destabilize the world and vowed to thwart such designs through protests and demonstrations. Whenever it appeared that the controversy would die down, Jhallus gave a new spin to the arguments and kept the wheel of controversy spinning. Elections only added more spin to the *Rodino* controversy, and the Kautukpur elections were no exception.

'What is the spin given to the Rodino controversy in Kautukpur?' asked Lattu innocently. Vartika gave a brief update as she said, 'Kappuswamy, the leading candidate, is merrily riding two boats simultaneously. He has decried Roti Research Inc., the largest company in the country, and demanded action against it. At the same time, he has promised to open more free *Rodino* shops in Kautuk Mandal. Guru Panchal, the candidate ranked number two, wants a ban on *Rodinos* and is touting Popat Canteens serving free *Dal-Roti* as a solution. Prachandika Dagar, or Prada, the leading woman candidate at number three, is all out in favor of the @UnCook Movement. The position taken by the candidates lower down the ladder gets weirder, but the opinion, on the whole, is neatly divided fifty-fifty.'

Sattu was not happy with the local politics and said,

'I think everyone has got it wrong. I may be the odd man out, but I am no adherent of the @UnCook Movement. My Popat makes fine *Dal-Roti*, and I sometimes fancy *Rodinos* as well. But at times I yearn for the simple, home-cooked *Dal-Roti* made of natural ingredients, just like my mother used to make.'

Mattu chipped in and said,

'Food is a matter of personal choice. Why should we politicize it?'

'Anything that has the potential to induce votes will eventually get politicized. If we don't politicize, we may as well go for a picnic,' replied Vartika.

The bulb was lit. Lattu beamed and said,

'That's exactly what we should do. Let us go out for a picnic—a real picnic focused on real food. That will be our way of de-politicizing and distancing ourselves from the *Rodino* controversy and the @UnCook movement.'

Kattu, as usual countered, 'These days, no one goes for a real picnic given the humongous choices of virtual picnics, and no one cooks the real food thanks to the @Uncook Movement. So what sort of real picnic do we have in mind, and how are we going to relate it to our manifesto?'

Y2K, who was keeping quiet so far, finally spoke up,

'I agree with Lattu's suggestion. It will be a novel and different way of dealing with the issues concerning food. I remember when I was a kid, there used to be a lunch picnic or a feast called '*Goath*' where a traditional dish called '*dal-bati*' was cooked and served. We can revive this long-lost tradition by inviting a few of our supporters for a '*Goshthi*' or conference over a lunch picnic or a '*Goath*'. My instinct tells me that '*Goath par Goshthi*' may turn out to be a hit.' Everyone concurred with Y2K.

Organizing '*Goath*' took some effort. Sattu found a scenic place in Kautukgram that was popular a few decades ago but had been in disuse for a long time. With great difficulty, he also found a '*Maharaj*', a fast-depleting tribe of chefs who specialized in traditional cooking. Invitees discussed politics as the Maharaj cooked '*bati*' over a slow charcoal fire and then dunked them into clarified butter or 'ghee'. As they ate delicious '*bati*' with slow-cooked '*dal*', the discussion shifted from politics to a range of topics like the benefits of 'pure ghee', age-old recipes, and traditional techniques of cooking.

While everyone concentrated on '*Goath*' or the feast, Vartika was focused on the outcome of '*Goshthi*'. She had invited Jholus from several local channels. The three Jholus who turned up had no interest in food but had a good nose for headlines. They waited till the end, when they pushed their mics toward Y2K, who had become proficient in delivering a speech on demand. Y2K made an impromptu speech.

'Friends, I thank you all for coming to this '*Goath*', which is a wonderful tradition that we have almost forgotten. It is not just a feast but represents a way of life that celebrates food that is simple, earthy, natural, local, and enjoyable. It is a reminder to us that food can unite by bringing together friends, family, and community. Unfortunately, politics over food is dividing instead of uniting us. My manifesto advocates eschewing politics over food. I stand for a 'Humans First' rather than a 'Politics First' approach. I believe that technology and tradition can co-exist. I have no cavil with the new social order, new trends, and new lifestyles. However, I also root for going back to our roots, our traditions, and our customs.

My manifesto, therefore, is committed to bringing the necessary balance to matters related to food. If elected, I shall declare '*dal-roti*' as a fundamental right. My government will also open 'Rehabilitation Centers for the Obese' to deal with the '*Rodino Syndrome*'. Like digital literacy, 'cooking literacy' will be made a mandatory subject to be taught in schools. Natural foods will be ensured a level playing field *vis-a-vis* sHmart foods by means of differential taxation. One day in a month will be declared a '*Goath*' day to be included in the list of optional holidays. And finally, your favorite dish, '*dal-bati*', will be given the status of 'Kautukpur Mandal State Dish', to be made tax-free whenever and wherever it is served. In the end, I exhort all of you to indulge in more of '*Goath par Goshthi*' and vote for Pigeon tonight.'

Out of Y2K's long-winded speech, all the Jholus picked up a common and concise headline for the day that simply said, '*Goath par Goshthi*'.

When Y2K and Vartika met in the evening at their favorite restaurant, it was busier than usual. Mr. Mahan was there to greet them personally and led them to a special table. When they were seated, he praised Y2K generously and said, 'Your 'Human Approach' speech was the best a politician could ever make regarding food. We are a fully *humanated* restaurant where only humans cook and serve. Your manifesto is a great encouragement for my kind of restaurant. As a token of appreciation for including food in your manifesto, dinner for you two will be complimentary until the elections last.'

After Mahan left, Y2K winked and told Vartika,

'Who said that an election manifesto is of no value? Our manifesto just paid off.' Vartika, too, replied happily.

'That is because we cleverly chose food as today's topic. After all, the way to a voter's heart is through his stomach.'

Vartika was vindicated in her assessment when voting results were announced, and Y2K improved his position by five ranks.

Chapter XXI

'You are looking stunningly beautiful in this dress,' complimented D2Y2 as Vartika arrived for the breakfast meeting.

'You just stole words from my mouth, D2Y2. But I must say that you have a great sense of appreciation,' added Lattu.

D2Y2, like all Popats, did have a good sense of appreciating beauty. For humans, beauty lies in the beholder's eyes. But for Popats, the beauty lay in the software embedded in them. They profiled every person they met and stored their attributes with beauty being one of them. In D2Y2's assessment, the beauty score of Vartika was ninety-five percentile which went up to ninety-nine on account of the yellow and green khadi silk dress she was wearing today, prompting the compliment. Vartika beamed and blushed a little, ignored the mild flattery attempted by Lattu, and returned the compliment to D2Y2 as she said,

'You are looking as smart as ever, D2Y2.'

This time, D2Y2 beamed and blushed a little.

How Popats looked was a matter of serious consideration when Popats were being developed. Popat prototypes were sculpted like a human body. Initially, Walnut Inc. toyed with the idea of shipping them like Adam and Eve, the way God had shipped humans to the earth, but knew better. Realizing that the casing is more important than what is inside, they hired a tech designer firm Terry, Harry & Marry, known as TH&M. The firm designed a proprietary garment that was dust-proof, weather-proof and did not need a wash. More importantly, it supported dozens of wearables. Wearables were low-energy IoT devices that incorporated sensors, cameras, and communication devices that enhanced the capabilities of Popats manifolds. Impressed with these functionalities, Walnut Inc. entered into an exclusive arrangement to use only the TH&M-produced 'smart Popat garments' which came to be known as *sParments.* D2Y'2 was donning one such sParment which made him look as smart as evcr.

Having lost the first opportunity of complimenting Vartika to D2Y2, Lattu grabbed another one. He opened the breakfast meeting discussion by saying, 'I compliment Vartika for her strategy of re-engineering the old issues of *roti*, *kapda*, *aur makan.* The first one about *roti* worked wonderfully well for us yesterday. Let us try the theme of *kapada*, or the garment, for today's manifesto agenda.' Everyone concurred.

Mattu carried forward the discussion as he said,

'The garment industry, no doubt, is one of the key drivers of the economy. The industry has done well to ensure that everyone in the world is clothed. The advent of Popats created a new demand, and the garment industry has evolved beyond recognition since then. Evolution, of course, is never without convulsion.'

Mattu was alluding to the social, cultural, economic, and technological changes that the smart Popat garments had triggered. Initial Popats were expensive but stylish. The rich owners presented their Popats with an attitude that said, 'My Popat is smarter than you'. This boomeranged when they were shown the mirror and realized that 'my Popat is smarter than me'. Louis & Lucchi (L&L), a company that catered only to the rich, was inspired to design a garment for humans that would be smarter than the smartest Popat garment. They hit upon the idea of making garments programmable using more extensive and powerful wearables. The L&L-developed programmable garments soon became a rage and were called Wonderments since they took the definition of style, looks, and smartness to a new level. Their basic Wonderment could display up to thirty programmed designs so that the dress looked new every day of the month. The expensive ones were connected to the designer Clowns, which enabled customization on demand as per size, physique, time, and occasion. The most expensive and exclusive Wonderments incorporated a mesh of optical wearables that helped in creating a programable image in such a way that a man with a paunch looked slim and a woman with plain features looked curvy. Wonderments ensured that there were only smart people all around. The longer the people wore Wonderments, the more convinced they became that they were smarter than they knew themselves to be. Trapped in their own image, they would not be seen without a Wonderment. The combination of sPartments and Wonderments, thus, led to a huge social, cultural, and behavioral change in the 2040s.

Kattu came to the point and asked Vartika,

'There may be personal, cultural, or social issues involved, but I don't see any political issue in how you dress.'

'Politicians don't look at the issues, they look at the opportunities. Our local candidates are quite adept in sensing and grabbing every opportunity of voterizing,' replied Vartika.

'What is voterizing?' asked a little perplexed Sattu.

'Just like in business you monetize an idea, in politics you voterize an idea, issue, or opportunity,' replied Vartika.

'And how our local candidates are voterizing the *kapda* opportunity?' asked Kattu.

'They are doing it on predictable lines. Only yesterday, Kappuswamy announced that if elected, he will make every person smart in five years. Guru Panchal is eying low-hanging fruits. He has promised to make the Wonderment imitations cheaper by half. Prada is more circumspect. She is promising a pair of glamorous Wonderments free to every couple who gets married. We can devise our own strategy to voterize.'

Y2K intervened,

'In our quest to voterize, we are unable to see the forest for the trees. Wonderments are one of the biggest data privacy and security risks. The wearables they use are optimized for style and not security. Hence, Wonderments are easy prey for unscrupulous hackers, compromising our privacy and data security. This makes us susceptible to fraud, blackmail, and other crimes. Data suggests that such incidences have increased manifold over the last few years due to

Wonderments. If I get the power, I would rather ban the Wonderments until all the data privacy and security issues are sorted out.'

Everyone concurred, but Lattu thought it better to elicit Y2K's opinion on sPartments as well. So he asked,

'Considering your uncompromising views on Wonderments, you may clarify your position on sPartments as well.'

'That is a question that has not received serious consideration. Today, there are more Popats than humans who need to be clothed. And all their garments come from a single source. Though sPartments are manufactured all over the globe, a hefty royalty gets paid to Walnut Inc. and TH&M for every piece of sPartment produced. Economists dismiss the huge payout as a natural corollary of globalization, but I see it as an example of neo-colonization. In my opinion, sPartments need urgent *desification* before our import bill goes out of control,' replied Y2K thoughtfully.

While everyone was mulling over how to proceed with the tough stand that Y2K was advocating, Vartika came up with a solution. She exclaimed,

'Guys, this is our MKG moment!'

'What is that?' asked everyone in unison.

'Remember that almost a hundred years ago, a certain Mohandas Karamchand Gandhi lit a bonfire of foreign clothes? He was protesting against the British Raj which was promoting the greed of foreign cloth manufacturers, crippling the local industry, monopolizing trade, and perpetuating enslavement. Today, the actors are different, but the story sounds similar. So let us try out the MKG model. I suggest that we organize a bonfire of Wonderments and sPartments in the evening at Pigeon Square to highlight our manifesto points on 'G for Garments'.'

Vartika's suggestion galvanized everyone as they discussed the plan to the minutest detail.

The Y2K gang managed to gather two dozen Wonderments and sParments for the bonfire and an equal number of onlookers in the evening. Sattu was in charge of sloganeering. He started with the usual repertoire of slogans like '*Inquilab Zindabad*'. He then added '*Mandal Neta Kaisa Ho, Y2K ke Jaisa Ho*', and '*Monopoly Nahi Chalegi, Nahi Chalegi Nahi Chalegi*'. As the tempo built up, he unveiled the punch slogan '*One Two Ka Four, Five Two Ka Ten, Wonderment Par Chahiye, Total Ban Total Ban*', which was picked up enthusiastically. As the slogans reverberated across Pigeon Square, Y2K ceremoniously lit the bonfire. When the slogans and the fire subsided, Y2K made a fiery speech demanding a ban on Wonderments and outlining steps he would take for the *desification* of sPartments.

Pigeon Square had not seen such a spectacle for a long time. For half a dozen Jholus who had gathered at Vartika's behest, it was a novel experience. They were familiar with an unruly crowd torching a vehicle but were witnessing a voluntary burning of personal items in a disciplined yet electrifying manner for the first time. Their headlines were mostly variations of 'Powerful Protest Against Wonderments and sPartments'. One headline, however, intrigued Y2K. It read, '*Neo-desi, Leo-liberal* Political Approach of Y2K'. Perplexed, Y2K asked Vartika,

'I understand the term '*neo-desi*' but for heaven's sake, what on earth is meant by '*Leo-liberal*?' Vartika laughed heartily as she explained,

'Leo-liberal is a term coined by some cerebral Jhallu. It means a person who has liberal leanings but adopts a muscular approach.'

Y2K was not sure whether such an approach would yield enough votes. He was, however, pleasantly surprised when, at the end of the day, his ratings improved by five ranks.

Chapter XXII

The Y2K gang had thoroughly enjoyed the bonfire experience at Pigeon Squire last evening. It had sent the political adrenaline soaring without any risk of getting arrested. When they gathered for the breakfast meeting, Lattu was the first to compliment Vartika as he said,

'Your MKG model worked wonderfully well yesterday. Continuing the theme of retrofitting '*Roti, Kapada, Aur Makan*', let us replicate the MKG model for *Makan* as well.'

Sattu responded instead of Vartika, and said,

'*Makan* or 'House for H' can surely be our agenda today. During the last two decades, we have witnessed a housing revolution unraveling. The cornerstone of this housing revolution is the development of a thousand planned urban resettlements, but MKG would be aghast seeing the smart houses in the smart city of Kautukpur. These vertical monstrosities are rightly criticized for creating virtual isolation and destroying community-living.'

Kattu not only disagreed with Sattu but started on a long explanation defending the developments in housing. During the mid-2030s, the housing sector entered a virtuous cycle phase, aided by new technologies. Massive green field cities were designed using AI technology that ticked every box on ease, convenience, and environmental conservation. The design ensured that the city generated as much clean energy as it consumed, recycled water, managed waste, and increased green cover. Newly minted Popat workers labored relentlessly day and night, speeding up the construction. New-age materials helped in cost-cutting. As every square meter of the earth got digitized, land sharks were eliminated. Savings in fossil fuels saw investment pouring into real estate. For the low-income group, the government chipped in with the '*Makan hai to Jahan Hai*' scheme, constructing affordable housing. As middle- and upper-income groups moved into smart houses, a huge inventory of old houses became surplus. As a result of the virtuous cycle, every citizen had a roof over his head by 2042.

'You sound as if we have attained utopia. But utopia is never realized because the definition of utopia changes with the progress mankind makes. Today, only one-half of our population enjoys the benefits of everything that is smart, including housing. This wide gap between those who have access to smart tech and those who don't, known as the 'smartech divide', is the most challenging problem of 2050. Addressing the issue of the 'smartech divide' is a matter of good politics and good economics. Unfortunately, you find the combination of good politics and good economics only in utopia,' lamented Mattu.

'I agree with you. Man develops technology to find solutions, and technology develops new problems for man. What was once a simple issue of internet access, known as the digital divide, has now metamorphosed into a 'smartech divide' that impacts every aspect of life. In the age of smart houses in smart cities, aspirational goals have shifted from a pucca house to a more comfortable dwelling,' surmised Lattu.

'Guys, we are entering into a territory of endless discussions. Can we stop and get back to the task of working out our manifesto agenda instead?' Vartika said it a little impatiently.

'We are doing exactly that, Vartika. Didn't we all agree that our manifesto will be worked out through discussions?' protested Kattu.

'Sometimes we need to give discussions a break. At any given point in time, half of the population is discussing the problems of the other half, while the other half is discussing the solutions offered by the rest half. And never the twain shall meet,' retorted Vartika.

'In that case, what is your grand suggestion, Vartika the strategist?' scoffed Kattu.

Vartika was cool as a cucumber as she replied,

'Well, we are going on an expedition to a hut.'

'Is that some kind of a joke?' commented Kattu.

'Not really. You may, however, call it a political gimmick. Every big-league politician indulges in this gimmick once in an election season. He visits a hut in a village, lunches there with his entourage, and clicks photos with the poor host. After the photo-op, he espouses the discovery made during this arduous expedition which is then widely publicized. In my view, an 'expedition to the hut' is a highly effective, low-cost-high-return political tool,' explained Vartika.

'But there are no more huts to be found in the whole of Kautuk Mandal since 2042,' pointed out Kattu.

'There are still a few hutment-like houses left in Kautukgram, and I have managed to inveigle an invitation from one of the house owners,' said Vartika.

'You are a great political strategist and we all look forward to the expedition you have planned,' conceded Kattu finally.

Before the meeting ended, Vartika briefed them on what to expect.

'Guys, our host today is an eighty-year-old proud farmer from Kautukgram. Don't be intimidated because of the *lathi* he wields. Don't mistake him for a *Neta* because he wears a *khadi* dress. Don't address him as 'Sir' because he likes to be addressed as '*Tau*.' Everyone took note and nodded.

The expedition to the hut turned out to be more than a pleasant experience. Tau greeted them warmly and his wife served a simple but delicious meal. The gang ate lunch sitting on the ground. They thoroughly enjoyed the experience and the conversation that followed. Tau had no interest in politics and was blunt in speaking his mind about politicians. After the meal, Y2K was offered a *Hukka* which he respectfully declined. It was time to talk business. Y2K put his best professional foot forward and said,

'Sir, we are working out an election manifesto incorporating the needs of the public. Today we are here to discover your views on the housing sector.'

'Am I a Discovery Channel?' replied Tau in a tone that had no hint of sarcasm but had an unsettling effect on the listener.

As Vartika glared at Y2K, he remembered the briefing to address him properly. Y2K corrected and said,

'Tau, I like your sense of humor. I meant to ask what are your expectations from the government on housing?'

'I have no expectations from the government,' replied Tau flatly.

'I am sure the government can do something for the settlements here,' said Y2K helpfully.

'I don't think the government does anything for us once the elections are over,' spoke Tau unflinchingly.

'I insist you tell us one single thing my government should do regarding housing if I get elected,' persisted Y2K.

'If you are insisting, then get an air-conditioner fitted in every house after you become a *lat saheb*,' replied Tau. Y2K had his answer and profusely thanked Tau as the gang trooped out into the courtyard.

Outside in the courtyard, they were met with three Jholus whom Vartika had managed to assemble for a photo-op. After the Jholus had clicked the 3D-HD pictures of Y2K with Tau, the mics were thrust before Y2K. By now Y2K had worked out his pitch and spoke with the practiced ease of a veteran politician.

'I had pledged to build my manifesto alphabet by alphabet based on an understanding of the problems faced by citizens on a daily basis. In that quest, I visited Tau today. I thank Tau from the bottom of my heart not only for his wonderful hospitality but for his wisdom and advice as well. I had a long chat with Tau about the needs of a common man. While every citizen in the Kautuk Mandal has a roof over his head, many still have to endure the vagaries of weather. Tau very thoughtfully suggested that the government should provide an air-conditioner for them. I realize that it is not just another ordinary demand but a representation of citizens' aspirations in 2050. It is also a timely reminder to us of the widening 'smartech divide' and the consequences it can have on society. Having addressed the basic needs of *'roti kapda aur makan'*, it is time for the government to shift gears and work to improve the quality of life of its citizens.

Accordingly, after having an engaging and enlightening discussion with Tau, I am happy to announce a *'Har Ghar AC, Ghar Ghar AC'* scheme that will strive to fulfill his dream and vision. I am sure that with Tau's blessings, the *'Har Ghar AC, Ghar Ghar AC'* scheme will go a long way in bridging the 'smartech divide' and improving the quality of life of our citizens.'

Tau did not understand much of what Y2K said but clapped nevertheless in appreciation of the articulate speaker. One of the diligent Jholu thrust the mic in front of Tau and asked,

'Tau, what do you have to say about the *'Har Ghar AC, Ghar Ghar AC'* scheme?' Tau had never faced a mic in his life but was not a person to be cowed down easily. Eager to match the rhythmic articulation of his host, Tau blurted out in his inimitable style, *'Raghupati Raghav Raja Ram, Sab Ko AC De Bhagwan.'* All the channels ran this quote from Tau along with the headline *'Har Ghar AC, Ghar Ghar AC'*.

It was not clear whether it was Y2K's scheme or Tau's tagline that hit the bull's eye, but Y2K improved his ranking by four positions that day.

Chapter XXIII

At the end of the tenth day of the month-long elimination round, campaign Y2K seemed to be doing better than expected. The Y2K gang was in a buoyant mood except for Mattu who was uncharacteristically worried. He waited till D2Y2 had served coffee and disclosed,

'Guys, I have to raise the red flag regarding the funds' situation. Our funds have bottomed out and we are not even halfway through our campaign. We have money left only for the next three days' campaign. We need to urgently raise funds if we want to survive.'

Kattu was quick to realize the problem and responded,

'Raising funds is a difficult task. Because an election is a high-risk and capital-intensive enterprise, no Bank will lend and only the dubious will invest. That is why eighty percent of the campaigns are self-funded. In fact, half of the time there is 'reverse funding' whereby the moneyed aspirant pays the established party for a ticket. Unfortunately, our candidate does not fall into such a moneyed category.'

'Is there any way to self-generate the funds and run a low-cost campaign?' asked Lattu innocently.

'Yes, but only three types of candidates can manage such a feat. One such type is a *Bahubali* who uses muscle power and intimidation to generate funds and garner votes. The second type is called *Daldali* who mainly indulges in the politics of mud-slinging as a low-cost campaign strategy. Lastly, there is a unique contender known as *Khalbali* who specializes in the art of rabble-rousing as a tactical tool to garner the funds and attract the votes. Fortunately, Y2K does not qualify to be in any of these distinguished categories,' replied Mattu.

'Then the only viable option is to try crowd-funding,' suggested Lattu, a bit hopefully.

Kattu was being practical when he responded,

'The interest of the public in electoral politics is like that of an App. They like it for free. In any case, targeting individuals for votes itself is a challenging job, so motivating them to contribute with funds would be very daunting. Data reveals that crowdfunding wins you elections once in ten years in one in a hundred Mandals. This dice is, therefore, not loaded in our favor.'

'Then tell the solution, Vartika. It is your domain?' implored Lattu.

Vartika, who had maintained a studied silence so far, spoke knowingly.

'The solution is obvious. As per the statistics, sixty percent of the election money comes from Industry. Under the circumstances, it is inevitable that we turn to the Industry for raising the funds.'

'But why would the industry give us the funds?' inquired Kattu.

'Well, the industrialists have their businesses to run and the politicians have elections to win. Therefore, the twain often meet for four reasons. The first and foremost reason is the need to 'speed' up things and the 'speed money' paid to the politicians does wonders. The second is the 'impede' tactic that sometimes makes the industry cough up precious election funds. The 'speed' and 'impede' game, however, can be played only by the established players who have the leverage of power or networking. Thirdly there is a statutory reason. Corporations have been mandated since 2037 to spend one percent of their profit on Corporate Political Responsibility or CPR. Lastly, in a rare case, an industrialist may decide to donate funds voluntarily without any *quid pro quo* for some altruistic reason,' explained Vartika in a professorial manner.

'A CPR funding can resuscitate our flailing campaign. A voluntary contribution will be more than welcome. But how do we go about it? Do we even have any chance at all?' asked Lattu.

'Luck favors the innovator. We are the political innovator and we once helped another innovator. Lady luck seems to be smiling on both of us,' replied Vartika mysteriously.

'Don't keep us in suspense. Tell us the details,' implored Lattu.

'Do you remember the case of vanishing paint on the first day of the campaign?' asked Vartika. Everyone remembered but none except Vartika had followed it up. And she narrated how the story unfolded.

The case of vanishing paint was dexterously handled by the Election Commission. But before being disposed of, it caught the attention of its Director. EC was facing a damages suit of ten million rupees filed by the topmost model Chapla Chopra on the grounds that the ink put on her nails during voting did not vanish for a whole month, keeping her out of work. In a dramatic move, EC announced that it will henceforth use the 'Golden Owl Paint' which will vanish in exactly twenty-four hours. Following this announcement, Chapla withdrew the case and became a brand ambassador of 'Golden Owl Paints'. This development was followed by a quick advertisement blitzkrieg in which acclaimed model Chapla could be seen playfully saying in her sensuous voice. 'Thanks to the 'Golden Owl Paint', I can change the color and paint of my house more often than I change my boyfriends.' Since the list of Chapla's boyfriends was not a secret, the advertisement hit the bull's eye, highlighting the immense potential of the once derided 'Golden Owl Paint'. People soon found more than a hundred 'use-cases' of the 'vanishing paint'. Within a fortnight, the fortunes of Vichitra Gupta, the founder of 'Golden Owl Paint', changed. From the verge of bankruptcy, he was on the road to becoming a unicorn.

The Y2K gang felt goosebumps realizing that they were the trigger behind this fascinating success story as Vartika announced,

'I have some good news for you. A grateful Vichitra Gupta has agreed to pledge enough funds to see us through the election.'

An elated Y2K finally spoke,

'That is a big relief. But is there any condition attached to the offer?'

'Yes, there is. The 'speed-impede' propelled donations are generally made under the table and outside public scrutiny. However, statutory and voluntary donations are informally regulated by the Association of Industrialists. They strongly advise their members to donate only to those candidates who are industry-friendly,' replied Vartika.

'That is ridiculous because everyone would proclaim to be industry-friendly in order to secure the funds,' asked Sattu.

'It is not so simple. To be considered industry-friendly, a candidate needs to be rated positive on the 'Eating Index' by TRAP.'

'I don't quite get it. What the hell is 'Eating Index' by TRAP?' asked Sattu, who never had any interest in politics.

'TRAP or the '*Tr*ansparency *A*bout *P*olls' is a rating Agency that specializes in electoral services. One of the services it offers is the '*E*valuation of *A*ttitude *T*oward *In*dustry in *G*eneral' or the Eating Index. The Index is considered to be the gold standard for industry friendliness. Hence the insistence on this rating by the Industry Association,' replied Vartika.

'That seems to be fair but what is the process involved and how do they rate the candidates?' asked Mattu.

'The Association pays the Agency a fee for sharing the Index. During the elimination round, the Agency organizes a food festival to which select candidates are invited. Besides the interested Industrialists, politics-hungry guests are also invited to the paid lunch or dinner where guest candidates make their tutored speeches and answer a few questions. Besides the speech itself, the proprietary AI algorithm of TRAP assesses the candidate on a hundred parameters to generate the Index. It may come as a surprise to you that very few candidates manage to qualify,' explained Vartika.

'So how do we join the party?' asked Mattu.

'I have made all the necessary arrangements. Y2K is scheduled to address a select gathering over dinner organized by TRAP tonight. TRAP already has the detailed profile of Y2K and every bit and byte of what he has said or done in public. All that is required of Y2K now is to say the right things tonight,' informed Vartika.

'That settles it. 'I for Industry' is going to be our manifesto agenda tonight and we can help Y2K prepare for it,' announced Lattu.

'We have so far neglected Kautukgarh and its problems. Let us begin by discussing what Kautukgarh wants,' suggested Mattu.

Kautukgarh was the area that developed around a lone hill on which once stood the imposing Kautuk Fort. As the power of the Kautuk Fort diminished, the area surrounding it became desolate till it was designated, developed, and promoted as an attractive Industrial Area. The industrialists and the entrepreneurs flocked to the resource-rich Kautukgarh Industrial area and a thousand industries of all kinds bloomed. With rising investment, production, and income,

Kautuk Mandal came to be ranked among the top twenty-five Mandals of the country by 2035. The decline, however, set in unannounced, and by 2050 Kautuk Mandal had slipped to a hundred-and-fiftieth position. Y2K echoed everyone's feelings when he declared.

'The state of the industry in Kautukgarh is a classic case of missed opportunity. Irrespective of whether we receive the funding or not, it should be our agenda to restore the health of our industry.'

Y2K was surprised to find full attendance at the event. The Chief Polling Consultant of TRAP introduced Y2K as a political entrepreneur trying to figure out the A to Z of an election manifesto. Y2K had five minutes to make his pitch and he began earnestly.

'My dear fellow citizens,

Kautukpur, Kautuknagar, Kautukgram, and Kautukgarh are the four pillars of our Mandal and we need to nurture them all. Unfortunately, Kautukgarh, which houses our industries and generates sixty percent of our revenue has been suffering from neglect, apathy, and misrule.

The industry needs support in terms of infrastructure, investment, and innovation. However, infrastructure in Kautukgarh is crumbling as represented by the potholes in the roads and a patchy 7G connectivity. Investment is fleeing because of multiple taxation and over-regulation. And innovation has no institutional support framework. To make it worse, the industry has not moved fast enough to keep up with the changes in technology. While the world has moved to Industry 5.0, we are still opposed to Industry 4.0 resulting in a constant decline in our competitiveness. For example, take the case of Vichitra Gupta, the innovator of 'Golden Owl Paint' which has the potential to put Kautukgarh on the global map. But he needs Industry 5.0 support which provides 'Manufacturing as a Service' enabling scaling up at minimum cost, time, and effort on a global level.

If I get elected, I shall ensure that the industry gets the support it deserves. Infrastructure will be maintained as per world-class standards using the technology. For example, drones would constantly monitor the road for potholes and order the Popat workers to repair them in less than an hour before any pothole becomes more than a centimeter wider. Our Mandal has a plethora of regulations. My government will do the ABC analysis and trim them to half. I must, however, warn you that the remaining essential regulations will be implemented strictly. And of course, my government will do everything in its power to facilitate the transition to 8G and Industry 5.0.

As told earlier, I am on a journey to discover the A to Z of the election agenda. And tonight, I stand for Industry.'

The applause was followed by a positive rating on the 'Eating Index' by TRAP. Vichitra Gupta kept his promise and announced generous funding support for the Y2K campaign. Contributions from two other industrialists came as a bonus.

After the dinner, Y2K and Vartika decided not to skip Mahan's restaurant and went there for coffee. As they sipped their favorite Coorg coffee, they looked up the local news channels. Breaking News of large donations to an upstart candidate was splashed on all channels. The taste of coffee was spoiled somewhat when Mungeri Lal aka *Netaji* appeared on one channel accusing Y2K of sitting in the laps of big industrialists.

When the voting results came, Y2K received enough negative votes to bring down his rating by one rank. Disappointed, he asked Vartika,

'Why this reversal in rating despite saying all the right things? I thought I did pretty well today.'

Vartika was sanguine as she replied,

'You really did well today in securing sufficient funding for the campaign. As far as the marginal drop in the rating is concerned, there are two reasons. Voters are generally wary of a nexus between industrialists and politicians since there is a very fine line between support and nexus. Your genuine support has apparently been misconstrued by some voters. Don't worry about it.'

'And what is the second reason for the drop in the rating?' asked Y2K.

'When you say the right thing, do the right thing, you almost sound boring. If you are a bore, your ratings stagnate. On the other hand, colorful criticism attracts some voters. Voters like their candidates to be colorful and interesting,' said Vartika in her mildly mocking manner.

'I shall try for the image makeover. In the meantime, would you care to walk in my boring company?' asked Y2K.

As they walked together, the deserted pathway echoed with their laughter and the chatter that had no hint of boredom.

Chapter XXIV

'Today's breakfast special is *Puran Poli.* This morning, I received a box of fresh and sweet *Puran Poli* from Shanta Bai accompanied by an even sweeter message,' announced Y2K and read the message aloud: 'Since you were not one of those employers who think of themselves as *Lat Saheb,* you are the right person to become a *Lat Saheb.* Count on my vote and support - Shanta.' Y2K was visibly moved when he said,

'Kindness shown by Shanta Bai is extraordinary since she was my maid whom D2Y2 replaced seven years ago. At that time, I was happy to replace her with D2Y2 because she was moody, used to cut corners at times, and went on leave unannounced. I feel bad today that the human angle involved in job loss did not bother me at that time.'

Sattu sympathized and said,

'I can understand the situation. We too let go of our Ramu Kaka after he had served us for more than fifteen years.'

Mattu generalized the discussion when he said,

'It is not about Shanta Bai and Ramu Kaka alone. The Popat technology has finished off eighty percent of all the jobs at the bottom and middle of the pyramid in the last two decades with cataclysmic consequences.'

Kattu as usual did not agree and said,

'That's not a fair assessment. A large number of jobs have indeed been usurped by Popats, Appus, and Clowns of various kinds. However, the new technologies have created a massive amount of new jobs as well. Have you ever heard of jobs in areas like ethical engineering, behavioral modeling, bionic materials, tactile communication, Popat training, and many more? Jobs are there, only the description has changed.'

'On the topic of new technology disrupting the job market, let me recount an anecdote,' joined Mattu and continued,

'In the early years of this century when large-scale computerization was happening, my father was worried about losing his job. My grandfather narrated to him the story from a 1957 movie 'Naya Daur' in which Dilip Kumar plays the role of a 'Tongawala'. He is pitted against the villain who introduces a bus service plying on the same route, threatening the livelihood of all the Tongawalas. Faced with protests from them, the villain agrees to withdraw the bus service if the humble Tonga defeats his bus in a race. Hero Dilip Kumar accepts the challenge and riding with some ingenuity and tenacity wins the race. This was a classic 'man versus machine' as well as a 'new job versus old job' conflict with the film script tilting toward the underdog hero. However, without delving into this conflict, my grandfather remarkably concluded that every man who takes up the challenge posed by change is a hero and a hero almost always wins.'

'I agree with your grandfather's conclusion. People who manage change are heroes and heroes in real life abound. For example, Shanta Bai is a hero to me. After she lost her job, she quickly found that she could not compete with a Popat. So she asked herself what she had accomplished that a Popat would not be able to. It occurred to her that she was able to manage her *bewda*[22] husband which was an exceptional ability. So she started conducting workshops on 'How to teach your husband a lesson' which soon became a hit. She then hired a Popat writer to author a book on the same subject 'How To Teach Your Husband A Lesson' which went on to become a bestseller. She is now a much sought-after Popat trainer, writer, and consultant,' shared Y2K.

Lattu picked up the example to show another facet as he said, 'I am glad that Shanta Bai lost her job. After all, why should a human being serve as a servant to a fellow human being? It is good that technology is substituting the job of a servant and elevating the value of human enterprise.'

Sattu had a different perspective though. He counter-argued,

'You are being selective in your argument. I'll give you the example of Ramu Kaka. After he lost his job, he too struggled and could find no work. A year later, he went into depression and now frequents the sanatorium. Change is welcome but it is never without a cost. When the human cost of change is enormous, change must be controlled.'

Lattu countered,

'You are now being a Luddite which will not help. Job apocalypse has been predicted many times but never

---

[22] *Drunkard*

materialized. On the contrary, every technological innovation has created more new jobs and we are witnessing the same thing now. Popats, Appus, Clowns, and associated technologies have created a whole new range of products and demands that did not exist earlier. As a result, there is a shortage of manpower that can take up the new jobs.'

Sattu was adamant as he said,

'You are now being a technophile without seeing the whole picture. What is worrisome is that the job decimation this time has been widespread over such a short period and its march continues relentlessly. Be it a blue-collar, white-collar, black-collar, gray-collar, or pink-collar job, all have been gobbled up. No color has escaped the job contraction. Even the gold collar jobs have seen reductions. The new jobs you are talking about are the orange collar jobs in the sunrise technologies needing new skills that most do not possess. How do you expect the smartech-challenged masses to take up such orange-collar jobs?'

Vartika intervened at this stage and said, 'Guys, let 'J for Jobs' be our manifesto agenda of the day. This means that instead of indulging in an academic debate, we take a political view of the job situation. Our opponents' response ranges from putting a total ban on Popats to raising the number of jobs even if those are dummy jobs. The number of jobs to be created varies from candidate to candidate but Guru Panchal takes the cake. He has promised to create so many jobs that every adult in Kautuk Mandal will have two jobs to choose from. It is high time that we also announce our job policy, lest we be left behind.'

Lattu was not keen to prolong the debate, be it academic or political. So he proposed, 'I have no idea of what the best political model should be to tackle the complex job situation of 2050. All I want is that it should be fair and workable, instead of being just populist. Let a rational policy be formulated by Y2K who is keyed in on both technology and politics by now. Since the presentation is as important as the recipe, let Vartika work out the presentation logistics of such a policy.' Others were equally keen to cut short the debate and concentrate on relishing the remaining *Puran Poli*, so they unanimously endorsed Lattu's suggestion. It would keep Vartika and Y2K busy for the whole day.

Vartika had planned to take out a rally from Pigeon Square to the Mandal Ministry of Labor and Employment. She enlisted the support of Shanta Bai and Ramu Kaka who managed to mobilize enough numbers for the rally. For a change, no slogans were to be raised in the rally. Instead, everyone wore a black band mourning the death of the jobs in a silent march. At the Mandal Ministry, there was no Gappu to sympathize with them but few Jholus had assembled on cue from Vartika. Y2K quickly took the stage as soon as the Jholus were well-positioned and began in his well-modulated voice

'Citizens of Kautuk Mandal,

Jobs undergo a cycle of life and death of their own. Man's ingenuity, which includes technological developments, generates jobs. And the same ingenuity destroys them as well. Therefore, do not mourn the demise of jobs for long. Instead, look at the job cycle with equanimity and with a new perspective. For me, that perspective is to put 'Humans First'.

Because the concept of 'Humans First' sounds so simple, it is often misunderstood. The 'Man versus Popat' and 'Jobs versus Progress' confusion stems from this misunderstanding. I have no cavil with Popats substituting jobs that are risky, hazardous, unhealthy, or unsafe. If we value human beings, we should reserve such jobs for the Popats. I even welcome Popats taking over the jobs that involve drudgery, slogging, and donkey work. I do not want a human being to serve as a servant to another human being. Popats can do that job very well.

Yet, such substitution inevitably comes at a cost to the affected humans. One way to minimize that cost is to train and educate people appropriately for the elevated new jobs. Therefore, if elected, I propose to open a new Kautukpur University of Popat Technology and several 'Centers for Reskilling and Up-skilling' in Smartech Technologies.

The job market is vast enough to accommodate everyone who is freshly skilled. However, that itself is not enough. Because, if we leave humans to compete with the Popats in the marketplace purely in terms of cost and efficiency, most will not be able to win and will be left behind. It is the State's duty to create opportunities even for those who are likely to be left behind. Therefore, if elected, I propose to introduce a 'Calibrated Job Reservation Policy For Humans'.

There are jobs that should be reserved for Popats and there are jobs where Popats must be barred. But the majority of the jobs are those which can be performed by both humans and Popats with equal ease. We should identify and reserve a certain percentage of such jobs for humans. The percentage of reservations can be calibrated based on social cost-benefit analysis. For example, a 20 percent reservation for humans may be introduced in the media by mandating the channels to employ one human journalist for every four Jholus. On the other hand, eighty percent of teachers should be humans to ensure that we do not deprive children of the human touch. On average, I am looking at fifty percent reservation in Jobs for Humans as part of my agenda 'J for Jobs'. I am sure that voters will overwhelmingly support my policy of calibrated reservation in jobs for humans.'

Just before winding up his speech, Y2K asked the audience to repeat his patented slogan thrice. Y2K called out 'I am Human' and the crowd raised their fists and shouted in unison 'Humans First'. The raised fists with black armbands in the background of rousing sloganeering provided exhilarating visuals for the Jholus. Their TRP-optimized algorithm played those visuals with the simple headline 'Y2K Demands Fifty percent Job Reservation For Humans'. The coverage did wonders both for the TRP of the channels and the ranking of Y2K.

When they met for dinner, Y2K was elated about reaching the number twelve position but Vartika seemed a little tense and worried. Responding to Y2K's inquiry, she replied somberly.

'You are now in the most vulnerable position and the knives will be out for you soon. Those above you would want to nip your challenge in the bud and those just below would try their best to dislodge you before it is too late for them. My experience in politics tells me that they will use every trick possible to thwart your march. Politics is neither love nor war and every trick in the trade is fair in Politics.' Y2K shrugged.

Chapter XXV

The knives came out earlier than Vartika had apprehended. That it was a day for the letter 'K' was only incidental.

An issue beginning with 'K' that would be worthy of a manifesto turned out to be trickier than expected. Sattu suggested the topic of kidnapping and killing. Kattu immediately rejected it stating that technology had made the exercise of kidnapping difficult and killings were more common in distant New York than in Kautukpur. Mattu came up with the idea of fixing 'Key Performance Indicators' or KPIs for politicians which everyone thought was brilliant. However, Vartika put it down as impractical and futile. She patiently explained that KPIs for politicians could never be formulated, if formulated they would never be accepted, if accepted they would never be enforced, and if enforced, the politicians would find a way around it. So why bother putting such an idea in the manifesto? Sattu thought over Vartika's discourse and suggested cautiously. 'Instead of rejecting the idea altogether, we can perhaps fly a kite.'

The bulb lit and Lattu excitedly announced 'I think 'K for Kite' can be a good idea for our manifesto.'

'Are you joking?' was Kattu's flat response.

'I am not joking. I am making a serious and sensible suggestion. When I was a kid, kites could be seen swooping and swirling in the sky all around this time of the year. However, even on *Makar Sakranti*, the day the sun transits into *Makar Rashi* or Capricorn zodiac, there was not a single kite to be seen in the sky? Would it not be nice if we revive the tradition of kite flying again?' replied Lattu eliciting immediate support from Sattu.

Sattu elaborated,

'It is not just about tradition or nostalgia. It is about going outdoors in the sun to let your spirit soar under the blue sky and have some innocent fun. As a boy, I used to spend hours catching falling kites or flying kites on the roof. For me, it was a sport that needed no team, no rivals, and negligible money. All it needed was a little time and an urge to have some fun. Sadly, such a simple sport has now become extinct.'

Kattu was scathing as he replied.

'The simple sport you are so eloquently talking about is a dangerous sport. Many mishaps have happened while flying or chasing kites from unguarded terraces or due to falling kites causing accidents on the roads. Hundreds of birds have been injured or even died due to entangled strands. The falling metallic string called *Chinese Manjha* has caused short circuits, power failures, and even electrocution. For this reason, *Chinese Manjha* is banned across the country and kite flying is prohibited in many Mandals.'

'That is not a fair criticism. We are proposing kite flying with safe practices only. For example, we can use cotton thread or

Sada Manjha and fly kites only in open fields away from trees and roads. That makes kite-flying pretty safe,' argued Lattu.

Kattu, however, was unrelenting as he responded,

'Even if you use good practices, it is still illegal to fly kites without a permit. You can be jailed or fined for kite flying.'

'That is ridiculous!' exclaimed Lattu.

Kattu looked at the incredulous expressions on everyone's faces with amusement and continued,

'Aren't you aware of the Aircraft Act 1934 which prohibits flying aircraft without a valid permit? Under section 2 of this Act, a kite is also included in the definition of an Aircraft, so legally speaking you need a permit to fly the kite. As per the amended provision in Section 11 of the Act, the penalty for flying so as to cause danger can be a fine of Rupees ten million or two years imprisonment, or both. No one took any notice of this section till drones and air-taxi services became pretty common which found kites to be a nuisance. In 2037, the first arrest was made under this Act for causing a mishap to a drone. After a few more accidents, more arrests and fines led to the discontinuation of kite-flying altogether. As Lattu rightly observed, not a single kite can be seen swirling and swooping in the sky now.'

'I think what happened is unfortunate and all the more reason to try and revive the vanishing hobby,' opined Sattu.

'I think we should obey the law and forget about kite flying,' maintained Kattu.

Y2K intervened to break the stalemate and said,

'I agree with the idea but Kattu has some valid concerns. Maybe Vartika can find a way around.'

Vartika indeed had a workaround which she explained,

'Remember the place where we assembled for a picnic. In 2035, permission was granted to use that ground for testing the implications of kite-flying on drones, air taxis, and similar devices. That permission had no expiry date, so we can legally fly the kites there.'

Having settled the trickiest part, Vartika assigned the rest of the logistics to Sattu.

The cottage industry of kite-making had long ago perished. However, with the help of a smart design and manufacturing facility, Sattu managed to procure a hundred ergonomically designed smart kites along with twenty cotton string spindles called *Chakri* within a few hours as per his specifications. The weather happened to be sunny with mild winds blowing at 15-16 Kmph, just ideal for kite flying. A decent crowd gathered creating a festive ambiance. Sattu was the one whose kites soared the highest. Lattu mostly kept busy giving tips, especially to female enthusiasts on how to fly kites. Kattu had not flown a kite ever. So he brought his Popat along to hold the Chakri and teach how to fly a kite. Even Vartika tried her hands with a little help from Y2K. The Jholus were watching the live kite-flying for the first time and were busy filming the merriment. There was, however, one human journalist present who did not fit. He seemed to be preoccupied and left before Vartika gathered everyone for an address by Y2K. She timed his address just when *Shikanji*, a freshly prepared spicy lemon drink, was being served.

Y2K was to the point as he spoke.

'Dear Kite Fliers,

Today is the birth anniversary of Kautuk Kumar, the great founder of Kautukgarh. A man of many talents, he was a great *Patangbaaz* as well. A scene depicting him flying a kite with his entourage is engraved in Pigeon Square. If elected, I shall declare his birth anniversary as the '*Patang Divas*' in his memory. A holiday will be declared to enable citizens to join in the kite-flying festivities. On this day, free Kites and *Chakri* will be distributed to children and coaches will teach them how to fly kites safely. In keeping with safe kite-flying practices, my government will also identify a few spots where no permits will be needed to fly the kites.

Please do not consider this 'K for Kite' agenda as merely symbolic or some kind of gimmick. It has a deeper objective in line with my 'Humans First' approach. In this smart world that we live in, a man is no longer a social animal but has turned himself into a self-centered specimen immersed in the virtual world. In a world where even the sun and the sky have been virtualized, outdoor activities like kite-flying will serve as a much-needed tonic. We also live in an age and time where hyper-competition has become the driving force of life. Every sport has turned into a battlefield where children are encouraged to fight and not enjoy. Kite-flying as a sport should serve as an antidote by letting your spirit soar high.

Today, I seek your vote in the name of the soaring spirit of we humans.'

Mr. Mahan complimented the Y2K-Vartika duo on organizing a kite-flying session which he had joined and thoroughly enjoyed. As they settled down to dinner, brief news appeared under the headline 'K for Kite - A Tradition Revived'. Scenes of kite flying were nicely interspersed with Y2K's speech.

'That was an inspiring speech you made,' remarked Vartika. It was the first time that Vartika had praised Y2K for his oratorical efforts. Y2K thanked her and instinctively reached out to her. Precisely at that moment, lights flashed, a camera clicked, and a human journalist suddenly appeared at their table. The journalist from Channel7 pushed a mic toward Y2K, and introduced himself. 'I am Himmat Joshi. You may call me HJ.' Without pausing, HJ asked, 'You speak eloquently on human relations. Would you care to tell our viewers what relationship you have with the beautiful lady?' Y2K reacted instantly with, 'That is none of your business, you xxxxx', and rose with rising rage. Before he could punch HJ, Vartika prompted him to sit down. While Y2K struggled to calm down, Vartika told HJ, 'Will you please let us have our dinner quietly?' HJ nodded and left.

Vartika's apprehensions came true when HJ appeared on the news channel a few minutes later. He began by presenting Y2K as the fast-rising star in search of the A to Z of his manifesto, and Vartika as an election strategist with exceptional charm and beauty. Y2K's brief electoral journey was covered with shots of both of them taking walks together. Then followed the scene with the pair kissing in the dark and the headline changed from 'K for Kite' to 'K for Kiss'. HJ then reminded his viewers of the kite-flying party organized by Y2K followed by a shot showing Y2K assisting Vartika in flying the kite. The scene then shifted to the restaurant showing Y2K holding Vartika's hand. After a few seconds of poignant gaps, Y2K's frame appeared delivering the punch line 'I seek your vote in the name of the soaring spirit of we humans.' At this point, HJ appeared again and asked in his vile tone, 'Would you vote for the soaring spirit of Y2K?' as the shots of Y2K and Vartika together kept repeating in the background.

The innuendo was clear and effective. Both Vartika and Y2K felt devastated and did not touch the food Mr. Mahan had so thoughtfully prepared. Y2K recalled the feeling of being followed when there was a blackout and Vartika kissed him goodnight. He also recalled seeing HJ in the crowd of kite fliers. HJ had shadowed his prey well and moved in for the kill with clever deception. Y2K cursed HJ loudly. Vartika too was taken aback by the vilification HJ had scripted and rued, 'Having got used to the Jholus attending our events, I had ignored the human journalist. Jholus are neither programmed to be devious nor can they acquire this level of deceit through their adaptive learning tools. Only a human journalist can be so unscrupulous and vituperative in his reporting. The sad part is that we may not be able to do much about it.' Both felt dejected and did not bother to wait for the voting results of the day. They left early and did not walk together.

By the time Y2K reached home, his ranking had tanked by twelve positions.

Chapter XXVI

The change in the air was palpable. Y2K and Vartika had clarified their position at the start of the meeting. Everyone understood but realized that convincing the public and recouping the lost ground would be an uphill task. The mood was that of anger directed toward HJ, the human journalist. Sattu gave vent to his frustration as he said,

'I spotted HJ yesterday. Had I known what he was up to, I would have given him a bashing he would have remembered for life.'

Kattu interrupted him and said,

'You may have to beat up another gentleman over there,' pointing to the frame of Netaji Mungeri Lal who had just now joined as a guest on the breakfast show of Channel7. Netaji was pompously flaunting his wisdom.

'I thank the channel for exposing the deplorable conduct of Y2K and his secretary. Had it happened in the UK, the cradle of democracy, he would have been forced to resign by now. In Kautukpur too, we consider our workplace as sacred which has been sullied by an imposter like Y2K. I demand that Y2K withdraw his candidature today. If he fails to do so, I shall be forced to file an FIR under section 294 in order to keep the politics of Kautukpur clean.'

A pall of gloom descended as Lattu reacted,

'Although Netaji makes no sense, his diatribe is a double whammy. If this coverage continues for another day, our ranking will plummet to a level from which we won't be able to recover. We have to do something quickly to arrest the slide.'

Mattu thought it over and suggested,

'I like Sattu's idea of beating up these scums but that will not be a very honorable option. I think the only option we have is to take legal action against these two gentlemen. Since we have no time to lose, I can arrange for a Lapat to join us in less than ten minutes.' Everyone agreed.

Lapats (*L*egal *A*ffairs Po*pat*s) were the Popats created especially for legal work. When they were first introduced in the market, lawyers promptly went on strike against their use. As a result, the number of Lapats remained restricted till 2042 when the 'Lapat Regulation Act' was passed under the 'ease of doing justice' policy. As per the Act, Lapats had to be certified by an AI committee of the Bar Council and were to be licensed exclusively to lawyers. The Act changed the life and fortune of the lawyers. Lapats did all the leg work as well as brain work for the lawyers. They interacted with clients, researched, drafted, and even argued in the courts. Litigants were happy because they got a standardized, convenient, and better legal service for which they did not mind paying a little more. Lawyers were happy because the on-demand legal services brought more business at higher margins for them. Lapats, however, did not come without a few drawbacks. They were not adept at obtaining '*tarikh pe tarikh*' since they could not fall sick and had no uncle or aunt to die occasionally. They were not deft enough in obfuscating the data and found it difficult to lie despite the tutoring. It was thus left to an individual lawyer to get the best out of his Lapat. In due course, how a lawyer mentored and handled his Lapat came to differentiate his practice.

Lapat320 joined the breakfast meeting just as D2Y2 was serving the second round of coffee. After introductions, Lapat320 made the opening remarks 'Thank you all for availing my legal services. I'll be charging you on an hourly basis. Any strategic advice will need the approval of my senior advocate and will be charged extra. While I was on my way, I went through the media coverage that is giving you an anxious moment. Having consulted all the databases, I am prepared and ready to answer your questions. Your time starts now.'

Sattu shot the first question.

'Can we sue HJ and put him behind bars?'

Lapat320 replied calmly.

'Privacy is your fundamental right and you can sue HJ for intruding on your privacy. However, HJ will simply argue that all the reporting was done under the program 'KYC' meaning 'Know Your Candidate' using the material available in the public domain. Based on this, he will be able to hide behind his 'right to inform' as a journalist. It is, therefore, highly unlikely that HJ will be put behind bars.'

Lattu was concerned about Netaji Mungeri Lal's attacks and asked,

'How about suing Netaji? He has openly indulged in character assassination.'

'We can certainly assist you in filing a defamation suit against Mungeri Lal. He will, however, use the freedom of speech argument as defense and 'tarikh pe tarikh' tactics to tire you out. At the end of this grueling match, the best you can hope for is an apology. I leave it to you to do the cost-benefit analysis.'

'How about the threats he has been issuing?' queried Lattu.

'Mungeri Lal will try to invoke section 294 of IPC to put pressure on Y2K. We can assist you in ensuring that he does not succeed in a court of law. But we can't do much about the collateral damage Mungeri Lal's action may cause.'

'Let me come to the point. If this vicious campaign by HJ and Netaji does not stop quickly, our ranking will dip to the level from which redemption will be almost impossible. Can we not somehow restrain HJ and Mungeri through the court?' asked Kattu forthrightly.

'The only way to get immediate relief, in this case, is to engage someone from the BNHKH panel,' replied Papat320 calmly.

'What the hell is the BNHKH panel?' asked Kattu

'Sorry, we Popats tend to use abbreviations very often. They are so much more convenient. Anyway, BNHKH means '*Bas Naam Hi Kafi Hai*'. I do not think you have the means to engage any one of those top-shot lawyers in the BNHKH league,' replied Lapat320 nonchalantly.

'What are we then supposed to do?' asked Sattu in exasperation.

'That is a million-dollar question for which I need to consult my senior. That will only take a minute. Please be warned that this strategic advice will be billed extra,' replied Lapat320 and went into a conversation mode using its in-built Concon. A minute later he was ready with the answer and said,

'Here is the advice, so listen carefully. Firstly, your core problem is that of perception which you are trying to fix through legal means. It's not going to solve your problem. Only an out-of-the-world idea can fix the problem. Secondly, your focus is on shooting the messenger. Instead, you should concentrate on managing the message. Thirdly, you need an election strategist and not a lawyer to tide over this crisis. If I am not mistaken, you have already got the best election strategist that this Mandal can boast of. Lastly, as agreed, you will be charged for all three pieces of advice separately.'

With that final piece of advice, Lapat320 handed over a detailed bill, thanked everyone once again, and made his exit. That left Sattu wringing his hands, Mattu staring at the hefty figure on the bill, Kattu scratching his head for a counterpoint, and Lattu not any wiser than he was. At last, Mattu remarked,

'Just now we paid a ransom only to be told what we already know.'

'Not really. Now at least you know the meaning of *'ghar ki murgi dal barabar'* quipped Vartika. Everyone laughed and the tension evaporated.

'On a serious note, we should focus on finding the right message as we have been doing so far. So, let us finalize today's message for our manifesto,' said Vartika.

'I think 'L for Legal Framework' is the right message for our manifesto today,' pronounced Lattu confidently. Everyone concurred and quickly authorized Vartika and Y2K to formulate a strategy for the manifesto as well as for dealing with the double menace called HJ and Mungeri. Vartika thought over for a minute and declared,

'We haven't held a single press conference so far. It is time that we organize one. Please assemble at the Press Club in the evening and leave the rest to me. Until then, avoid any contact with human journalists. I also suggest that while leaving, use the backdoor exit.' Everyone complied.

The press conference was crowded with all the channels present in anticipation of an opportunity to grill Y2K and Vartika. 'Maybe Y2K will announce his withdrawal today,' muttered HJ to another journalist. They were however taken by surprise when Vyoma appeared in her virtual avatar and took center stage. Flanked by Y2K and Vartika, she looked regal and imposing in her space apparel. 'This changes the optics,' muttered HJ to himself. He had no choice but to listen.

Vyoma began,

'Ladies and Gentleman,

When I look at the vastness of the universe, affairs on the earth look trivial. Yet, the heart and mind of an astronaut is always grounded to the earth. I have deep connections with Kautukpur. Naturally, I have been watching the election activities in Kautukpur with keen interest. More so, because my husband happens to be one of the candidates. However, I was distressed to see the slanderous reporting and low level of politicking over an issue that should have been nobody's concern except mine. I absolutely love and support both of these two wonderful people sitting by my side.' She paused, clasped Y2K and Vartika's hands, and raised them together for all the Jholus to take the pictures. She then continued,

'The activities of HJ and Mungeri Lal have caused immense distress to me. If these two gentlemen do not render their apology by the end of the day, I shall be compelled to file a suit against them in the International Court of Space.'

A hush fell in the hall as the implications sank into HJ's clever mind. The International Court of Space was established in 2045 to protect the interests and well-being of space citizens whose population had grown substantially in number. It operated out of a large spaceship in geosynchronous orbit and had come to be known for its stringent laws. Earthlings who were sued could be ruined merely by fighting the case. The fines imposed were astronomical and a month's jail in space was considered worse than the '*kala pani*' imrisonment in Andmans on Earth. '*Astronauts se panga nahi lene ka*' was the prevailing wisdom. HJ was a wise man. He quickly and quietly left the press conference to draft an apology. Vartika observed it and knew that Mugeri Lal too would fall in line.

Relieved, she thanked Vyoma and prompted Y2K to take up the manifesto agenda of the day.

Buoyed by Vyoma's presence and performance, Y2K felt confident and composed as he addressed the press:

'Friends,

In 1993 a movie dialogue '*Tarikh Par Tarikh, Tarikh Par Tarikh, Tarikh Par Tarikh Milti Rahi....Lekin Insaf Nahi Mila My Lord*' famously captured the unwelcome side of our legal system. It is a matter of shame that even in 2050 our legal system remains infected with the *Tarikh Par Tarikh* syndrome. Twenty-five years ago, fifty million cases were pending in the lower courts, with each Mandal having an average of fifty thousand cases. That figure remains unchanged in Kautukpur even today. We have witnessed tremendous progress in every sphere except for legal administration which remains an island of ineptitude and a relic of inefficiency.

To wipe out the pendency, the rate of disposal of cases must be much higher than the rate of institution of new cases. Since this fundamental issue is not addressed by the conventional approach, the wait time for justice has been increasing steadily. Justice delayed is justice denied. Fortunately, Popat technology can ensure that justice is neither denied nor delayed. Japats or the *Judicial Affair Popats* are designed specifically as judges to man the courts and deliver judgments. They have been successfully deployed in some countries. Our Constitution Amendment 2045 also empowers Mandals to deploy Japats in lower courts and constitute hybrid benches in other courts.

The introduction of Japats has been resisted on the ground that a machine cannot sit in judgment over a human. Japats of today are much more than simply machines and possess all the qualities that a judge should possess. They not only have comprehensive knowledge of the law but can also learn from experience. They are impartial, incorruptible, and scrupulous in following the law. More importantly, they need no holidays, have no lineage, and can be appointed in any number without generating controversy or turf-war. The diffidence in using this smart technology, therefore, is unwarranted, especially when the amendment also provides enough safeguards. For example, an appeal against the judgment of a Japat will lie only with a human judge. In the case of a disagreement in a hybrid bench, the judgment of a human judge will prevail.

Keeping these factors in mind, if elected, I shall constitute enough Japat courts to clear the entire backlog in one year. These courts will work 365 days a year in two shifts to ensure that justice is delivered on time. To further improve efficiency, I shall also mandate the total elimination of the use of paper. To support the needy, the Mandal government will also offer free help from the government-appointed Lapats.

In short, my manifesto agenda 'L for Legal framework' is to shape the legal framework in a manner that will ensure 'Ease of doing justice' to deliver 'Just in time justice'. I am sure the 'Ease of doing justice' achieved by the Lapat and Japat ecosystem will lead to enhanced 'Ease of doing business' and 'Ease of living'.

I appeal to the citizens of Katukpur to vote for me to make it happen.'

Post-conference, HJ and Mungeri Lal were banished from the channels and the headlines talked of 'Ease Of Doing Justice', 'Just In Time Justice', 'Japat-Lapat Tango', and 'Y2K Promises To Clear Legal Backlog In One Year'.

Miraculously, instead of sliding further down, Y2K improved his rating by three positions when the polling for the day closed.

Chapter XXVII

The breakfast meeting began in the usual atmosphere of carefree exuberance. Recalling the worried, angry, and frustrated mood of yesterday, Lattu quipped, 'After yesterday's episode, I now realize that even a day can be a long time in politics. We must thank Vartika for pulling off the miracle,'

'Oh, it was just a simple strategy that worked. Miracles are actually happening in the world of medicine these days,' replied Vartika modestly, pointing out to the news program that was narrating the advances in medical science over the last quarter of a century.

Vartika had reason to believe in the miracles of medicine. A few years ago she was diagnosed with a rare form of cancer. Fortunately, nanobots detected and repaired the damaged cells immediately while the nanomedicine worked to remove the genetic deficiency. She was declared hale and hearty within a week. Not only Vartika, the rest of the gang too had their own stories of miracles to tell. Kattu was happily eating pancakes but he was not allowed to do so till 2037 when stem-cell therapy cured his Type1 diabetes by regenerating beta cells in the pancreas that produce insulin. When Mattu's brother needed a kidney transplant, he didn't have to run around for a kidney donor, it was simply bioengineered and 3D printed. Lattu had his head spinning frequently which got fixed with the help of an AI-assisted neuromodulating device. Sattu was thankful that gene editing had cured his son of a hemophilia disorder that could be life-threatening.

While they were busy sharing the miracles of medicine, Lattu remembered the manifesto and declared, 'Let us make 'M for Medicine' as our agenda today.' Kattu immediately opposed and said,

'Medicine is a noble profession. Why bring politics into it?'

'Politics is about good, bad, ugly, and everything in between. So, why keep the medical world outside its scrutiny? To be more precise, let us discuss the state of medical setup in Kautuk Mandal and how should we shape it?' replied Lattu and found muted approval.

Mattu thought over it and said,

'You are making a fair point. So much has changed for the better and yet there is a feeling of slight unease somewhere that needs to be assessed and addressed.'

In response, Lattu embarked on a long discourse,

'How do you assess the change in isolation? Just like in every other field, big data, computing, bionics, and AI are driving medical science with unimaginable results. The approach itself has changed from reactive and curative to predictive and preventive care. Everyone now sports a few electronic tattoos that generate data about vital functions. The real-time data coupled with the medical history, lifestyle data, and genome data is processed by licensed medical-Clowns using predictive algorithms. If anything is amiss, your friendly 'Doctor Popat', or Dopat, appears to physically examine and prescribe treatment. Dopats have brought back the concept of the family physician, so much so, that I see my Dopat more often than my children.'

Lattu was not exaggerating. The transformation brought by technology had enabled 'treatment at home' possible in most cases, making traditional hospitals redundant. Internal sensors, wearables, electronic patches, miniaturized devices, and on-demand immersive consultation obviated the need for a hospital bed. Only in dire emergencies, patients were ferried by an air ambulance to a hospital. Hospitals of 2050 resembled more like vast control centers which housed licensed Clowns, and boasted of new departments like Genomics, Bionic Organs, Nanomedicine, Brain-Computer Interfacing, and Organ-Cloning. They were mostly manned by 'Healthcare Application Updated Popats' called Happus. More than ninety percent of surgeries were done by surgeon-Popats and hospitals employed more Popats and Happus than humans.

Sattu intervened before the discourse could go further and said,

'The problem with the new medical set-up is that it has taken humans out of the equation. Doctors do no more than play golf. In fact, I played golf with my doctor friend this morning. He worries that humans will soon be out of practice and will therefore lose the ability to further improve, innovate, and invent. That means the progress will soon plateau and new problems will overwhelm the medical system.'

Comments from Sattu inspired Kattu, as he added,

'The other problem is that of bias distorting the whole medical ecosystem. In the earlier system, pharmaceutical companies used to invest heavily in discovering a new drug and market extensively, sometimes even unethically. Doctors used to prescribe all kinds of medicines, mostly in excess of the need and without care for the after-effects. This bias has been transplanted and magnified in the new system. Assisted by AI, pharmaceutical companies are now discovering a new medicine every day, which speedily reaches the market after the trials simulated on computers. Because of the flooding of medicines and acquired bias, Dopats always prescribe newer, costlier, and excessive medicines. Excess medicines complicate the existing problem, leading to even more medicines being administered, creating a vicious cycle. Sadly, nobody bothers to arrest this vicious cycle.'

'I have a more serious problem with the system. All the advances have been hailed in the name of cutting costs and making healthcare more affordable. In reality, the reverse has happened since the benefits of cost reduction are unevenly distributed. Ultimately, your wealth index, your power quotient, and the worth of your Insurance policy determine the treatment you get. Miracles elude those who can't afford,' said Sattu forcefully.

It was now Mattu's turn to raise concern. He said,

'We should also worry about the dark side of the medical world. The incidents of deaths or mishaps caused by negligent production or administration of drugs are not unknown. Negligence may be an aberration but is a crime nonetheless. What is alarming is the intentional use of medicines in a crime, most exemplified by the M-Gang who specialize in 'murder by medicine'. Just like a contract killer who tracks his prey, and chooses his gun, time, and place to deliver the fatal shot, the M-gangster hacks the medical database, and chooses his medicine, time, and place to give the shot that proves fatal. I think such cases should be dealt with an iron hand.'

Vartika, who was listening patiently so far, intervened,

'Guys, I agree with all that has been said. However, voters are more influenced by action, even if symbolic, rather than by informed discussions. A good political strategy is to highlight such incidents. In the past three weeks, there have been three deaths that can be attributed to excess medicine, lack of medicine, or misuse of medicine. I, therefore, call such deaths as 'Muder by Medicine'. What we can do is to stage a candle march in protest against 'Murder By Medicine'. Other candidates too will jump on the bandwagon of 'M for Medicine', but we get the first-mover advantage.'

As agreed, the Y2K gang started the candle march in the evening from Pigeon Square and many joined them on the way. By the time they reached Jantar Mantar, enough crowd had gathered and Jholus had taken their position. After observing two minutes of silence for the three departed souls, Y2K took the mic and spoke,

'Citizen of Kautukpur,

A hundred years ago, life expectancy in our country was only thirty-five years. Advances in medical sciences and their integration with smart technologies have increased the average life expectancy in 2050 to a hundred years. That is a miracle of medicine that all of us should salute.

To consolidate these gains, my manifesto pledges to give Kautukpur a new medical university dedicated to genomics, nanomedicine, bionics, robotics, and many more upcoming technologies. I also promise to open a medical research center that will bring together medical practitioners, engineers, and data scientists to create and provide the most efficient system of healthcare in Kautukpur.

Besides making promises, I also wish to invite your attention to the dark side of this noble profession and give voice to every citizen's concerns. Today, we have gathered to protest against the 'Murder by Medicine' and condole three deaths in three weeks that could have been averted.

A man died a few weeks ago due to excessive medicines. Many called it an act of unintended murder, but no cognizance was taken because greed, negligence, and incompetence are usually well tolerated by the system. I would, however, ensure that such practices are regulated and corrected.

Paradoxically, the lack of medicines was the cause of another death last week in Kautukpur. Such cases routinely happened in the past but are unacceptable in 2050. It is my agenda today that the miracles of medicine do not pass by the needy. If elected, I shall ensure that every citizen has access to the medicines whenever and wherever needed.

Lastly, we witnessed a mysterious death three days ago which has been allegedly linked to the M-Gang. From the preliminary evidence gathered so far, it appears to be a murder by medicine. Sadly, a few of the candidates have sprung up in the defense of M-Gang while a few others are advising not to politicize this issue. I deplore such misleading posturing and demand quick investigation and exemplary punishment of the perpetrators.

'M for Medicine' in my manifesto stands for a safe, secure, accessible, and affordable medical system for all the citizens of Kautukpur.'

After listening to Y2K, Jholus wondered how they could miss the newsworthy potential of the three deaths Y2K had mentioned. They decided to compensate for it by highlighting the candle march and Y2K's speech. Jhallu from the channel which ran a documentary on 'miracles by medicine' in the morning held a spirited debate on 'Murder by Medicine' in the evening. HJ from Channel7 redeemed himself by running an *expose* on M-Gang that had succeeded D-gang under the headline 'Dial M for Murder'. Many candidates in the fray woke up to the new opportunity for politicking and began chasing the Jholus for a few bytes. Jholus, however, chose to supplement Y2K's speech with comments from experts in a white coat and a decorative stethoscope. Soon, the viewers knew more about 'M for Medicine' than the experts themselves.

When the votes were counted for the day, Y2K was back in the business, having improved his rating by two positions.

Chapter XXVIII

By 2050, Popats had come to occupy a unique position in the lives of humans. To humans, they were more than just pets or servants. They were neither friends nor relatives. They were constant companions but had no attachment. They were neither rivals nor partners. The human history of a million years had no parallel or precedence to define such a relationship. Yet, within a decade, humans had effortlessly assimilated Popats into their social life. A small reflection of this was that in a social or friendly gathering, Popats almost always were the most common topic of small talk.

D2Y2 was the envy of everyone in the gang. It was only human that they would find someone else's Popat better than their own. Kattu was in a somewhat similar mood when he said,

'D2Y2 is so cool and my Popat is so irritating. He has become too argumentative.'

'Popat and argumentative is an oxymoron,' commented Lattu.

'He must have learned the art and science of arguments from you,' said Sattu without a hint of malice.

'Unlike humans, a quick fix for behavioral problems of Popat is easily available. Your problem of argumentative Popat can be solved simply by upgrading with a 'Yes Sir' Appu,' suggested Mattu.

'I did upgrade with the 'Yes Sir' Appu and regretted. Once, while admonishing in a moment of anger, I said, 'Am I a fool?', and my Popat immediately replied, 'Yes, sir'. Since then, I have kept the 'Yes Sir' Appu in the deactivated mode,' confided Kattu.

'I wish we could deactivate the 'Yes Sir' mode in humans as well. Then cronies like Mungeri Lal would be better persons to deal with in politics,' rued Y2K.

'Cronyism is deeply ingrained in our culture of favoritism and influence peddling. For example, Mungeri Lal is a Kappuswami crony because he used Kappuswami's influence to get a Popat distribution agency as a favor,' elucidated Sattu.

'Don't forget that Kappusawmi himself is a product of nepotism who derives all his influence and political heft from his cousin Appuswami who in turn has inherited his political party from his father Tappusway,' elaborated Mattu.

'In that case, why don't we make 'N for Nepotism' as our agenda for today,' concluded Lattu. Everyone concurred.

Discussion on nepotism was particularly gratifying for Vartika as she explained,

'Rumor is being spread by Guru Panchal that Y2K is a proxy candidate of Kappuswamy. Therefore, raising the issue of nepotism will be very opportune to counter such rumors.'

Sattu always saw beyond the election strategy. He articulated,

'Nepotism is unfortunately deeply rooted in all walks of life, be it politics, bureaucracy, judiciary, entertainment, or private enterprise. To be honest, we all indulge in nepotism of some form or the other. Therefore, we resent but we also acquiesce, overlooking even the grave acts of nepotism in the public sphere.'

'I couldn't agree more with you. Nepotism is like cancer. Technology has found a cure for cancer but it has no cure for nepotism,' chipped in Mattu.

Lattu, the CTO, always championed technology. So he defended.

'Technology may not cure the cancer of nepotism but it can arrest it to some extent. Most tasks are nowadays automated, cutting out the delay, inconvenience, and inefficiency. Instant availability of information has enhanced transparency. A large number of human resource functions are now routinely delegated to Popats and Clowns with outcomes based on data, rules, and algorithms, reducing the scope for discretion and favor. We can perhaps strengthen these processes further as part of our agenda.'

Kattu always looked for a counterargument. So he rebutted,

'Technology is not the panacea for all the ills. It has its side effects too. Algorithms carry forward the originator's biases and are prone to manipulations. AI-based outcomes may not always be the best when you are dealing with humans. Spotting a talent, spark, or innovation is beyond the capacity of AI. Learning from their masters, Popats have now started creating their own closed-loop Popat networks which are akin to our old boy networks, leading to apprehensions of spreading a new kind of favoritism that will only bolster the culture the nepotism in the future.'

Mattu always tried to do the balancing act. So he intervened and said,

'Your point is well taken. The benefits of technology plateau after a certain point. Polity has to ultimately evolve based on education, consensus, and ethics. However, in the context of today's manifesto agenda, we do not know what to advocate. So let us leave it to Vartika to strategize.'

Vartika responded,

'Everyone preaches against nepotism but it can be eradicated only if we practice what we preach. Politicians specialize in telling others what to do. For a change, let us tell the voters what we shall do. I propose that we all take an oath today not to practice nepotism in public life and exhort all others to do the same.' Everyone concurred.

As planned, the Y2K gang assembled in the evening at Jantar Mantar. Vartika was able to gather a bunch of Y2K supporters as well. As soon as three Jholus had taken their position, Y2K began his speech.

'Citizens of Kautukpur,

I am here today to campaign against the menace of nepotism in our polity. The term nepotism comes from the Latin word *nepos* meaning nephew. In India, we use the wider term *BhaiBhatijavad* and its practice is also more widespread. We find *BhaiBhatijavad* all around us but its practice in politics is particularly glaring. It is corrupting our organizations and corroding the very institutions that sustain us. This disease is now threatening to infect the Popat world as well which we have freshly and assiduously built over the last decade. Therefore, if elected, I shall constitute a *'BhaiBhatijavad Unmoolan Committee'* which will work for the eradication of nepotism from our polity with a wider jurisdiction that will cover the Popat world as well.

My manifesto agenda, 'N for No to Nepotism', is committed to the clarion call given by our local poet, 'Kavi Kautuk Kumar', whom I quote:

'Suno suno o sattawalon, janta ki fariyad ko, khatam karo khatam karo, Bhaibhatijavad ko.'

In keeping with the spirit of this slogan, I implore all of you to work toward the eradication of nepotism from public life. Without naming anyone in particular, I appeal to the citizens of Kautukpur to vote out all the candidates who are known practitioners of nepotism.

I believe in practicing what one preaches. Therefore, in order to reiterate my commitment to the manifesto, I shall take an oath today not to indulge in any act of nepotism and request each one of you to do the same.'

Y2K then raised his hand in the manner of taking an oath and read out loudly.

'I, Y2K, solemnly take an oath that I shall not indulge in any act of nepotism while performing public duty and that I shall work assiduously for the elimination of nepotism from our polity.'

Having taken the oath to a huge round of applause, Y2K invited his gang and the supporters to take the same oath individually. At the last count, three dozen people took the oath. Impressed Jholus ran the headline 'Y2K campaigns against nepotism' and Jhallus debated whether the Y2K campaign against nepotism was politically motivated and what impact the Y2K manifesto would have on the poll ratings of some of the candidates.

At the end of the day, the efforts put up by the Y2K gang did have some impact. For the first time in two weeks, Kappuswamy lost his top position and Y2K improved his ranking by two positions. Y2K was in the reckoning once again.

Chapter XXIX

Breakfast meetings had become relaxed and livelier with improved ratings of Y2K. Lattu was back to cracking his PJs. He started the banter by asking,

'How do you make out a Popat from a human?'

When no one answered, Lattu volunteered,

'Give each one an onion to peel. The one who does not cry is a Popat.'

Encouraged by a little laughter, he cracked another PJ.

'How do you make out a Popat from a politician?'

'The one who does not shed crocodile tears is a Popat.'

The laughter this time was a little more appreciative, so Lattu continued,

'How do you make out a Popat from a voter?'

'The one who does not protest over the onion prices is a Popat.'

This time Kattu put his foot down and said,

'Enough of the PJs, Lattu. We are here to discuss serious politics amid an impending election. So be serious.'

Enjoying the hot onion uttapam and onion sambar that D2Y2 had served, Lattu, however, continued in the same vein.

'Okay, let us talk about politics seriously. Politics is like an onion. It has layer after layer and leaves a foul smell in the mouth if eaten raw. However, if cooked well with the right ingredients, it delivers.'

Everyone seemed to be unimpressed with this profound culinary statement and continued to nibble at their onion uttapams. Seeing this, Lattu delivered his final punch line.

'Light up a Lattu and respond, you morons. Onions are right now trending as hot potatoes. I, therefore, suggest that we cook up some 'O for Onions' for today's manifesto menu.'

'You do have a knack for finding the right issue with the right alphabet at the right time,' responded Vartika appreciatively and continued,

'Research shows a strong correlation between onion prices and election results. Out of a thousand Mandals, four hundred Mandals are considered highly sensitive, four hundred are moderately sensitive, and only two hundred are immune to onion prices. In the sensitive Mandals, if the onion prices rise beyond a threshold, the probability of an incumbent losing the election is more than ninety percent. If there is a glut in the market, discontent amongst the growers inversely affects the feel-good factor by seventy percent. Ninety-five percent of the successful candidates make some kind of promise about controlling onion prices. The moral of the research is that talking about onion economics makes good politics.'

Kattu was not impressed with the analysis and said,

'This is stale research and I do not agree with your conclusion either. The problem is not that economics affects politics. The problem is that politicians spoil good economics. We are the largest producer, consumer, and exporter of onions in the world. We have AI technology that can assess global, national, and local demand and work out an optimum strategy for onion production, distribution, and pricing. However, politicians, profiteers, and hoarders find ingenious ways to spoil the broth.'

Sattu supported Kattu for a change and said,

'I agree. A few years ago, there was a dip in production because Gappus failed to arrange artificial rains despite the drought. Two years ago, there was a shortage despite sufficient production because some hoarders broke into the supply chain software. Last year, onion procurement prices crashed as profiteers connived with politicians to manipulate the pricing. This year's price rise is being attributed to incompetence in inventory management by Mandal, creating an opportunity for *Netas* to jump in. Kappuswamy has already announced a ban on exports, while Guru Panchal is promising the free supply of a bag of onions to every household. Prachandika Devi, or Prada, has been holding a protest rally for the last ten days as if the slogans would scare away inflation. It is a tragedy that despite so much attention, no one is talking about fixing the actual problems.'

'Leave alone fixing it, there is one problem that politicians aren't even aware of. When we were kids, we used to eat *Kautukpur Kanda*, the local onion, which was distinctly red and uneven in size. Today, all the onions you get are white and of almost uniform size but with no flavor. The Kautukpur onion is almost extinct. We are fast losing biodiversity due to unmindful commercialization of technology like genetically modified crops, and the Kautukpur onion is only a small example of the plant diversity that is vanishing,' protested Sattu.

'Commercial technology is a tradeoff between present fulfillment and future dangers. For example, demand for onions has shot up by ten times in the past fifty years. Without the use of technology and its large-scale commercialization, you can't meet this demand. In the process, indigenous variety gets pushed out of the market. All you can do is preserve it for sentimental reasons,' said Kattu.

Y2K finally spoke up, 'We need to preserve biodiversity, not for sentimental reasons, but for well-founded scientific reasons. Thank you for the discussions. I get the hang of what we need to do regarding the agenda on onions. Vartika may perhaps tell us how we go about it.' VC explained her plan for the day before they dispersed.

The gang met at Jantar Mantar in the evening. Looking at the small crowd that had gathered, Vartika was pleased to note that the brand Y2K was slowly catching up. Everyone in the crowd was given a packet containing four Kautukpur onions and some seeds. A pigeon was printed on one side, and the other side of the packet read: 'Join our Onion Mission, Vote for Y2K's Pigeon'. Jholus found the Onion Mission slogan interesting and interviewed people randomly on their opinions about onions. Finally, they settled down to record Y2K's speech.

Y2K spoke briefly,

'Citizens of Kautukpur, The common man today is going nuts over the rising prices of onions. In response, my fellow candidates are shedding a few tears and making tall promises which you all know will come a cropper. Instead of making promises, I would like to propose solutions. The solution to the underlying problem is multilayered like the onion itself. These layers include the use of the right technology, planning, execution, pricing, and distribution. I propose to set up an 'Onion Planning Clown of Kautukpur' which will not only accomplish these tasks but will also formulate real-time strategies to counter profiteers and hoarders. Only a combination of technology and good governance can deliver sustainable results. If elected, I will deliver both on technology and governance.

Talking of technology and governance, it is my duty to speak about the problems of the future as well. Fast-declining biodiversity is perhaps the biggest challenge mankind may be facing in the future. Vanishing Kautukpur onion is only a small example. This flavorful but unevenly shaped vegetable was the staple diet of the common man till a few decades ago but now is not grown commercially at all. At this rate, it will be extinct in the next few years. It is futile to promote it as a commercial crop, but it can certainly be promoted for growing in home gardens and vertical farms. The state should not give free onions, but teach its citizens how to grow them. Accordingly, my government will push to increase vertical farms that will not only produce indigenous varieties but contribute up to twenty percent of production which will act as a price stabilization factor.

Friends, the solution ultimately lies in working together. Vote for me and give me an opportunity to work together with you.'

Jholus lapped up Y2K's manifesto recipe on onions and the audience liked their headlines. But the most impressed was Mr. Mahan whose restaurant consumed copious amounts of onions. He was fond of the Jonathan Swift quote 'This is every cook's opinion – no savory dish without an onion'. So onion was the star ingredient of every dish he served to Vartika and Y2K. Vartika, however, was adherent to the second part of the quote that said 'But lest your kissing should be spoiled, your onions must be fully boiled' and kept the dishes garnished with onions at bay. Notwithstanding her aversion to raw onion, she was confident that the little talk of onions in the manifesto would surely stir up some excitement in the voters. She was vindicated when the voting results came in and Y2K improved his position to move to number ten.

Chapter XXX

When D2Y2 informed the Y2K gang that the breakfast meeting had been canceled, none protested. They had been working continuously since last fortnight so the unexpected break was welcome. None even pressed D2Y2 for a reason.

The reason for Y2K, however, was not a break, but the breakup. It literally came as a bolt from the blue in the form of a message from his wife, Vyoma. Y2K read the message again and again, half hoping that the message would disappear. Even on the hundred and first reading it didn't. It read.

'In a few weeks, we would be completing twenty-five years of our marriage. I, therefore, felt the urgency to reflect upon what life has in store for both of us.

In the early years of our marriage, I would often complain that you did not give me enough space. As destiny would have it, I now have the whole space to me. Having spent nine out of the last ten years in a spaceship, I consider it my home. That makes the possibility of our making home together rather remote.

Life in space is in stark contrast to that on Earth. There are no storms, no hustle and bustle, no rush, and no noises.

All you have is a deep silence and a vast darkness. That can sometimes be very lonely. I have shared those moments of loneliness with Andrew, a fellow astronaut, looking together at the big blue earth from space. In one of those moments, I fell in love with him. He proposed some time ago, leaving me at the crossroads, literally between the moon and the earth.

The idea of breaking up with you was a classic duel between heart and mind. My mind told me to get back to earth and my heart implored me to fly and reach out to the moon. In the end, I decided to listen to my heart. That most certainly will break your heart. I am sorry. Hope you will forgive me for being heartless.

The notice for divorce will reach you soon after you receive this message. We have decided to get married in a spaceship according to Hindu rites. It will be the first traditional Hindu marriage in space. The logistics of taking seven rounds around the fire in the presence of a priest in the spaceship will take quite a bit of planning and time. So the announcement of marriage will come well after the election concludes.

Your decision to contest the election gave me hope that you would be able to find a new purpose in life. Just as I have moved on, I fervently hope that you too will be able to move on in life, for which I wish you the very best.

Vyoma.'

Having read the message for the nth time, the enormity of what Vyoma had written finally dawned upon Y2K. Stunned, he kept sitting without knowing what to do. After a while, resigned to his fate, he reached out to his Lapat to file a 'no contest' reply to the divorce notice.

Like everything else, the process of divorce had metamorphosed by 2050. There was a humongous increase in the number of divorces in late 2030 as the rise of Popats compounded the already complex relationship equations that most humans found difficult to cope with anyway. The *'pati patni aur woh'* triangle, the usual culprit in the marriage, became unmanageable with Popats playing the triple role of a friend, confidant, and spoilsport with utmost imperfection. Another knotty equation of *'sas-bahu'* got even more insoluble with Popats not knowing whether to follow the instruction of the mother-in-law or daughter-in-law. As a result, they frequently went into an overload condition known as the *'sas-bahu and Popat'* conundrum. However, more tragic than the cases of triangular or quadrangular relationships were the cases of relationships turning singular, as loneliness and isolation engulfed the whole society. Problems like the increasing rate of divorce was a direct consequence of it.

The human relationship is too complex for technology to understand, let alone master it. Yet, it is the technology that humans resort to for dealing with the consequences of technology. Not surprisingly, AI was put to use in streamlining and managing the process of divorce that had come under strain. In 2040, the data scientists came together and discovered that marriage was just a state of zero or one. It was either workable or non-workable. So they devised a marriage-workability index that could be derived using big data, supplemented by AI-generated analysis. If the resultant value was below the threshold, marriage was considered unworkable and divorce was promptly granted by a 'Marriage Bureau Clown'. In the case of Y2K and Vyoma, the workability index was found to be below the threshold value and the divorce came by the evening.

It was the end of the process that hit Y2K hard. Despite being far away, he had always felt attached to Vyoma by the invisible bond of marriage. It was like floating along a spaceship without losing contact in a no-gravity zone. When the divorce came, he felt as if that spaceship had made a course correction, leaving him to hurtle down into the big dark space with seemingly no end. Feeling utterly rudderless, helpless, and clueless, Y2K took to drinking till he finally collapsed.

Chapter XXXI

The next morning, Y2K was not in his senses, and D2Y2 dutifully conveyed this condition to his gang. Y2K was known for his disciplined habits, but every man was entitled to a drinking bout once in a while. Though they felt a little concerned about his condition and a little about the election campaign, they decided to wait for one more day. Vartika thoughtfully put out a press note stating that the Y2K team was doing a mid-way appraisal of their manifesto and would resume the daily alphabetic agenda soon after conducting a ground survey.

By afternoon, the effect of alcohol wore off. As he sobered up, the reality of separation from Vyoma hit him again and the feeling of floating around in space without any anchor came back. When D2Y2 reminded him of the incessant calls and queries about the campaign meeting from his gang, his immediate reaction was to get away from it all. All he wanted was to float away in the dark space and relive his pain. So he instructed D2Y2 to fix no meeting, make no appointment, and take no call from anyone. He then switched off his Concon and locked up his *Adda*. Having ensured that he would not be bothered by the outside world, Y2K resumed his drinking.

When the same story repeated on the third day morning, everyone in the gang was seriously concerned. D2Y2 had apprised them of Y2K's binge drinking. From D2Y2's account, something seemed to be troubling Y2K. They wanted to help but had no means of finding out what was bothering Y2K. His rating had slipped by eight points and looked set to go down further. The gang held an emergency lunch meeting in which they ate less, worried more, and finally authorized Vartika to do whatever was needed.

In the evening, just when Vartika was feeling frustrated at not being able to find a way out, she received a brief message from Vyoma. It read.

'I am unable to get in touch with Y2K. D2Y2 tells me that he is in bad shape. I am distraught at the thought that I am responsible for his condition. I broke up with him and the divorce came through two days ago. Y2K has not been able to handle the shock and needs help. The only person who can assist and anchor him right now is you. Hope you can help him out. Vyoma.'

Vartika desperately wanted to reach out to Y2K. Now that she knew the reason, she frantically tried to think of a solution. The problem was that Y2K was still not communicable and was refusing to even meet anyone from his gang. She thought of calling a cop, a medic, and even a shrink but dismissed such ideas immediately. Going incommunicado was not a crime and binge drinking over two or three days did not warrant hauling him up to a rehabilitation center. Y2K needed counseling, a shoulder to cry on, and time to heal. He had none of these luxuries. Vartika thought over the impossible situation and finally hit upon a strategy. She called up one person who could help.

Chapter XXXII

It was rare for D2Y2 to attend to a doorbell and even rarer to find a smiling man clad in a pure white cotton dress with a tilak on his forehead. A quick look-up from his database told D2Y2 that the visitor was Professor Ashwini Acharya, the famed astrologer, popularly known as Guruji. D2Y2 greeted him and said,

'Namaste Guruji. I am sorry to tell you that Y2K is not meeting anyone.'

Guruji smiled and replied,

'That is alright D2Y2. I am not here to meet Y2K. I have come here only to give him *Prasadam* and my blessings.'

Having been trained in Indian traditions and ethos, D2Y2 had turned into a fine '*sanskari*' Popat. D2Y2 reckoned that taking *Prasadam* to Y2K would not amount to disobeying his instructions. So he respectfully let Guruji in and offered him a seat and a glass of water.

Prasadam was a piece of sweet called *laddu* and a marigold flower that D2Y2 carefully took to Y2K who had sobered up a little by that time. Y2K touched the flower to his head, folded his hands in prayer, and ate the *Prasadam*. He had not eaten well enough for the past two days and *laddu* felt divine. When Y2K had finished eating the *Prasadam*, D2Y2 told him that Guruji wished to give him blessings. Y2K was in no mood to see anyone but his *'sanskar'* forbade him to refuse the blessings of a Guru. Even in his disoriented state, he went out and as per custom, touched Guruji's feet. Guruji smiled and simply said,

'Be happy, son.'

Y2K in his depressed state responded,

'Thank you Guruji for your blessings but there is not much to be happy about.'

Guruji smiled again and said,

'That depends on your perspective. If you look at life as *Prasadam* from God, it can be bliss. Otherwise, it can be a drag. In life, you may not be able to shape the outcome but you can always shape your outlook.'

'That is easier said than done, Guruji,' murmured Y2K as a tear appeared in his eyes. Before he knew it, the tears swelled as the suppressed pain came out. Guruji sat in silence, letting him cry. Before Y2K could feel embarrassed, Guruji said,

'It is alright, son. Even a tough guy needs to cry sometimes. Now that you look even more disheveled than earlier, I have some more *Prasadam* for you.'

Y2K smiled as Guruji gave him another *laddu*. His mother used to make similar *laddus* and he felt like a child again while eating the second helping of *laddu*. Miraculously, after devouring the *Prasadam*, Y2K felt energized and in control of himself.

Y2K recalled his first meeting with Guruji and asked,

'Guruji, Thank you for being so kind to me. However, I am curious to know what brought you here. How did you know that I was in distress? Was this meeting preordained? Can I do something for you?'

Smiling as ever, Guruji replied,

'There was no divine intervention. There were no regular updates on your manifesto continuously for three days. My concern was confirmed by a call from Vartika. To answer your other question, let me remind you of our first meeting. I predicted that you would be amongst the final two contenders in this election. I came here to make sure that my prediction does not go wrong. By offering you *Prasadam* and my blessings, I was merely doing my *Karma*. Now it is up to you to follow your *Karma*.'

Y2K reflected for a moment on what Guruji had said and replied,

'I get your message, Guruji. You just reminded me of what *Bhagwadgita* teaches us. I promise I won't run away from my *karma*.'

Guruji blessed him again and left. He had accomplished what no other counselor could have.

After Guruji left, Y2K sat in a contemplative mood for a while but did not take to the bottle. Instead, he switched on his Concon and called Vartika. He was sober and sincere when he said,

'I am sorry for being so rude. Would you still care to join me for dinner tonight?' Vartika was delighted to hear his voice and gave her usual reply.

'Are you asking me for a date or a business meeting?'

Y2K replied, 'Maybe both,' and it felt like the old time.

When they met for dinner, they didn't talk much about the election. Mahan was glad to see them again and served his best food. Y2K was famished and ate voraciously. After dinner, they decided to take a walk. It was a moonlit night. They walked together silently as if not wanting to disturb the tranquility of the night. On the way, Y2K noticed a bench. They sat down and stared at the moon and the stars. Y2K imagined Vyoma circling somewhere up in the sky and the memories came flooding back to him. Y2K didn't know why, but he opened up to Vartika. He told Vartika about Vyoma, his courtship, his marriage, his divorce, and his nightmares about hurtling down in the dark space. Vartika just sat there listening to him quietly. Then on an impulse, she reached out and gave Y2K a long, passionate kiss.

The moonlit night was tranquil again, and Y2K felt at peace with himself.

Chapter XXXIII

The Y2K gang was glad to be back to the daily meeting after a break. Y2K apologized for his behavior and was quickly forgiven. As D2Y2 served coffee, the discussion cautiously turned to the election campaign. The four-day hiatus had been bad for the Y2K campaign. Vartika summarized the scene as she explained,

'I have some bad news and some good news. The bad news is that we are down by twelve points in the rankings. The good news is that brand Y2K is still holding. Voters are curious to know what will come next in our manifesto agenda. We have elicited more suggestions than we can handle.'

Vartika updated Y2K further on the election scene.

'Most of the election buzz is happening around the big three who are now intensely fighting to occupy the number one position in the ratings. There have been rallies by Kappusway and Guru Panchal at the Ramlila Maidan over the last two days and Prada is holding her rally tomorrow. Prada, who is currently at number three, hopes to jump to number one by announcing a total prohibition policy in her Ramlila Maidan rally.'

The bulb lit and Lattu had his idea. He proposed,

'Why don't we preempt Prada by announcing our plan for imposing prohibition as today's manifesto agenda for alphabet 'P'?

Mattu responded,

'I think that is a good idea. As per my data, about thirty percent of the Mandals are against the prohibition while thirty percent fervently support prohibition. In the remaining forty percent of the Mandals, advocacy of prohibition is known to result in varying electoral dividends. Judging by Prada's plans, Kautukpur voters seem to be inclined to vote for prohibition this time. Prompt support for prohibition may do wonders for our sagging ratings.'

Kattu was immediately up in arms and reacted.

'Prohibition has never been known to be successful. While it sounds good in theory, it invariably leads to a win-less, lose-more situation. The government loses revenue, the alcohol economy goes underground and crimes increase. All this happens in the name of social gains which are not measurable.'

Sattu was a staunch supporter of prohibition. He argued,

'Social benefits of prohibition should not be dismissed lightly. When lives are wasted and families are devastated, the cost cannot be measured. The old social structure has withered away and an age of loneliness has ushered in. This has led to a doubling of alcohol consumption in just one decade. In my opinion, we have reached a tipping point where only total prohibition can save the social order from collapsing.'

'What you are arguing is repackaged Volsteadism that is simply irrelevant in 2050,' protested Kattu. Sattu stood his ground and said,

'Call it by whatever name, but the case in favor of prohibition is not irrelevant. Take for example Y2K's recent problem. He would have been better off if there was prohibition.'

Vartika intervened and said,

'Let us not get personal. Only Y2K can decide what would have been better for him.'

Y2K at this point took a stand and responded,

'I think I am entitled to comment on this issue. Respect for one's choice should always be at the core of our social structure but the cost of choice should not become burdensome on society. Current policies on prohibition do not minimize the cost, they merely transfer it. Therefore, what we need is a smart policy that uses smart technology to help optimize the cost.'

'Technology has only helped in increasing consumption of spirits. How can it be used to curb consumption?' asked Sattu.

Y2K replied,

'The crux of the problem is excessive, irresponsible, or uncontrolled drinking. Therefore, reasonable curbs may be imposed on an individual's freedom to drink if it is found that it will be harmful to his health or financially ruin him or his family. So far, moral sermons have fallen on deaf ears and policies have failed in enforcing such a responsible drinking habit. But now we have a technology nicknamed '*smart dhakkan technology*' that can enforce responsible drinking?'

Dhakkan is also used as slang for an idiot also. Sattu immediately caught on to the incongruity of the term as he derisively said,

'Never heard of a smart *dhakkan* and can't fathom how will '*smart dhakkan*' technology help in enforcing the exalted goal of responsible drinking?'

Y2K calmly replied,

'Let me explain. Let us say each bottle of alcohol is equipped with a '*smart dhakkan*', which is a smart cap fitted with an IoT device. Every time you want to pour a drink, the embedded IoT device will identify you and check with a 'Drink Controller Clown' that can be set up by the government. This Clown assigns a drinkability threshold limit based on your income and health condition. If you cross this limit, the '*smart dhakkan*' won't let you pour the drink. Mission accomplished.'

Sattu was skeptical and said,

'Not really. There will be many practical difficulties. For example, you could ask your friend, who has not crossed his drinking limit, to pour an extra drink for you.'

'Why bother? If you are lucky enough to have such friends in the friendless world of 2050, no one needs to worry about your well-being.'

'What if bottles without smart caps still find their way into the market,' enquired Mattu.

'That can be controlled in many ways. Lower taxes for bottles fitted with smart caps will not only cover the slight increase in the cost but also price out the ordinary ones. The logistics and distribution chains can be programmed to reject the handling of ordinary bottles. Repeat attempts to get a drink beyond the threshold limit can trigger an alarm initiating a visit from a counselor. Even then, if a person is found to have crossed the threshold limit, his insurance cost can go up, social benefits can be cut down, and a case for sending him to a rehabilitation center may be initiated. Overall, the approach would be more assistive and less punitive. A test run has already been conducted in some towns with encouraging results. Kautukpur can be the first Mandal for full-fledged implementation of smart prohibition,' explained Y2K.

'I think this scheme can work, both for the public and for our campaign. Let 'P for Prohibition' be our smart agenda today,' surmised Vartika and proceeded to explain plans for the day.

Y2K returned to Pigeon Square in the evening to announce his grand plan for smart prohibition. In his speech, he more or less repeated what had been discussed in the breakfast meeting. At the end of the speech, a pigeon-shaped drone made a grand entry presenting the prototype of a '*smart dhakkan*-equipped bottle' and a banner pronouncing 'Pio Smartly, Jio Smartly'. Yet another drone carried a banner exhorting 'Support Y2K's suggestion, Prohibition by *Smart Dhakkan*'. The spectacle provided ready-made headlines for Jholus and Jhallus debated endlessly on the topic of smart prohibition powered by '*smart dhakkan*' technology.

It all augured well for Y2K as he recouped some of his lost ground. By the end of the day, his ranking had improved by four points.

Chapter XXXIV

The breakfast meeting had regained the earlier vibrancy but Kattu seemed to be off-color. His Popat had become faulty, losing some of its mobility and memory. As a result, that talking, walking and thinking marvel had turned into a machine that resembled an old man barely able to lift his finger. The service center at Kautukpur could not repair it since not only did the moving parts which were like living organs had to be replaced, but memory had to be restored in a manner that the accumulated data and knowledge were neither lost nor compromised. They advised Kattu that restoring his Popat was akin to performing a major surgery on a human body. Likewise, there was a queue for such a delicate and specialized operation with a waiting time of more than three months. For Kattu, even a day without Popat was like an eternity.

'I am barely surviving with the help of Concon but poor Concon is no substitute for a Popat. I do not know how I can pull on without my Popat for so long. The queue at the central repair facility is killing me,' complained Kattu.

'I fully understand your tribulations but have no worries. Where there is a queue, there is a way. If you want to jump the queue, all you need to do is take recourse to one of the three laws of queue management. These three laws depend upon *Jan-pahchan, Pakwan, and Vijay Dinanath Chauhan,*' commiserated Sattu.

'I know the first law of jumping the queue is to look for a '*jan-pahchan*' or an acquaintance. The second law is about the power of '*pakwan*' or the bribe. But what the hell do you mean by the third law related to '*Vijay Dinanath Chauhan*'?' enquired Mattu.

'Oh, that was a little riddle. Vijay Dinanath Chauhan was the name made famous by Amitabh Bachchan in a Bollywood movie. It was Amitabh Bachchan who unraveled the third law of jumping the queue in another movie in his iconic dialog '*Hum jahan khade ho jaate hain, line wahi se shuru hoti hai*'. This law is the most effective in managing a queue but unfortunately applies only to celebrities, VIPs, Netas, Bahubalis, and criminals. Now that I have solved the riddle of queues for you, you can take your pick,' explained Sattu with a straight face.

'I neither appreciate your sense of humor nor endorse your advice,' retorted Kattu.

'In that case, you may perhaps consider buying a new Popat instead of getting the old one repaired,' suggested Mattu.

'Buying a new Popat is not only expensive but there is also a long queue of three months for the delivery. And it takes another three months to train a new Popat according to your needs,' replied Kattu pensively.

'In that case, you may resort to the fourth law of queue management which simply states that 'wherever there is a queue, there is a quota'. A quota gives you instant redemption.

The only catch is that you need the help of a Gappu, Neta, or middleman who knows how to mine the quota,' said Sattu.

'You are talking as if we are living in the 1970s when the queue and quota were the normal way of life. Things are drastically different in 2050,' intervened Mattu.

'It may seem so, but our past tends to resurface in new forms all the time. For example, the queue and quota system is simply a manifestation of constrained resources and constraints never disappear. They only take new forms. The problem is that humans can never learn to distribute resources fairly and without any discrimination. Hence we see the urge for queue jumping and quota creation,' said Lattu rather philosophically.

'The problem in 2050 is even deeper than that. Humans have outsourced eighty percent of the activities to machines like Popats and Clowns. With their ability to learn, they have acquired eighty percent of human characteristics which may or may not be the best that humans possess. It is, therefore, no surprise that Popats and Clown now practice the art of queue jumping or quota mining with greater ease than humans,' warned Mattu.

'That is a serious issue. I think 'Q for Queue and Quota' can be a farsighted agenda for our manifesto,' suggested Lattu.

Y2K liked what Lattu had proposed. Concluding the point his colleagues had made, he said,

'There is a social, economic, and political cost attached to how the queues and quotas are managed. Progressive societies strive to minimize this cost. If Popats and Clowns are allowed to manage such activities, this cost can spiral and we may end up creating a regressive society. I believe that the issues of queue and quota should be left to us humans to deal with and Popats or Clowns should be kept out. If I get elected, I shall bar Popats and Clowns from handling such issues.' Everyone concurred.

As usual, Vartika was consulted and came up with a plan on how to make the point. She suggested to *Gherao* the office of 'Kautukpur Popat Corporation' or KPC that handled the sales and service of Popats for the whole of Kautuk Mandal. The idea of a Gherao against the 'Queue and Quota system' of KPC met with an instant protest from Lattu who thought that a Gherao was illegal and immoral. Mattu also opposed it as he felt that Gherao was a counter-productive tool that discouraged businesses. Sattu, however, justified the Gherao as a means of fighting unjust or unfair practices. Kattu chose to be neutral saying that the practice of Gherao had become irrelevant in 2050 because Popats had replaced the workers everywhere and Popats were not allowed to Gherao.

For the first time since the campaign began, there was a serious difference of opinion amongst the gang members. Vartika, however, was undaunted and said,

'Let us think in terms of strategy and not in terms of legality, morality, or practicality. No politician ever comes to power without having a Gherao in his CV. I concede that frequent, aggressive, or violent Gheraos are foolish but an occasional gherao brings you to the forefront. I think it is the right time we gheraoed those who manage the Popats and project Y2K as a leader who can fight.' Y2K was not convinced but did not want to be seen as a passive leader either. He acquiesced and the rest came around as well on the condition that the Gherao would be peaceful.

The Gherao against the 'queue and quota system' was peaceful but noisy. Vartika was able to recruit two dozen volunteers, most of whom did not own a Popat. They were the ones who made most of the noise and enjoyed it. The lone Gappu managing the KPC was flustered and made a hasty exit from the backdoor. Y2K termed the retreat by the management of KPC as his victory and vowed to set things right once elected. It was the first Gherao of this election and easily made the headlines. The hustle and bustle of a Gherao pushed Y2K's agenda of 'Q for queue and quota' to the forefront and earned him a jump in the rankings by two positions.

Chapter XXXV

A side benefit of the Gherao was that the repaired Popat was delivered to Kattu the same day in the late evening hours. Kattu was elated. The restored Popat worked well but by morning Kattu had noticed one problem. His Popat had forgotten how to perform Pooja or any religious ritual for that matter. It was not without any reason.

All Popats initially came in three versions – religious, secular, or atheist. Being a self-proclaimed atheist, Kattu had originally ordered the atheist version. His mother took an instant liking to the newly acquired Popat despite its religious orientation and set about teaching the Popat what she knew of her religion. She had faith but not extensive knowledge. Poapt had access to knowledge but no faith. In the end, faith triumphed, and Kattu's Popat turned religious, just like his mother. After his mother passed away, Popat continued her legacy. Popat's religious devotion rubbed off on Kattu, who soon ended up being a practicing religious person.

Kattu now wanted his restored Popat to be exactly the same as his mother had left him to be. The refurbished Popat had been restored back to the atheist version. Without his mother's help, reversing Popat's thinking was going to be a herculean task. He was sharing his problem with his friends as he remarked gravely

'Religion is a combination of beliefs, biases, practices, and faith. They can easily be taught to a machine, except for faith. Everything rational can be digitized but not the faith.'

'Let it be. No two Popats evolve similarly just as no two humans practice religion identically. Religion is a journey an individual undertakes to find the meaning of life. You sometimes need a Guru or a guide on this journey. A Popat can be a guide, but it can never be a traveler like a human Guru,' commented Mattu philosophically.

'The problem of 2050 is that we have forgotten our journey, having outsourced it to the Popats. Today, you will find only *Thopats* performing every religious function at every religious place,' lamented Sattu.

Thopats were the 'Theologically oriented Popats' trained by the preachers who could perform the pooja in a temple, proclaim the call to *namaz*, or deliver a sermon in a church. Since Thopats could perform such duties with greater finesse, regularity, and efficiency, priests and preachers gradually receded in the background. By the late 40s, almost all religious places were manned by Thopats. Bigger religious entities that had many affiliated preachers developed and indoctrinated their own Thopats. The AI indoctrinated Thopats attracted more followers and competition ensued. A few Thopats became star performers, raising both money and an army of ardent followers. This attracted politicians, always on the lookout for money, power and followers. Politicians of Kautukpur were no different. The trinity of Kappuswamy, Guru Panchal, and Prada had already forged alliances with the entities whose Thopats had a large number of followers. Many others waded into this game as well attracting niche followers. Mid-way through the election, the nexus between politics, religion, and technology was complete.

Lattu was quick to realize the implications as he remarked, 'How could we be so ignoramus to overlook religion? Let us make up for it by keeping 'R for Religion' as our agenda today.'

Sattu was up in arms immediately as he said,

'I do not recommend it at all. Mixing religion with politics is outright dangerous.' Unexpectedly, he found support in Vartika, who was a rare strategist with a conscience. She bemoaned,

'Mixing religion with politics may be disastrous but mixing religion and politics together with technology can be catastrophic. The mixture of religion, politics, and technology has turned the votes into a commodity that can be sold, exchanged, or traded in the currency that is called favor and power.'

Lattu said, 'What option do we have except to join the rat race? In politics, you can't remain aloof from a problem.'

None in the group had a deeper political insight than Vartika who replied,

'I disagree with you, Lattu. Politics is all about creating a problem. But, smart politics is about remaining aloof from the problem thereafter. Good politics is to talk about a solution to the problem and Positive politics is about walking the talk. You can take your pick.'

Sattu responded,

'We all are in this business of election for the sake of supporting good and positive politics. So let us talk about a solution in our manifesto rather than be a part of the problem to buy some votes.'

It was time for Y2K to react. He said gravely,

'I couldn't agree more. As a first step, we need to break the stranglehold of theological Popats and Clowns by banning them from all the religious places and functions in public. I propose it to be a part of the action plan in our manifesto concerning 'R for Religion'.' Everyone concurred and left the details to Vartika and Y2K to work out.

As planned, they all met in the evening at Kautukeshwar temple. Kautukeshwar temple was the oldest temple in the Kautuk Mandal, sitting on top of a hill around which the Kautuk Fort was built. Being the presiding deity of Kautuk Mandal, it had seen glorious days before gradually falling into disuse and disrepair. It was one of the few remaining temples where a Thopat was not appointed, mainly because the RoI did not justify it. It was also the reason why Vartika had chosen this venue to gather Y2K's supporters who were pleasantly surprised by the beauty and serenity of the place. Kattu was appointed the priest for the evening and he conducted the prayers in traditional *Sanskrit* with an aplomb. As the gongs played and the prayers were chanted, the atmosphere turned electric. Though Y2K and his gang prayed for success in the elections, not a single word about the election was uttered till they remained within the premises of the temple.

It was only when they had descended a hundred steps and reached a clearing that Vartika signaled the Jholus to join in. It was time for an impromptu election meeting. Y2K jumped onto a step and calmly addressed the small crowd that had gathered as if on cue.

'Citizens of Kautukpur,

Welcome to this old and forgotten temple. When I was a kid, I used to visit this temple every week with my grandfather who would tell me the stories about Kautukeshwar, our presiding deity. In many ways, this temple reminds us of our stories, our history, our way of life, and our religion. For this reason, whether I win this election or not, I shall strive to restore the old glory of this temple.

However, if I win this election, I do have another pledge to fulfill in the name of my agenda 'R for Religion'. That pledge is to ban all the Popats and Clowns from religious places and functions in public, in line with my policy of 'Humans First'. Many of my friends may find such an act antithetical to spiritual progress, citing reports that religious activities more than doubled during the last decade owing to the Thopats and Clowns. But do we call that progress?

We have outsourced our prayers to Popats and religious functions to Thopats. We visit our temples and churches virtually and relish the oratory of Thopats over the wisdom of the saints. We have allowed Clowns to interpret our scriptures and religious institutions to become Corporations manned by machines. Religion and spirituality distinguish humanity from *Popatdom.* Let us not allow the machines to obliterate our religion, stultify our spirituality, and manipulate our beliefs. The mixture of politics with religion has always been poisonous. Let technology not make the poison more potent. I humbly seek the blessings of Kautukeshwar to give me the mandate to implement my manifesto and follow the path of 'Humans First'.'

Religion of Jholus was TRP. They saw potential in Y2K's approach toward, 'r for religion', but found the gravitas of Y2K's statements difficult to translate in their headlines. So they tailored the headlines which read 'Y2K to ban religious practices', 'Y2K stokes religious sentiments', 'Y2K's communal agenda to ban Thopats from religious places', 'Popats have no right to practice religion, says Y2K', 'Mandal will build Kautukeshwar temple, pledges Y2K'. Jhallus too jumped into the manufactured controversy and hotly debated whether banning Thopats was secular or communal. While the Lappus could not decide such knotty issues, everyone on the panel, which mostly included the spokespersons of the top trinity, ended up denouncing Y2K.

Sitting in Mahan's restaurant for dinner, Y2K was amused watching the coverage being dished out in his name which was only remotely connected with what he had said. The only authentic serving was the food which was pure vegetarian in deference to Y2K's visit to the Kautukeshwar temple. The highlight of the menu was the dessert 'R for Rosogulla' which Mr. Mahan claimed was the favorite dish of Kautukeshwar deity. He told Y2K that he would offer eleven kilograms of Rosogulla to the deity if Y2K won the elections.

As Y2K and Vartika finished their dinner, the poll results came in. Y2K had unexpectedly gone up in the ranking by four positions. While Vartika attributed the healthy jump in the rankings to the hype created by channels and the vociferous criticism of Y2K from his rivals, Mr. Mahan was sure that it was the promise to offer Rosogullas to the Kautukeshwar deity that had done the trick!

Chapter XXXVI

D2Y2 diligently compiled a local news summary daily for Y2K to glance at while sipping his morning tea. The kidnapping of Ketan Mahajan had been the top news item for the last several days. Ketan Mahajan was the same Property Tax Inspector who had visited Y2K sometime back. Y2K remembered him as an officious but affable person who even turned up for his cricket match. Ketan had not been found as yet, despite concerted efforts. According to the latest news, the case was being closed after the Leopat (Police Popat) in-charge of the case had filed a report that it had reached a dead end. Y2K was angry and concerned. He made it a point to discuss this issue in the breakfast meeting.

'Ketan's kidnapping case is bothering me and I am concerned about his safety and security. We should think of doing something about it,' said Y2K.

'I agree with Y2K. The safety and security of the citizens is the first duty of the State. We should make it our manifesto agenda for today,' supported Lattu.

Kattu as usual had a different perspective and said,

'I would like to help Ketan but I don't think that making it an election issue will do much either for Ketan or our campaign.

Safety and security are not much of a concern in 2050 due to the huge technological advancements. Statistics show that crime has practically disappeared. The success rate in solving crimes has gone up to ninety percent and ninety percent of them are solved within twenty-four hours. Common citizen has never felt so secure and safe.'

Kattu was not exaggerating. By 2042, the policing scene had changed drastically. For every thousand citizens, there was one Leopat policing the streets. More importantly, Leopats could not be bribed, they did not discriminate, and were never lax. Moreover, every inch of public space was covered by some kind of observation device and the Leopats monitored them twenty-four by seven from huge control rooms of smart and not-so-smart cities. Even then, if a crime got committed, it was promptly solved, mostly using electronic monitoring, surveillance, or snooping. Electronic monitoring was more than a century-old practice that had proliferated with every advancement in technology. The advent of AI gave a different dimension to it. So much so that even if you sneezed, someone somewhere would know that you did. The power of AI and Popats backed by electronic monitoring and surveillance was enough to overpower the criminals. As a result, by 2045, 'Virtual Meta Police' consisting of Leopats and Clowns were managing the responsibility of handling crimes as an accepted routine.

Sattu, however, had a different view as he pointed out,

'It's not always a hunky-dory situation. Statistics on crime have improved because technology has taken care of petty crimes and petty criminals. But smart criminals know how to dodge the technology. So the remaining ten percent represent the big-time crime that the machines can't solve.'

'I agree with you. Take for example the case of Ketan itself. He was kidnapped in broad daylight many days ago. Yet, all the Popats and Clowns put together have not been able to find him. The news today is that after mounting the biggest snooping operation in the Mandal, Virtual Meta Police has come to a dead end and has filed a closure report,' said Sattu.

'How can the case be closed? It involves the safety and security of a citizen. According to the grapevine, the mafia is behind the kidnapping, and cracking down on the mafia would have perhaps cracked the case,' opined Mattu.

'Machines do not know the grapevine. They only know the data, programs, precedents, rules, processes, and tools at their disposal. In the last five years, machines have solved every single case of kidnapping in less than a day by using legal interception, AI, and location-based tools. Their ultimate tool is the identity chip that every adult is embedded with. In the case of an emergency, the location of this chip is enabled and then the rescue operation is a cinch. Unfortunately, in this case, surveillance data has yielded no clue and the identity chip is inaccessible. Without a digital trail, it is a dead-end. So the Police have decided that resources can no longer be allocated for something that will not yield any result,' explained Kattu in detail.

'That is ridiculous. The safety of a citizen cannot be dealt with in such a mechanical manner. The case cannot be closed till we find Ketan. We need to do something about it,' insisted Y2K.

'A dead case can be revived only through a court-trial or media-trial. We can try on both the fronts. Let us approach the Court first thing in the morning and appeal against the closure of this case. Let us also make the issue of 'Safety and Security' a part of our manifesto agenda for the day. Finally, we can hold a press conference in the evening to highlight our agenda in general and Ketan's case in particular. We can thus hope to kill two birds with three stones,' suggested Vartika. Everyone agreed.

Vartika managed to hire a prominent human lawyer Daruwala from the election funds. Courts in 2050 had become super-efficient. Daruwala managed to get the urgent petition heard in the morning itself. The Mandal Police told the Court that it had an impeccable record of solving every single kidnapping case in the last five years. This case was an outlier. In the absence of a digital trail, all possible efforts were leading to a dead-end, exhausting the precious resources of the department. Therefore, the Clown who made decisions on resource allocation was right in recommending the closure of the case. Daruwala disputed the facts. He maintained that the kidnapping had been carried out by a mafia whom Ketan planned to expose. The mafia knew exactly what investigations Virtual Meta Police would carry out and had planned accordingly. They apparently had influenced the Gappu-in-charge as well to look the other way when the case was being buried quietly. The Judge was unimpressed, observing that it was all hearsay.

This was the moment Daruwala was waiting to seize as he raised his pitch and argued,

'Mi Lord, I am not here to argue on the basis of hearsay which we all know is inadmissible in law. I am here to argue on a point of law whether machines can be allowed to decide on matters concerning the safety and security of a human. We have outsourced the task of our safety and security to the machines because they are efficient and convenient. We like them in this role because they do not display the vices that humans have. But do the machines have the compassion that only a human being can have for a fellow human being? More importantly, do the machines have the ingenuity that humans can display in a tough situation? When faced with a dead-end, machines will give up, but human ingenuity will work around it and find a way. Human ingenuity may mean out-of-the-box thinking. Or it may mean working on hearsay, intuition, hunch, or just a blind lead. Machines have not yet been able to duplicate human ingenuity. That is the reason I pray for human intervention. The law may not be clear on this, because law always lags behind technological advancements. But when the question involved is that of life and death, will it rely on the efficiency and processes of a machine or allow human ingenuity a chance? Simply put, will the court put Humans first or Machines first? I rest my case here My Lord,' concluded Daruwala.

The Judge, who was about to dismiss the petition, was suitably impressed by Mr. Daruwala's concluding remarks and passed a brief order,

'This court normally would not interfere in operational matters such as this. However, a point of law regarding the safety and security of a citizen has been raised. Admittedly, the law needs to evolve on such issues. Under the circumstances, I find no harm in accepting the applicant's plea for human intervention. If the applicant approaches the Inspector concerned for further investigation by him instead of closure, he will give due consideration to such a request and make an unbiased decision.'

Y2K was elated by the decision but Vartika warned that it was only half a victory since the ball was now in Inspector Godbole's court. Y2K approached Inspector Godbole with the court's order but he was unimpressed. The Department had already taken a decision and he saw no need to overturn it. Godbole was more receptive when Y2K explained the Mafia angle but was still undecided. Y2K needed to advance a more convincing argument. Remembering that flattery sometimes is more convincing than a convincing argument, he appealed in his most flattering tone.

'Inspector, it is a question of life and death for Ketan and only you can help him. I know your capability. If you decide, you can find Ketan even if he has disappeared in the thin air or vanished under the ground.'

Inspector Godbole sat thinking for a few agonizing minutes and suddenly asked Y2K, 'Did you say under the ground?' As Y2K nodded, Godbole got up and dismissed them by saying, 'Thank you for coming. I shall let you know of my decision before your press conference.'

Inspector Godbole need not have informed Y2K since he was all over the channels before Y2K's press conference. As it turned out, Inspector Godbole was way smarter than his sloppy demeanor suggested. When Y2K mentioned 'under the ground', Godbole suddenly realized that a digital trail could vanish only in an illegal underground dwelling. Due to the space crunch, a large number of such dwellings had come up in Kautukpur. All such units were regulated and were mandated to have connectivity but illegal ones could remain offline and undetected. Finding such illegal underground dwellings was difficult if they had no digital presence. Inspector Godbole reckoned that all of them would need to install an air ventilation system. A quick check revealed that apart from those installed in the registered units, five more such systems were installed. These five were obviously illegal underground dwellings. Further check revealed that one of these five illegal units was ordered by a mafia member. Confident of the kidnappers' location now, Inspector Godbole organized a raiding party and rescued Ketan Mahajan unharmed.

Inspector Godbole was not only gracious in acknowledging Y2K's role, he sportingly delivered Ketan to Y2K's press conference on Vartika's request. Ketan was the star attraction of the press conference. He narrated the story in great detail and profusely thanked Y2K. It was then left to Y2K to conclude. Y2K stuck to his manifesto agenda and briefly spoke,

'Friends, Ketan's case is a reminder that we can never take for granted the safety and security of our citizens. It appears to me that we have abdicated this onerous responsibility and handed it over to the machines. I have nothing against the Leopats and Clowns. They have done a fine job. However, the question of life and death cannot be decided by statistical considerations or resource allocation algorithms. Such questions must be decided by humans and all actions related to safety and security must be guided by 'Humans First' approach. The court observed today that the law has not yet evolved on such aspects. If I get elected, I shall enact appropriate laws to ensure that the safety and security of citizens always comes first and remains in the hands of humans.'

The unusual kidnapping, courtroom drama, mafia link, and ingenuity of Inspector Godbole made up a riveting story that played out on the channels throughout the day. The role of Y2K in unfolding this story too got noticed along with his call for putting 'S for security and safety' in focus once again. It was enough to earn Y2K a jump in his rankings by four points.

Chapter XXXVII

Y2K had a premonition that D2Y2 would bring bad news in the morning and it did. Late last night, news came of the untimely death of Shubhrant Singh Shekhawat, an upcoming and popular actor known as S-cube. Officially, it was declared a case of suicide. His 'Thought Mining' alerts were cited as evidence to suggest that he was having suicidal tendencies. However, his kith and kin claimed that his girlfriend abetted the suicide since 'thought mining' also suggested that S-cube was planning to ditch her. A few of his friends claimed that the big project S-cube was working on had been 'thought mined' and led to his murder. Since K-cube was S-cube's mentor, there was a strong local connection which kept half of the Kautuk Mandal riveted to the unfolding drama on news channels. It was therefore no surprise that by morning, the big trinity of Kautuk Mandal comprising Kappuswami, Guru Panchal, and Prada, had taken diametrically opposite positions on the tragedy. While one of them blamed the Government for not acting on alerts about suicidal tendencies, the other demanded immediate arrest of his girlfriend for abetting the suicide, and the third called for setting up an inquiry commission to investigate the conspiracy hatched by his enemies.

'It is appalling that the trinity is doing politics over a tragic loss of life,' observed Sattu with some disdain.

'You are absolutely right. We should perhaps keep out of this controversy and let the law take its course,' said Mattu.

'But did you notice that the underlying common link in all the theories floating around in this case is 'Thought Mining'? I think this is a larger question that needs to be politically discussed and addressed. Maybe we can make it our manifesto agenda for today,' said Lattu. He looked around for the response and found none.

'Maybe we need more discussion on it,' added Lattu quickly. The discussion went on for a while with opinions evenly divided on whether thought-mining was a bane or boon.

Thought mining, as opposed to data mining, was a relatively new technology that had its origin in the medical sciences. The discovery of neurons and understanding of the electrical activity of the mind enabled medical science to treat patients suffering from brain diseases, mental illness, and neurodevelopmental brain disorders. The advent of AI, Bionics, and Neuronics greatly expanded the scope and understanding of the human mind and its thought process. Soon, the devices used for this purpose became smaller, more powerful, and non-invasive. By the early 2040s, thought as a unit could be coded and decoded, read and edited, added or deleted, stored and transmitted.

Harry Hemrajani was amongst the early entrepreneurs and investors to recognize that 'Thought' was the new oil that could be mined for gold. In 2041, he founded a 'Thought Mining' company named TEA Corporation. 'TEA' here was an acronym for '*T*hought *E*xploration and *A*nalytics' and the Corporation's logo was an inverted tea cup with a single drop falling from the cup. The TEA Corporation truly marked the breaking away of this technology from the shadow of medical science into the world of pure commerce and business. By 2045, the TEA Corporation had become the fastest-growing company in the world and was counted among the top ten most valuable companies.

The success of TEA Corporation was built on its flagship 'Thought Mining platform' that powered two revolutionary products 'Thoughtware' and 'Thoughtvice'. Thoughtware enabled the direct conversion of thoughts into machine code and by the mid-40s was threatening to replace the old archaic technology called software. Thoughtvice was the generic name for the new generation devices that interfaced the human mind with the outside world. Thought mining coupled with 'thoughtware' and 'thoughtvice' spawned a thousand new services and a thousand new enterprises bloomed. As thoughts became a commodity, Indians monopolized the thoughtware services, Chinese mastered the thoughtvices, but Americans had the last laugh as they got to keep the cake.

As the 'Thought Economy' grew, many of the companies offered use cases that were difficult to categorize as legitimate or illegitimate, legal or illegal, desirable or undesirable, ethical or unethical. From marketing companies to insurance companies, all used thought mining extensively. No deal or contract ever went through without either party using inputs from the thought mining. The employers deployed thought mining to hire the right employees and keep an eye on them. Employees in turn used the same technology to find out what the boss thought of them. Ideas were conceived or stolen, built or destroyed, using TEA Company's products. By 2045, most corporates were clients of the TEA Company.

From corporations, technology soon entered the personal space. The most common use case was for someone to find out what affair his or her partner was having or planning. Mind games between the daughter-in-law and mother-in-law took on a new dimension since using thought mining they would know in real-time exactly what they thought of each other. The list went on and on as people became addicted to such mind games.

'I think we are being thought compromised. I did a routine sanitizing exercise this morning and found a suspicious device that can snoop on thoughts,' announced the generally quiet D2Y2 while serving a second round of coffee.

'Welcome to the elections 2050. The technology that was the exclusive preserve of US presidential elections has now percolated down even to the Mandal level,' mused Kattu. The irony was not lost on everyone present. In the 2042 US presidential elections, the winning candidate extensively used Thought Mining technology which was promptly termed as 'Thoughtgate'. Wiser to the advances in technology, the other party's candidate used 'Thought Mining 2.0' in the 2046 elections. Thought Mining 2.0 employed the 'Push' technology which could effectively push a particular set of thoughts in a subject's mind. The detractors called it AI-powered brainwashing which was immoral and unethical. They tried to impeach the President but nothing came of it since there was no law against the new technology which was originally invented to help mentally and physically challenged people.

'I am not enamored of Thought Mining technology. I am even more wary of its 2.0 version. I agree that technology diffusion is now happening at a rate faster than one can imagine and is even helping us in many ways. But that is no excuse for using it unethically anywhere. Take this case of thought snooping on us. I don't know who exactly is behind this. But whosoever is involved must be condemned,' said Sattu.

'I think we should protest against the whole thought mining technology in general and this incidence of thought snooping in particular,' suggested Lattu.

'I am afraid any such protest would have no impact. Once technology makes inroads into our lives, it is impossible to banish it. As far as the election is concerned, there would not be many takers for the ethical pitch. Remember, everything is fair in love, war, and the elections,' opined Mattu.

'In that case, Vartika should tell us what to do,' proposed Lattu.

'If an active protest is not going to work, then let us try out passive resistance. Passive resistance was the favorite tool of Gandhi and nobody has ever won an election without using the name or game of Gandhi,' replied Vartika.

'How does passive resistance fit in here?' asked Lattu.

'You all agree that nobody will pay attention if you protest that someone is thought snooping on you. But what if we voluntarily invite them to come and 'thought snoop' on us for a change?' suggested Vartika.

'That surely will fire but how do we pull it off?' asked Lattu again.

'Well, I have a simple plan,' said Vartika and went on to explain it.

As per the plan, the Y2K gang assembled on the other side of the Kautukeshwar Temple hill which had a maze of caves. The Y2K gang was to spend an hour meditating inside the caves. Outside the caves, Vartika's favorite five Jholus were present. Vartika had given each of them the same type of snooping device that had been discovered by D2Y2 in the morning. Jholus had been invited to thought snoop on the whole Y2K gang and they had jumped on the opportunity. Unfortunately, however hard they tried, they could not record a single thought despite the open invitation to do so. The reason was that the cave system was the only place in the whole of Kautuk Mandal that was not digitally accessible. Moreover, meditation meant calming the mind, reaching a state of peace devoid of any thoughts. With the intensity of thoughts drastically reduced due to meditation, there was nothing that could be snooped.

While the Jholus struggled to snoop, a good crowd gathered outside the cave. As Y2K came out of the cave, a loud cheer went up in the air. It was time to give a speech. Y2K, in a measured and calm voice, spoke,

'Citizens of Kautuk Mandal,

Once upon a time, our home was our castle. That myth was broken long ago but our mind still remained our castle. Technology like Thought Mining has breached that last fortress as well. I concede that technology like Thought Mining can do plenty of good but I am equally convinced that the results of the though privacy breach have not always been pleasant. The tragic suicide case of S-cube highlights this dilemma. Sadly, the response of my rivals has been to sidestep the ethical questions and do politics over the tragedy. Instead of doing politics over a tragedy, we should be asking questions about the tools of the tragedy. Notwithstanding the support it has garnered, I call Thought Mining technology a tool of tragedy. Thanks to its unbridled use, the divorce, suicide, and murder rates have gone up. Now no one trusts anyone anymore and everyone keeps aloof for fear of spilling his thoughts. Thoughts are the new asset but loneliness is the price we pay. I, therefore, exhort all of you to wake up and resist before this price becomes too high.

And how do we resist it? By demanding a ban on it? Maybe not. What I advocate is proactive regulation. As a rule, any emerging technology should be categorized as fit for a ban, fit for hard regulation, fit for soft regulation, or fit for forbearance. In my opinion, the thought mining technology is fit for hard regulation. If I get elected, I shall enact tough laws to preserve the sanctity and integrity of thoughts. I shall also ensure that the use of Thoughtware and Thoughtvices happens under the strict regulations and oversight of a regulator. In case any ethical questions arise, they will be immediately referred to the 'Humans First Commission'. Thought Mining is a risk to the very fabric of our society. Let us, therefore, treat it with due caution. Today's symbolic exercise in passive resistance was to underscore this simple agenda of 'T for Thought Mining' and I thank you all for joining me. Let us all control our thoughts through meditation and not through the technology of Thought Mining.'

Though the audience applauded Y2K, Jholus did not think that the idea of strictly regulating Thought Mining would excite the viewers. However, the optics around the cave, the appeal of meditation, and the fact that the Y2K gang could successfully beat their thought-mining efforts in an open challenge, made up for TRP-worthy stories. Their stories gave Y2K a consolation advantage of one position in the ratings.

When Y2K and Vartika met for their regular dinner meeting, the question of their future together and not the poll rating was on their mind. Thought Mining would have told them that they were now in love with each other. But having eschewed the use of such technology, they had to depend on their heart which knew the answer but was afraid to ask the question. Though the matter was concerning the heart, and the heart was willing, the mind told them that election time was not the best time to discuss the matters of the heart. When faced with such a delicate question, they did what all good politicians do. At the back of their mind, they decided to put the burning question of their future together on the back burner.

Chapter XXXVIII

As the thirty-day-long qualifying period was nearing an end, it was natural for the Y2K campaign committee to take stock of where they stood and what their rivals were doing. Y2K was now back at the tantalizing twelfth position in the polls. According to Vartika, their campaign was on track and if they kept their nerves, Y2K was sure to reach the next round. Lattu, on the other hand, felt that the time was ripe to go for a final push to become a lead challenger to the Trinity.

'We have carried out almost every activity from the standard political tool-kit, except holding a rally at *Ramlila Maidan.* Take the case of Harsh Havaldar, known as Don H2, who was originally seven ranks below us. However, after yesterday's Ramlila Maidan rally, he is sitting pretty, well above us,' said Lattu.

'For a successful rally at *Ramlila Maidan*, you need a huge crowd. In 2050, you won't see a single soul on the road for days altogether. So mobilizing a large crowd is out of the question. The only alternative is to get a large number of *Ubiqs* to attend the rally. I must say that Don H2 exploited the '*Ubiquitization*' technology to the hilt to get some legitimacy and respect,' commented Sattu.

'*Ubiquitization*' that Sattu was referring to, was the new technology feature initially introduced in 7G in 2042. It enabled the presence of a subscriber anywhere through a 'Ubiquitous humanlike virtual image' known as '*Ubiq*'. Although the technology was far from the tele-transportation as known in fiction, it was much more than the mundane 3D holographic presence. The new concept was developed as a stepping stone toward the omnipresence of humans. Many people thought that the technology was inspired by the movie 'Avtar' while some were reminded of 'Narad' from Indian mythology. Philosophical-minded scholars saw it as a representation of 'duality' while the religious-minded quoted scriptures to claim that it was all a '*mayajal*'. Whatever be the inspiration or interpretation, the technology was truly transformational.

'Ubiquitization' was transformational because it was adapted as a productivity enhancement tool. You could be at home, with your Ubiq in the office, with a customer in the field, and also with your girlfriend, all in real-time with real-life experience. It was an expensive and capital-intensive service but true to its name, it soon became ubiquitous. Besides making sales pitches, having multiple affairs, and crowding tourist places, people found many innovative ways of using this technology.

Ubiquitization technology particularly came in handy in politics as well. Politicians now could hire as many Ubiqs as they could afford, to hold rallies, sit on a dharna, or mount a protest. They proved to be quite effective too, since Ubiqs could sit through the long winding speeches without batting their virtual eyelids. Successful *Ramlila Maidan* rallies were a testimony to their efficacy.

However, Kattu, as always, had a question.

'If you count the total attendance in all these rallies so far, it would add up to almost three times the population of the whole Kautuk Mandal. The same Ubiqs are spotted in all the rallies. Is it not a farce? Is it not the time to put a stop to the 'ubiquitization of politics'?' asked Kattu.

'This question was raised but was rejected by the courts on the ground that any such restriction would amount to infringement of the right to freedom of speech, assembly, and movement,' explained Sattu.

'That is fair enough. But what about the use of Ubiqs in political protests? Has it not revived the culture of protests?' persisted Kattu.

'Nothing wrong with that. Technology has democratized the whole process of political discourse. You can now organize a protest anywhere for any duration by hiring Ubiqs through specialized agencies. These agencies even give you SLA for uninterrupted service since the lathi-charge or tear gas by the police can't deter the Ubiqs. Most analysts believe that Ubiquitization has strengthened democracy since the Ubiq protesters are peaceful by design,' replied Sattu.

'The reality is always more complicated. You should know that the Police are unable to control Ubiqs since they don't possess the special U-gun needed for shooting the Ubiqs. On the other hand Gangsters or the DDWs (Devious Digital Warriors) employed by the gangsters possess plenty of them and are not shy of using them. This has given rise to a new kind of virtually dirty politics. So democracy is back in danger,' mused Mattu.

'In my view, 'U for Ubiquitization' qualifies to be our agenda point today. The only problem is that I am confused as to what the real issues are and what stand we should take,' said Lattu. The breaking news at that point interrupted further discussion which could have cleared their confusion.

The Jholu covering the sensational news in the morning was excited to the brim of his programmed capacity. It all started with a woman whose Ubiq was being stalked by another Ubiq. Her numerous complaints to the authorities in this regard were of no avail since there was no law regarding a Ubiq stalking another Ubiq. The harassed woman foolishly hired a local gangster who assigned a DDW (devious digital warrior) to take care of the problem. The DDW shot the stalker Ubiq. It so happened that the stalker Ubiq, who was shot dead, was that of the brother of Don H2.

Don H2, aka Harsh Havaldar, was no ordinary gangster. He was one of the four Dons of Kautuk Mandal, each of whom controlled the territory of Kautukpur, Kautuknagar, Kautukgarh, and Kautukgram respectively. Don H2, who controlled the 'Gangs of Kautukpur', was incensed at the virtual murder of his brother and ordered a reprisal. His DDWs went on a shooting spree in the rival gang's territory, virtually murdering thirty-six Ubiqs. The rival gang quickly mobilized its members, who then confronted Don H2's gang. The confrontation turned into a brawl with fisticuffs and hockey sticks. Soon the real guns came out and two gangsters died before the Jholus arrived and the police followed to intervene.

Three dozen virtual murders and two real ones were a serious matter that soon turned into a political slugfest. While Don

H2 was an independent mafia star with political ambition, the other three 'Gangs of Kautuk Mandal' owed allegiance to the Trinity. Inevitably, further course of action was taken over by the politicians. Kappuswami promptly termed the whole incident as the clash of oppressed and oppressor, a conflict between rural and urban, and a fight for the downtrodden. Guru Panchal announced huge compensation to those who had lost their Ubiqs. Prada declared all three dozen dead Ubiqs as martyrs and promised to build a memorial for them.

The gang of Y2K was appalled by the turn of events and left it to Vartika and Y2K to respond. Y2K with the help of Vartika drafted a memorandum to the EC, demanding immediate arrest of the gangsters, disqualification of Don H2, a ban on Ubiqs till the elections, and an independent probe to punish the guilty. When Y2K emerged from the EC office after submitting the memorandum, Jholus were already stationed there. Y2K readily obliged them by reading out the memorandum and then supplementing it with a byte

'Gentleman,

Today's tragic incident is a manifestation of the criminalization of politics, trivialization of politics, and ubiquitization of politics. Ubiquitization is a new phenomenon that we should take note of. May I remind you that the condemnable incident started with an incident of virtual stalking for which our system provided no adequate remedy. There are hundreds of such problematic situations that a new technology like Ubiquitization throws up and we simply ignore their ill effects. If I get elected I shall work on my agenda 'U for Ubiquitization' aimed at developing appropriate SOPs, laws, rules, and regulations to deal with its ill-effects. Having said that, I must admit that the rules and regulations can only regulate technology and not human conduct. Therefore, the onus is on us to regulate the criminalization and trivialization of politics. You may or may not vote for me. But I appeal to all of you to neither vote for the gangsters nor for those who shelter and mentor the gangsters.'

Y2K's memorandum to EC perhaps went to a virtual dustbin but his byte given to the Jholus outside the EC office was picked up by most of the channels. It was not clear whether Y2K's agenda for 'Ubiquitization' caught voters' fancy or not, but his appeal to vote against the gangsters found enough takers. Voters' sentiment led to Don H2 crashing down by five positions. The net result of all this was that Y2K still managed to improve his rating by one point.

Chapter XXXIX

'Why does D2Y2 look so sad?' asked Mattu as he sipped his coffee. Popats were not supposed to have feelings or emotions. However, they were designed thoughtfully to display expressions that were appropriate to the context. That way, they looked more like humans and less like the boring and primitive robots of the early 2030s. Of course, the display of feelings by Popats was always measured. They laughed softly, talked softly, never got angry, and never sulked. The emotive AI technology had evolved enough to subtly convey contextual meaning without being disobedient, disrespectful, or rebellious.

That imperceptible expression of sorrow in D2Y2 could be attributed to the much-talked-about P3 murder case. P3 in this case meant 'Popat of Pappu Pasha'. In a fit of rage, Pappu Pasha had mercilessly beaten P3. The beating of P3 was so severe that the Popat Clinic declared P3 as brought dead, instead of dysfunctional or irreparable. It became the first official death of a Popat in Kautukpur and immediately attracted the media's attention. The News channels dug out evidence of Pasha beating P3 and played the clips showing P3 asking for mercy from his master. These clips of senseless and uncontrolled violence triggered public outrage. A thousand Ubiqs gathered in Jantar Mantar demanding the arrest of Pappu Pasha. A group called 'Friends of Popats' (FoP) that opposed the slave-like treatment of Popats and advocated equal rights for Popats promptly joined the issue.

The FoP termed the death of P3 as murder and filed a petition in the Court seeking life imprisonment for Pappu Pasha. They argued that Popats were virtual humans and P3's death by beating was an open-and-shut case of murder. For that, Pasha deserved to be punished with life imprisonment. The defense, however, contended that since Popats were not born, they could not die. Hence Pasha could not have been tried for the murder of a Popat. Moreover, P3 was solely and privately owned by Pasha, and under no law, Pasha could be punished for destroying what he solely and privately owned. Much to the disappointment of FoP and many others like Kattu and Mattu, the Court upheld the defense's arguments and absolved Pasha of all the accusations.

Kattu was his scathing self when he said,

'Funny that we have an Act against cruelty to animals, but we condone cruelty against Popats who are virtual humans.'

'It is a complex issue that we are facing for the first time. According to me, it is a social and not a legal issue. You rightly said that the Popats are virtual humans. So the core question is how to deal with something virtual. Of course, we need to remember that virtual is real in 2050,' opined Lattu.

'I agree with virtual being real. Today, humans have embraced the virtual world with a vengeance. The connected world has disconnected us from the real world. More than ninety percent of our interactions are with Popats, we prefer to use Metaverse instead of the real world, our leisure time is consumed by Vunics and Concons, and Ubiqs have become our alter-ego. The society we live in today is rightly called a virtual society. While human society has evolved over thousands of years, we have had only a decade or two to develop the norms for a virtual society,' commented Sattu.

'Then 'V for Virtual Society' should be our agenda for today. As a society, we have developed values, morals, ethics, etiquettes, and practices to a fine degree of refinement. But in 2050, we should rethink and redefine the same while dealing with the virtual world. For example, violence has no place in civil society. But how do we treat the violence which is perpetrated upon a virtual entity? That is the gap we need to bridge for an evolving virtual society,' said Lattu.

'That makes sense, but taking up such an agenda will yield no political dividend. After all, Popats have no voting right,' commented Mattu, who always looked at the cost-benefit analysis.

'We need not look at the rating and voting all the time,' protested Kattu.

'I agree. Our manifesto should be forward-looking and articulate our vision for the virtual society. As usual, we can leave the details to Vartika and Y2K,' suggested Lattu.

'My view is that we don't politicize this issue. We can also eschew the usual protest path. Instead, we may take an unconventional and subtle route to convey our message. May I suggest that we all join a '*Nukkad Natak*' this evening at Pigeon Square?' proposed Vartika. Everyone agreed.

Street theater was an art form that had virtually vanished since the virtual world became dominant. Vartika had stumbled upon a small group called *'Nukkadbaj'* that was trying to preserve the tradition of street theater. The murder of P3 gave them a perfect script and Vartika's timely support enabled them to stage the drama at Pigeon Square. On Vartika's nudging, Y2K was made the chief guest for the show. The street play turned out to be short and captivating, in which a pliant Popat pleaded with Pasha 'Don't beat me Master' in a soul-stirring manner before dramatically collapsing in the last scene. After acknowledging the applause, the play director asked Y2K to say a few words. Though the request for 'few words' was never taken literally by the politicians, Y2K decided to be as brief as he could be. He slowly spoke.

'My dear citizen of Kautukpur,

It was a privilege to watch such a fine play that has brought into focus the dilemmas we face every day. As highlighted by the play, we are witnessing the birth of a virtual society and that process is irreversible. Therefore, we need to have a vision for this transformation. I have always advocated the policy of 'Humans First'. That policy should be taken forward with the objective of becoming 'Better Humans'. In my manifesto, therefore, 'V for virtual society' stands for the vision of 'Humans First, Better Humans' in a Virtual Society. Whether I win or not, I pledge that I shall always be guided by this vision.'

There was polite applause for Y2K's few words. Jholus could find nothing worthy of a headline, though they thought that 'Humans First, Better Humans' was an interesting tagline.

Only one channel gave coverage to the street play and Y2K's tagline.

Even Mr. Mahan was unimpressed with Y2K's performance and told Y2K, 'Whatever little you spoke was a bit heavy stuff for me. You should have kept 'V for Vegetarian' as today's agenda. That would have brought you plenty of votes.' 'I seriously thought of including 'V for Vegetarian' in my manifesto but decided against it since I am a fan of your 'V for Vindaloo Chicken',' replied Y2K as he devoured the Vindaloo curry. The voting results reflected Mr. Mahan's perception. For the first time in many days, Y2K's rating did not improve. A disappointed Vartika digested the results, looked at the curry thoughtfully, and said,

'The selling point of this dish is the good amount of spices put into it. Today we presented a decent dish but did not put any spice. I should have known that the lower the amount of spice, the lower the poll rating.'

'Let us not always be obsessed with the voting and the rating,' repeated Y2K as they got up for their usual walk together. Vartika nodded and smiled. At that point in time, being together was all that mattered.

Chapter XL

Lattu had come to believe that he had a nose for picking up the topics that would connect with the voters.

'After focusing on contemporary topics, let us revert to the old and time-tested issues,' suggested Lattu.

'I thought we had already exhausted them. In any case, they may not be so relevant,' observed Kattu.

'The hot topics for elections in the 2020s were *'bijli, pani, and sadak'*. Out of these, we haven't covered *'pani'* or water at all. So 'W for Water' can be our obvious agenda for today,' proposed Lattu.

'I agree that water was a hot topic in the 2020s. It was even predicted that there would be wars over water in the 40-50s. Nothing of that sort happened. Technology saved the day. IoT and AI now help conserve enough water. Water supply is managed intelligently, leaky pipes are a thing of the past, and every drop that can be recycled is recycled. When all this is not enough, artificial rain comes to the rescue. I think water as an election issue has lost steam,' countered Kattu.

'Count on a politician to create a crisis and another one to keep the crisis alive. Kautukpur is a prime example of this.

Kappuswamy has been demanding that all the water of river *Kautuki* be controlled by a Kautukpur Gappu so that Kautuk Mandal gets the maximum water. Guru Panchal is promising to extend the scope of free water to almost everyone. Prada is promising 'Rain on Demand'. Water seems to be making waves in the political circles,' mused Mattu.

'Politicians are known to be oblivious to the dangers of what they demand or promise. If an upstream Mandal politician controls the river flow as per his whims, downstream Mandal may either be flooded or parched. If water is made available free of cost, no one, including the Popats, will care to control the consumption. We have already seen that the 'Rain on Demand' in two Mandals caused floods in the third Mandal. We must understand the pitfalls of a populist agenda,' urged Sattu.

'I agree. On an essential and emotive issue like water, we need to be constructive and not just populist,' said Lattu.

"How do we do that?' asked Mattu.

Leave that to Y2K and Vartika was the consensus.

As planned by Vartika, the Y2K gang met at *'Kautukmahal Baoli'* in the afternoon. *Kautukmahal Baoli* was an old system of underground water storage that was built near the Kautukpur Fort more than eight hundred years ago to quench the thirst of Kautuk Mandal. It was an intricate and imposing stepwell structure. Although the water it stored had almost dried up and the structure had become dilapidated due to disuse and disrepair, it had not lost its grandeur. Restoring it to its old glory needed a lot of time, money, and Popatpower. Y2K vowed that if elected, he would press for the restoration and renovation of this *Baoli.* For the time being, however, he urged his gang to start with cleaning and repairing a few steps themselves. They were still at it when the Jholus arrived. Jholus had come to rely on Y2K to give them an interesting and different headline every day. Jholus had hoped that Y2K would not disappoint them today as well.

A handful of people had joined them on the call for '*Shramdan*' or community labor. As they got tired and halted for rest, Y2K saw the opportunity to make a small speech. He rose and spoke,

'Citizens of Kautukpur,

Thanks for joining me in this small *Shramdan* initiative. This magnificent *Baoli* hasn't seen so many visitors in a long time. But, once upon a time, it was the lifeline of this town where men and women gathered to fetch water. As the popular saying goes, the *Baoli* ensured *'har ghar pani, bhar bhar pani'*. However, plentiful water in every home became a distant dream as we forgot how to conserve and manage the water resource that is precious but limited. Technology saved the day and provided us with alternate means of supply but our thirst would soon outpace it. Even as Technology enables us to exploit new water resources, the old water bodies have dried up. While smart Technology can prevent wastage, it cannot control the unbridled and thoughtless ways of humans. As a result, we have a water crisis looming large that everyone is trying to ignore. Today's agenda of 'W for water' is to call everyone's attention to this looming crisis.

To address this crisis, we need to find local solutions, go back to the basics, and rediscover our traditional practices.

As a first step, we must rejuvenate our water bodies and harvest the water by all means including the age-old system of *Kautukmahal Baoli.* Therefore, If I get elected, I pledge to restore this great *Baoli* to its old glory and put it to use again. I promise to revive lost water bodies and increase the green cover. I promise to strengthen the use of technology but keep it in sync with the environment. I promise to eschew politics over water and rely on tech-based management. In short, I promise to bring *'har ghar pani, bhar bhar pani'*.'

Slogans in politics are as important as solutions. Y2K had found a nice slogan and used it effectively. At the end of his speech, he shouted *'har ghar pani'* which was followed by the audience's reverberating response of *'bhar bhar pani'*. Jholus liked the slogan as well and repeated it on their channels as much as Y2K had done. The footage of the Y2K gang cleaning and repairing the steps of *Kautukmahal Baoli* helped. But it was the slogan *'har ghar pani, bhar bhar pani'* that catapulted Y2K to the tenth position, his best ranking so far.

Chapter XLI

'What is going to come out today from your bag of old tricks for winning the elections?' asked Mattu jocularly.

'Well, calling out interference from the CIA was one trick that repeatedly clicked in the good old days,' answered Lattu with a straight face.

'Are you seriously suggesting the CIA's involvement as an election issue?' exclaimed incredulous Kattu.

'That will be too far-fetched because no one takes the CIA seriously these days. Its competence and influence have declined since the rise of smart tech. Earlier, the CIA understood technology but not humans. These days it understands neither. It has ceded the space to a few private entities, more specifically to the Xi International,' explained Lattu again with a straight face.

Xi International was founded in 2035 at a time of great volatility when big Corporations were falling like a pack of cards. CEOs of fourteen of the top twenty Corporations of the world met to discuss not only their survival but the continuance of their dominance in the future. They concluded that their long term profitability depended on efficiently turning and leveraging the wheels of Power across the globe. Traditional methods of influencing power centers had become ineffective and new methods had to be found to manage the power centers globally. So the 'Big Fourteen' decided to collaborate and form an organization that they named after the fourteenth letter of the Greek alphabet 'Xi'. The stated mission of the Xi International was to promote 'Peace, Progress, and Prosperity'. Critics claimed that the unstated mission was to promote 'Profitability, Power, and Predictability' worldwide for the fourteen Corporations.

Xi International grew exponentially on the back of large endowments from the big Fourteen. What distinguished it from similar organizations was the focus on leveraging the technology. Xi operated the largest Clowns in the world, hired the largest number of researchers, and employed the largest number of Popat volunteers called Popateers. Best PhDs in the field of AI, thought mining, and Ubiqs worked for Xi. Admirers of Xi claimed that their ingenious use of smart technology and astute deployment of Popateers helped in strengthening democracies worldwide. Its research-based advocacy, data-based analysis, and AI-based solutions for governments promoted economic growth, peace, and stability. Critics, however, claimed that besides organizing countless protests, Xi had a leading role in toppling thirty-six elected governments, installing fifteen dictators, deposing three despots, and instigating more than a hundred ethnic or religious riots by 2050. Only a few believed such critics.

Sattu was one of those few who believed the critics of Xi. As evidence, he pointed out the rising profitability and the dominance of the 'Big Fourteen'.

'The rising profit of the 'Big Fourteen' is par for the course and the least of the problems. What is worrisome is the new architecture that Xi is cementing,' said Mattu. He was referring to the much touted '*P*eace, *P*rogress, and *P*rosperity *P*roject *I*mplementation through *S*tructured *S*upport' program of Xi, derisively called *P4iss.* The program was based on the simple architecture of Gappu, Clown, and Popat operating in tandem to optimize well-defined objectives which in this case were profit, power, and predictability. While every system worked to maximize profit or power, Xi put a premium on predictability. It believed that profit and power were sustainable in the long term only if the events affecting them could be predicted effectively. *P4iss* architecture implemented predictability by making the system pliable in an optimum manner. While critics attributed all the political upheavals to the *P4iss* program, Xi denied its involvement in any such activities and maintained that its role was apolitical.

'In addition to the architecture, the added problem is its ambition. It is rapidly expanding its footprint to every nook and corner of the world. It is feared that within the next twenty years, Xi with the help of their *P4iss* program will be ruling the world. As I said, the 'Architecture' will have the last laugh,' said Sattu.

'That is an unfair assessment borne out of the perception that someday machines, algorithms, and AI will enslave humans. Such perception has been cultivated by popular fiction and movies and has nothing to do with reality,' countered Kattu.

'May I remind you that such predictions have come from some responsible quarters who understand the technology and have the foresight? It is therefore important that every thinking person is aware of such risks. For that reason, let us make 'X for Xi International' as our manifesto agenda for today,' interjected Lattu.

'Politically, what position should we take? Do we openly support Xi like Kappuswamy, shake hands with Xi when convenient like Guru Panchal, or maintain a studied silence like Prada? Or, should we oppose Xi like some fringe groups do, just because it is a foreign entity?' asked Kattu.

'Maybe we should ask Vartika about it,' replied Lattu.

Vartika was lost in deep thought. For the first time, She looked uncertain as everyone looked at her for answers.

'I am afraid I have no answers for you on this one,' answered Vartika rather uncharacteristically. Sensing her unease, Y2K took a position and spoke,

'We need not hold Xi responsible for everything evil and we need not oppose them merely based on apprehensions. A lot of what they do and say is good. But I do not trust their *P4iss* program which is opaque and non-transparent. I am opposed to the use of Popateers and external Clowns in the elections. I am also opposed to external interference in matters of governance. These may have unforeseen consequences. If we are not careful today, then 'Architecture' will surely take over the world in thirty years, if not in twenty years. And Xi may very well be its vehicle,' said Y2K.

Everyone agreed though Vartika seemed non-committal. It was Lattu who came up with the idea of holding a peaceful protest at Xi International's recently opened office.

They stood in protest against Xi International for two hours holding placards that drably said 'Xi, Go Back'. Another placard proclaimed 'We want Truth and Transparency, Not *P4iss*'. The protest turned out to be a non-event as no crowd gathered and no Jholu turned up. Lattu prepared a press release exactly on the lines of what Y2K had so effectively said in the meeting but only one channel took notice. It ran the headline 'Xenophobia against Xi' and berated Y2K for opposing Xi on unsubstantiated grounds.

Y2K was dejected by the response, especially by the strident criticism of one channel without hearing him out. Even the excellent *Xacuti*, that Mr. Mahan had prepared keeping in mind the agenda 'X', failed to lift his spirit. Vartika did not help either since she seemed to be too preoccupied with her thoughts. When the poll results came, negative votes brought down Y2K's ranking by one. After dinner, both walked together in gloomy silence as Vartika remained in her brooding mood. Y2K tried to figure out a song that would lift the spirits. He could think of none.

Chapter XLII

Around breakfast time in the morning, there was a commotion at the entrance of Y2K's apartment building which was unusual. Two persons accompanied by three Popateers had gathered there and started shouting slogans against Y2K. Their shouting turned a bit abusive when the Y2K gang arrived. One of them even tried to block Vartika. It was D2Y2 who in coordination with the security escorted them safely to the meeting. Half an hour later, they dispersed. A stone was hurled at Y2K's apartment window as a parting gift, but it failed to make any dent.

Y2K wanted to give a chase but Vartika advised against it. D2Y2 had quickly found their identities. They were the aides of Sholay Singh, a candidate ranked sixth in the current race. Though visibly shaken, Vartika had quickly gathered her wits. She explained that the whole episode was meant to demoralize the Y2K gang. Their intention was also to provoke Y2K into a direct engagement which would have been counterproductive for Y2K. Y2K was furious but saw merit in Vartika's reasoning. So he called up Inspector Godbole who enquired if anyone was hurt or anything was damaged. When Y2K answered in negative, Inspector Godbole advised him to ignore the Yahoos.

'One may ignore an individual Yahoo but we should all be concerned about the rising trend of Yahooism in politics. Sholay Singh is not an isolated case. I can recount three incidents involving politicians from yesterday alone. Supporters of Don H2 burnt an autonomous vehicle. Two candidates ranked in the top ten abused each other on a Jhallu show. Karan Kalia, who is ranked fifth, gave yet another display of his crass and boorish nature when he threw chappal at his opponent. It is high time that we do something about rising *Yahoogiri* in politics,' said Sattu.

'To begin with, let us make 'Y for Yahooism in politics' as our manifesto point for the day,' suggested Lattu.

'Aren't you going a little overboard on this issue? Politics is not a preserve of super genius or gentlemen alone. We should give space to all,' countered Kattu.

"We do strive to give space to all. Ours is a tolerant society. But don't you think we should draw a line somewhere between what is acceptable and what is not?" asked Mattu.

'How do you draw such a line? Earthiness in politics may be criticized as crassness and one's assertiveness may be dismissed as boorish behavior. You may even paint political exuberance as aggression or violence. It is dangerous to tread into behavioral politics by being judgmental,' persisted Kattu.

'There is no need to be judgmental. Social and Political Science has advanced enormously in the last two decades, thanks to AI. Even for Yahooism, we have an objective and scientific measure called the Yahoo Index. The good news is that it was developed by our own Professor Yash Mohan from Kautuk University,' said Mattu.

'Bad news is that the Yahoo Index landed Professor Yash briefly in jail. During the last election, he published the Yahoo score of a few candidates. They promptly filed a defamation suit under the Defamation Act 2013, claiming that they had been insulted and that their election prospects were irreparably damaged by the Index,' informed Kattu.

Lattu lit up on this piece of information.

'I think an individual's behavior is none of our business. However, *Yahoogiri* pollutes the politics. Therefore, voters have a right to know and evaluate the behavior of their representatives in public space. I suggest that we support the publishing of the Yahoo Index for all the candidates daily, just like the Air Quality Index. It will clear a lot of air in the political circles by being a deterrent to *Yahoogiri*. If that requires an amendment in the Defamation Act, our manifesto can promise to do that as well,' suggested an animated Lattu.

'Your suggestion is well taken. But how do we advocate our agenda today?' asked Sattu.

All eyes turned to Vartika.

'We seem to have forgotten Hyde Park. It so happens that Professor Yash is speaking there in the evening on the very same subject of *'Yahoogiri in politics'*. For a change, Y2K can listen to a speech rather than make a speech. Later, Y2K can extend his support and announce little steps he will take if he wins. Lattu has already elaborated these steps to be incorporated in our manifesto,' replied Vartika. Everyone agreed.

Professor Yash, jocularly known as 'Yahoo Master', was an authority on the subject and articulated the Yahoo-Index well. Post-lecture, Y2K engaged with him in an animated discussion and made a little speech that everyone applauded. Even Jholus took note of 'Yahoogiri in politics' and came up with headlines like 'Y2K promises to expose Yahoos in politics', 'Y2K takes on Yahoos', 'No room for Yahooism in politics' and 'Welcome voices against Yahoogiri in politics'.

While serving the special dish 'Y for Yakhni', Mr. Mahan told Y2K that it was for the first time that somebody was raising an issue like *Yahoogiri* in politics and he welcomed it. He was used to dealing with Yahoos in his restaurant but saw no reason why the public should suffer the ruckus created by the Yahoos in politics. Like Mr. Mahan, many more voters were equally fed up with *Yahoogiri* in politics. Their votes improved Y2K's ranking by two positions.

Chapter XLIII

Y2K was tantalizingly placed in eighth position on the last day of the qualifying round, considered as the quarter-final round. Barring a disaster, the rank was good enough to take him to the next round but not good enough to ensure entry into the final round. However, it was a performance much better than anticipated which made the meeting atmosphere relaxed. As soon as D2Y2 served coffee, a banter between Sattu and Kattu ensued.

'For the last so many days, Lattu has been making suggestions and Kattu has been asking questions. For a change, let Lattu ask a question and Kattu make the final suggestion of this round,' said Sattu.

Lattu immediately took up the challenge.

'I have been wanting to ask a question which may seem rather odd. All the leaders tell their voters what they will do in their manifesto but why don't they tell what they will not do, once elected to power?' asked Lattu innocently.

'That's because no politician will ever tell you what he has up his sleeve. A leader reveals his true colors only when he is in power,' answered Sattu.

'Also because a politician's job is to sell the dreams. Like the clever salesman of an untested product, a politician never tells about after-sale service,' added Mattu.

'I think the real problem is that most politicians are clueless about what to do and what not to do. They simply throw a stone in the water and hope that it will not sink. Who cares if the hope of the public sinks as well?' said Sattu.

'I think you are exaggerating and demonizing the politicians. Most of them are clever and well-meaning people. They are humans and all humans make mistakes. How are they even supposed to know in advance what not to do?' defended Kattu

'That is simple. They can always take the help of an AI platform that will tell them what not to do. The best such platform that I know of is called '*Zimbastic*' and the best thing is that it is local,' said Lattu.

'Let us then make 'Z for *Zimbastic*' as our agenda point of the day,' announced Kattu triumphantly.

Zimbastic was a platform developed by Professor Zahoor who specialized in the study of African nations. He was particularly fascinated by the story of Zimbabwe, a beautiful country. At the time of its independence, it had a strong economy with a Zimbabwean dollar trading higher than the US dollar. By 2030, a million Zimbabwe dollars were needed to buy one US dollar. Such a steep downfall could not be attributed to one single reason. For Professor Zahoor, Zimbabwe presented a classic case of 'what not to do' in politics and governance. He used deep learning from this case study to build an AI platform that told politicians and policymakers 'what not to do'. He named his AI Filter Platform 'Zimbastic'. Some found it fantastic while others called it bombastic, but it worked. In 2041, Zimbabwe became the first country to use it extensively and was able to turn around its fortunes by 2044.

'I have heard of this platform but in 2045 it got banned worldwide. I don't know why?' wondered Sattu.

'That is because of three reasons. Firstly, the mother-in-law syndrome. No one wanted a Platform whose only job was to tell you what not to do. Secondly, though brilliant, it was an individual effort. There were no investors, no big corporate supporters, and no interest groups who would take an interest in backing up a platform that had no axe to grind. Thirdly, it was fiercely opposed by Xi International. *Zimbastic* was diametrically opposite of Xi in concept, methodology, and purpose. Xi told you what to do but *Zimbastic* told you what not to do. Xi suited politicians for pedaling their dreams but *Zimbastic* mostly poured water on them. Pretty soon Xi realized that *Zimbastic* was a threat and campaigned for its ban by telling the whole world that it was a tool of interference in internal governance. They succeeded without much difficulty,' explained Kattu.

'If we filter all the promises and actions of the leading candidates through the *Zimbastic* platform, most of them will fail the test. What a pity it got banned,' rued Sattu.

'Well, nothing prevents us at least from voluntarily submitting our manifesto for filtering. We can also pledge to validate all our policies and acts through this platform. If we decide to go ahead despite failing the test, we shall make public the reasons for doing so. It will ensure that we don't make too many mistakes once we get elected,' suggested Kattu. Everyone agreed.

As suggested by Vartika, Y2K met Professor Zahoor in the evening at his modest residence. The aged Professor was pleasantly surprised at the renewed interest in his pet project. He was even more surprised when a few Jholus, arranged by Vartika of course, turned up for an interview. They took pictures of Professor Zahoor and Y2K together and asked questions about the banned Platform which they thought was newsworthy. One Jholu asked, 'Will the revival of Zimbastic not lead to the rule of the machine, for the machine, and by the machine posing a threat to democracy as alleged by its critics?' Professor replied in the negative explaining that it was a passive AI platform, unlike the Clowns which were active AI platforms. Moreover, unlike the 'Architecture', it was a 'standalone' 'one-way' platform. Hence it could pose no threat to the authority of humans. Another Jholu asked Y2K whether his pledge to use the platform would conflict with his vision of 'Humans First, Better Humans'. Y2K clarified that 'It was the age of 'Platforms' and a Platform that ensured that we didn't move backward actually complemented his vision. Moreover, advance warning over the consequences of your actions always makes you a better human and better leader.

Jholus interpreted and presented the answers in their own way. One of them headlined it as 'New paradigm of Platform Politics', another simply said, 'Y2K revives the banned *Zimbastic*', and yet another read, 'Tango of Politics and Platform'. However, all the channels ran a byte from Professor Zahoor who said,

'In today's scenario when every politician has thrown caution to the winds, Y2K emerges as a ray of hope. Because he promises to use the *Zimbastic* platform, He will at least not lead our Mandal to disaster.'

Y2K ended the final day of the grueling qualifying round in seventh position, riding on the generous endorsement from Professor Zahoor.

Chapter XLIV

Reaching the round of twelve, also called the quarter-final round, was a victory of sorts. As soon as the Y2K gang had gathered, they demanded *laddu.* Big or small, it was customary to distribute *laddus* on any political victory. Y2K was relieved to see that D2Y2 had arranged enough *laddus* ready to be distributed. *laddus* made the mood celebratory. Even Vartika took a second helping of *laddus.*

'Guys, take as many *laddus* as you want since we shall be burning all the excess calories during the course of the day.' She said, gulping down her *laddu.*

'Are you planning to organize a race or a boxing match?' asked Lattu.

'No, something simpler. We are going to undertake a *Padyatra* for the two days of this round. The *yatra* will commence from Pigeon Square right after this meeting and conclude at Jantar Mantar tomorrow,' replied Vartika.

Padyatra was quite a popular tool in politics till the 2030s. A seasoned politician would undertake a yatra when he had nothing worthwhile to do. He would also embark on a yatra if he had too much on his plate. He would not only go on a yatra when he was down and out but bask in the glory as well by undertaking a yatra. Whether in power or out of power, yatra was a routine fixture for a politician. Though termed as a 'journey on foot', the leader had the flexibility of using a vehicle of his choice. Leaders walked only as much as they liked and usually made others to walk. Yatras were launched ostensibly to educate or contact the masses. By 2040, however, the masses were educated enough on almost every subject and generally did not want to be contacted by other humans, let alone the politicians. With the virtual world having a complete sway, *Padyatra* had gone out of fashion almost a decade ago.

'*Padyatra* or any other yatra for that matter is a dying tradition. Why do you want to undertake such an exercise now?' asked Kattu

'Just a matter of strategy, recommended by my intuitive AI tool. Remember that this is a 'maro kato' or a no-holds-barred round in which every remaining candidate attacks every other candidate. You survive by pulling down your rival. In this fierce fight, it sometimes pays to abandon the battlefield. Remember that even Lord Krishna adopted this strategy and was called 'Ranchhoddas' for his strategic acumen,' explained Vartika.

'I do not understand the strategy part but it is a good idea to try and revive a dying tradition,' opined Sattu who seemed to be quite happy with the idea of a long walk in nice sunny weather.

'If I recall, *Padyatras* used to be of many varieties with different themes and fancy names. So, what name and what theme have you thought of?' enquired Lattu.

'Let us call it a 'Manifesto Yatra' with the focus on our Manifest-2050. A yatra may look old-fashioned but the idea is to reinvent the old. If nothing else, it will at least keep you fit for the next round,' replied Vartika.

Team Y2K was perhaps the fittest election campaign team in Kautuk Mandal. They started on Padyatra from Pigeon Square without much fanfare. Despite Vartika's efforts, no Jholu turned up to cover the start. After all, an outing by walking was no big deal. Undeterred, the Y2K gang walked earnestly with folded hands, occasionally shouting slogans like 'vote for Y2K' or 'jeetega bhai jeetega, Y2K jeetega'. The slogans got no response and the team could hardly meet any voter in person.

In a turn of fortune, the team Y2K finally got noticed in the evening.

As predicted by Vartika, the fierce war with no holds barred started sooner than expected. Fifth-ranked foul-mouthed Karan Kalia, KK to his supporters, appeared on a morning show and abused all the rivals ranked above him. This incensed the fourth-ranked Vellu Prasad, called Vella Vellu Prasad or V2P by friends and foes alike, to no end. He launched an equally offensive tirade against KK and all the rest. Since Prada was his immediate rival, she came in for special attention. In the heat of the moment, he used a few unparliamentary words for Prada. In a counterattack, a furious Prada singled out V2P, reminding him that he had 'one leg in the grave and two hands in the cash vault'. She was referring to V2P being caught in a corruption case unearthed by new technology. Since then V2P had become the most vocal opponent of technology. Anyway, while talking about corruption, she also included the name of Guru Panchal. Taking note, Guru Panchal called Prada names and tossed the corruption charges onto Kappuswamy. Supremely unconcerned Kappuswamy berated all the other candidates calling them unworthy of any position. This started a chain of allegations and counter-allegations all over again.

While all the Jholus and Jhallus were gleefully reporting the escalating war of words, one of them pointed out a lone candidate, Y2K, walking on the streets on a mission. Instead of indulging in a war of words, he was being constructive. Instead of talking about rivals, he was talking about the manifesto. Instead of being rude or aggressive, he was humble and sincere. The stark comparison impressed many who voted Y2K to the fifth position as day one of the quarter-final round ended.

The significance of the jump in Y2K's ranking was not lost on other candidates and they all decided to take to the road the next day.

The first one to go out on the road was Don H2 with his team of thugs who went about reminding people of the dire consequences if they didn't vote for the Don. They, however, lacked the finesse and were soon caught on camera and were forced to retreat. In the meantime, KK marshaled his fire-spitting troops. He carefully avoided Don H2's territory and in the process found himself face to face with V2P's supporters. V2P, who eschewed technology, had armed all his supporters with *lathis* and a mantra '*meri lathi, meri marji*'. The V2P supporters did not hesitate to follow their leader's mantra and beat up KK's troops who fled even before Inspector Godbole could turn up. On another front, Prada had called Guru Panchal a misogynist and marched to his office with a crowd. Sensing trouble, Guru Panchal fled from the back door, only to marshal his supporters against Kapppuswamy. He was confronted by Netaji Mungeri Lal, the favorite troubleshooter of Kappuswmy. Mayhem ensued again, till Inspector Godbole appeared on the scene and both sides dispersed. The leaders then took to issuing statements condemning each other in general and the police led by Inspector Godbole in particular. The war of words that had spilled onto the streets became a war of statements and further spilled into the studios of Jhallus.

'Somethings never change' commented Y2K as he watched the day's proceedings while having a quiet dinner with Vartika at Mahan's. The rankings however did change. V2P got pushed to fifth position followed by Don H2 and KK. While all these gentlemen suffered penalties on account of negative votes, Y2K surged ahead to the next round with an improved ranking at number four.

Chapter XLV

'Reaching the semi-final round of the election looks surreal to me, given the fact that none of us had any idea about politics,' said Lattu as he gulped down *motichur*, a finer variety of *laddu* which D2Y2 had thoughtfully arranged beforehand.

'Beware that our political skills are going to be seriously tested in this round,' replied Vartika.

'How?' Y2K asked in concern.

'Now that only six qualifiers remain in the field, the situation is ripe for fixing, *jod-tod*, and deal-making. Rivals will form new alliances in exchange for money, power, or position. Negotiation, persuasion, intimidation, and temptation will be the tools of the trade employed. Equations will change, votes will shift, and the fortunes will swing,' said Vartika.

'I do not subscribe to this kind of politics. I joined the race with the intent to promote clean politics. I shall not be part of any horse trading or dirty dealing,' said Y2K firmly.

'That's fine Y2K. There are a few offers but I have already put up a 'not for sale' board,' replied Vartika quietly.

'The million dollar question is what do we do now?' asked Mattu.

'Nothing. We have worked tirelessly for more than a month. So we take a day off,' replied Vartika.

There was bewilderment at Vartika's suggestion but a break was welcome. They had no better suggestion to make anyway. They all agreed and dispersed.

Y2K had been so busy that he had not had a long conversation with D2Y2 for over a month. Now that he had nothing to do, he decided to have a friendly chat with D2Y2. It always worked.

'How am I doing D2Y2?' asked Y2K.

'You are doing fine. Better than expected. Good luck to you for this round,' replied D2Y2.

'I do need a huge amount of luck. I am stuck in fourth position and don't know what to do to improve. On top of that, Vartika has advised everyone to take the day off as if a miracle would happen,' grumbled Y2K.

'Patience is a big virtue in politics. And miracles do happen if you grab your opportunity,' said D2Y2.

'Cut those sermons, please. Right now I do not see any such opportunity arising unless you are referring to horse-trading as an opportunity,' said Y2K impatiently.

'Okay. I'll be realistic and give you my analysis. It all boils down to '*Hawa*' or the wind. Unless the wind changes in a particular candidate's favor, current rankings correctly reflect the probability of his or her winning the election. So everyone is trying to create a strong enough wind to ensure smooth sailing through the remaining round,' replied D2Y2.

'How?' asked Y2K.

'It is a simple mathematics of combination and permutations. If the top two candidates combine to fight, it will be an invincible combination. But it is also the least likely combination. If any of the top two combines with the third-ranked candidate, this combination will also be impossible to defeat. However, Prada who is ranked number three, is very unlikely to join hands with any of the top two. If she does, her chances of winning in the future diminish to almost zero. That leaves you at number four. If any of the top three can enroll your support, he or she has a high chance of winning. But the problem with this permutation is that you are not available. Next, you may try and enlist the support of those below you and become a credible challenger but that will not happen. You do not have as much heft and wherewithal as the top three who are already trying to enlist the support of the fifth or sixth by hook or crook. The situation will be clearer by the evening. Till then, you have very little option but to wait,' summed up D2Y2.

'Thanks for the update but I still don't get it. Tell me something that will make me feel better,' said Y2K.

'You will feel better if you push the elections out of your mind and think about your future with Vartika,' advised D2Y2, almost like his mother would have.

Y2K was startled by D2Y2's perceptive observation. Though his relationship with Vartika was no secret, he had not yet proposed to her. That was something he kept postponing. He was sure of the feelings they had for each other but a nagging doubt kept bothering him. Events during the election had brought them closer but will the bond last post-election when life would be back on the mundane track? Y2K longed for Vartika and felt uneasy at such a thought. He decided to propose to her soon after the elections were over. Having made up his mind, Y2K felt better and went to sleep. His dreams were interrupted when D2Y2 woke him up for dinner with Vartika.

Vartika looked as stunning as ever when she arrived for dinner. Looking at her, Y2K forgot about the elections. 'Winning the elections is not as important as winning Vartika's hand' he thought to himself. Y2K was brought out of his reverie when an agitated Mahan asked him,

'Have you heard about the unholy alliance between Kappuswamy and V2P? As if that was not enough, Guru Panchal has tied up with Don H2. Everyone is talking about the money changing hands and promises being made for powerful positions in the government. I haven't seen such a low point in politics. They are even trying to justify it in the name of numbers.'

Mr. Mahan had become an ardent fan of Y2K and it was touching to see his concern. Vartika consoled him saying,

'When mathematics overrides ethics, politics is bound to become negative in value. But don't worry Mr. Mahan. Y2K will try to do his best for Kautuk Mandal. I am sure things will turn for the better with support from citizens like you.'

Mr. Mahan seemed a bit unconvinced, but Y2K was convinced that Vartika had something up her sleeve.

Vartika broke the suspense only after the dinner was over.

'I am afraid we have to cancel our post-dinner walk together. Someone is waiting for a secret midnight rendezvous with you,' she said.

'Who and why?' asked a perplexed Y2K.

'Prada wants to meet you to discuss the possibility of bringing synergy in the ongoing election campaign,' was Vartika's cryptic answer.

'Not interested,' said Y2K tersely. He saw no point in meeting with his rival. In any case, he had come to cherish the quiet post-dinner walk with Vartika and did not want to miss it tonight either. Vartika, however, was adamant.

'Never say 'No' in politics. At least not at the outset and not when you are on the backfoot,' chided Vartika. Y2K had no choice but to agree.

Meeting with Prada was one-to-one and a full drill was carried out to ensure privacy. Prada was a sharp, intelligent, and ambitious woman. She had a stern-looking demeanor but could turn on charm when she wanted to. She welcomed Y2K profusely but quickly came to the point.

'I am sure you have done the electoral math. It is almost certain that we shall lose this round unless we join our forces,' said Prada.

'Yes, I am aware of that eventuality,' replied Y2K tentatively.

'I admire the way you have worked your way up from the bottom. In recognition of your talent and potential, I offer you the chance of being my deputy if you step down in my favor,' offered Prada.

'I have not come this far to cut a deal and withdraw. It would be like cheating the voters who have voted for me,' replied Y2K firmly.

'Would it be fair to your voters to let Guru Panchal or Kappuswamy win?' asked Prada.

'Why don't you ask that question to yourself and consider stepping down in my favor?' replied Y2K rather audaciously.

Prada was all grace and said,

'Anything is possible in politics so long as you are realistic. I am your senior in politics and I am ranked above you. Give me a realistic reason why should I step down in your favor?'

'The vote gap between us is less than three percent and the momentum is in my favor since my graph has been consistently going upward while yours has been almost flat,' reasoned Y2K.

'You are mixing facts with optimism and not reason. It only makes the situation intractable,' said Prada in diplomatic exasperation.

'The only way to come out of this intractable situation is to have a fair and evenly balanced option. We can decide who will step down by tossing a coin,' said Y2K, almost on an impulse.

Prada was taken by surprise but quickly gained her wits. She was a seasoned politician ready to take her chances. 'If I win the toss, Y2K will not retract. If I lose, I can still find a way around to wriggle out and put up a fight,' she reasoned to herself.

'Let us then toss the coin and decide,' announced Prada. This time Y2K was taken by surprise. He was not very comfortable about the offer he had just made and was hoping that Prada would refuse. He thought about the difficult situation and said,

'I do not want to be accused of making a backdoor deal. Let us go to the public, and explain what we are doing and why, with full transparency. Then we can toss the coin in public to decide who will stand down.'

Prada was dumbfounded at this bizarre suggestion. She looked at her rival with renewed respect. She will have to now take her chances fairly and honestly.

'I agree. Let us go ahead with your suggestion. Our teams can work out the details,' replied Prada.

The Breakfast News next day was agog with the Y2K-Prada agreement. The headlines varied from 'Politics reduced to a child's play' to 'A new paradigm in politics'. The news generated a high quotient of curiosity and even a higher level of betting. To keep the level of interest high, Vartika held a mini press conference in the morning to announce that the 'toss-ceremony' would be held in Pigeon Square in the evening in the presence of the media and the whole world. The novel Y2K-Prada deal got wide publicity as Jholus vied with each other to cover the details while comparing it with the deals stitched by Kappuswamy and Guru Panchal.

Vartika had taken it upon herself to make elaborate arrangements for the toss. A big stage was set up at Pigeon Square on which a ring-like area was demarcated to facilitate the toss. A neutral umpire was hired along with a battery of commentators and a popular anchor. Before the appointed time, supporters of both Prada and Y2K marched in the Square shouting slogans. As Prada walked onto the stage, a hundred bunch of balloons were released to showcase her election symbol 'Balloon'. The anchor introduced her in glowing terms. When Y2K joined from the other side, a hundred pigeons were released to remind everyone of his election symbol. Anchor introduced Y2K equally profusely. As per the script coached by Vartika, the anchor asked Prada,

'What is the reason for forging such an alliance?'

'Both of us are opposed to the candidature, policies, and governing style of Kappuswamy and Guru Panchal. If we do not fight unitedly, we will be handing them the victory on a platter and letting down our voters,' replied Prada.

'Why have you chosen this method of settlement?' asked Anchor, turning to Y2K.

'It is to show our commitment to transparency and fairness in governance. If you indulge in backroom dealing, fixing, and maneuvering, you are unlikely to bring transparency and fairness in governance,' replied Y2K.

'What kind of an alliance is this? Have you worked out a common agenda?' asked the anchor again.

'The alliance is unconditional. We respect each other's views and whosoever wins will be free to implement his or her manifesto and policies,' replied Prada.

'Something without a *quid pro quo* in politics is unheard of. Has money changed hands or have you come to a mutual understanding for names on some positions of power?' asked the anchor pointedly.

'Absolutely no. Had money changed hands, we would not have been standing here. There is no secret understanding about the nominations either. Our understanding is that the winner will be free to make nominations as per his or her choice to be able to provide an accountable government,' replied Y2K.

As the anchor exhausted her pre-scripted questions, the umpire took over and tossed the coin. Prada called 'Heads' and lost the toss. In a boxing match style, the umpire raised Y2K's hands and declared him a winner to thunderous applause. Again, a hundred pigeons were released and a new slogan coined by Vartika reverberated '*Prada Y2K ek hain, inke iraade nek hain*'. Prada read out an appeal to her supporters to vote for Y2K and Y2K thanked her for it. Before dispersing, the supporters of Y2K and Prada marched together to Jantar Mantar raising the slogan '*Prada Y2K ek hain, inke iraade nek hain*'. The verdict of Jholus, as reflected in their headlines, was that '*Hawa*' had positively turned in favor of Y2K.

When Y2K and Vartika arrived for dinner, they found Mr. Mahan in an upbeat mood. He was vindicated when the results were announced. Y2K had managed to beat Guru Panchal to reach the final round.

'I was sure that Y2K would innovate something and reach the final round,' said Mr. Mahan, as he opened Champagne to celebrate.

Y2K smiled at his most ardent supporter's faith in him and wondered what if he had lost the toss.

Y2K would not have lost the toss, courtesy of Vartika. Y2K had innovated well but had put Vartika in a spot of bother since the toss could go either way. So, she summoned technical help. A sensor, AI-processor, camera, and a powerful blower were combined in a tiny device and fitted beneath the stage. As soon as the coin was tossed, the AI-powered computer calculated that it was going to be 'Head'. A tiny whiff of precisely calculated, calibrated, and directed air pressure had silently turned it to 'Tail'.

As everyone congratulated Y2K and celebrated, no one noticed how perturbed Vartika was.

Chapter XLVI

To celebrate the occasion of reaching the final round, D2Y2 had arranged a whole array of sweets but Vartika would have none of it. The breaking news in the morning was that after Guru Panchal's defeat, Don H2 had shifted allegiance to Kappuswamy. Taking note of the new development, she initiated the discussion as soon as coffee was served.

'Last night, we had the momentum with us but Kappuswamy's latest maneuvering has given him a slight advantage. It's going to be a tight finish and we have a lot of work to do in the remaining two days,' said Vartika.

'What is your plan Vartika?' asked Lattu.

'Nothing very original. We stick to the old traditional way this time. We will end our campaign with a grand rally at *Ramlila Maidan* tomorrow,' said Vartika.

Ramlila Maidan was where local drama troops enacted Lord Ram's epic fight between good and evil. The usually twenty-day-long Ramlila had been reduced to just a few hours by the 2030s but the grandeur and technical excellence had increased multifold. By 2040, with the help of Popat Actors, Virtual Reality, and AI pyrotechnics, *Ramlila* had advanced so much that it became mostly a *Lila* with very little *Ram* left. In any case, *Ramlila* ground was hardly associated with *Ram* since most of the time it was used by politicians for their rallies where drama was aplenty but the difference between good and bad usually got obliterated.

Every Tom, Dick, or Harry could not afford to hold a rally at *Ramlila Maidan.* A rally here meant that you had arrived at the local political stage. Though technology had brought many changes in politics, the basic format of a rally at *Ramlila Maidan* had not changed even by 2050. There were, however, few challenges that the Y2K gang could immediately think of and wanted Vartika to clarify.

'To begin with, we need a celebrity for our rally at the *Ramalila Maidan,*' said Sattu.

'We can manage with local celebrities like K-cube and Professor Acharya, *aka* Guruji. Besides, the idea is to present Y2K himself as a rising celebrity,' replied Vartika.

'How do we gather enough crowd? We don't have the wherewithal to hire a large enough crowd,' queried Kattu.

'Crowd hiring, both of people and Ubiqs, is routine for such rallies but we may not have to resort to such a tactic on a large scale. Thirty days of our campaign has given us many supporters who will pitch in with the mobilization part. However, to be on the safe side, I have engaged the best and the most discrete professional service provider for top-up purposes only,' responded Vartika. There was a minor debate on the ethics of hiring the crowd but Vartika prevailed in the end.

'What about the catering?' asked Sattu.

'There is no one better than Mr. Mahan for this purpose and he has been very kind to give us the deepest possible discount for *chai-samosa*,' answered Vartika.

'We have very limited funds, so we have been very frugal in our campaigning so far. How do we fund such a huge expenditure now,' asked Mattu in worry.

'Not to worry. Remember Vichitra Gupta, our largest donor? Considering the rise and rise of Y2K, he has agreed to fill the gap in our budget,' replied Vartika, much to Mattu's relief.

'Logistics apart, what will be the theme and what shall we focus upon in this rally?' enquired Lattu.

'Y2K has repeatedly expounded the 'Humans First, Better Humans' policy and we stick to that. Additionally, I propose to release 'Manifesto-2050' as a book during the rally,' replied Vartika.

'That is a great idea. But while we concentrate on our rally, what will our rival be doing?' asked Kattu.

'Good question. Having held a rally at Ramlila Maidan only yesterday, Kappuswamy can't counter us with another rally. So he will look to disrupt our rally, perhaps through Don H2.'

'What do we do then?'

'Y2K should take on Kappuswamy directly in his speech at the rally. Till then we keep restraint. Inspector Godbole is on our side and he'll take care of any sign of trouble,' replied Vartika.

Inspector Godbole did take care of any potential trouble over the crucial two days. He reduced his reaction time from one hour to ten minutes, took the miscreants by surprise, and prevented any serious incident. Rest was achieved by Vartika's meticulous planning and Y2K gang's hardwork. Crowds turned up from unexpected quarters and Jholus certified the rally as mammoth. Vartika had contracted the best of local talent for a song and dance show to keep the crowd entertained. K-cube added to the glamor quotient. The crowd recalled Astrologer Guruji's prediction of Y2K reaching the final round and listened to him with rapt attention. Professor Zahoor presented a Zimbastic-proof certificate to Y2K's Manifesto-2050. Everyone connected with the manifesto was invited to the stage and the book 'Manifesto 2050 – Humans First' was released amid big fanfare.

The stage was now set for Y2K to deliver his final speech of the campaign. He spoke in his customary measured tone.

'Citizens of Kautuk Mandal,

Just about a month ago when I decided to fight the election, I had no idea of what it would entail. But I joined the campaign wholeheartedly with a desire to serve, a willingness to learn, and an intent to bring about a change for the better. As I embarked on this journey, you guided me, mentored me, and encouraged me. It is your love, affection, and support that has brought me to the final round in this election. Thank you all.

Only yesterday, my worthy opponent had tried to dismiss me as a novice and a newcomer by saying '*jane kahan kahan se aa jate hain yeh log*'. While I deprecate such a low level of discourse, I readily and honestly agree to the charge of being a newcomer and even a novice. After all, I am only forty-two days old in politics. However, being a newcomer and a novice can sometimes be a blessing. Not being bound by the burden of expectation, ambition, or legacy has enabled me to make some right choices.

While my worthy rival has made tall promises, I make none. He claims he would perform miracles if elected. Since I don't have *Aladdin's Chirag*, don't expect miracles from me. His ploy is to play with your emotions. I prefer to engage in a rational discourse. He keeps in mind his vote bank, but I keep in mind the interest of the whole Kautuk Mandal. He takes technology for granted. I grant that technology has its challenges. He lives in 2050 with a mindset of 2020. I live in 2050 and think of 2070. His mission is 'Power First', and my mission is 'Human First'. It is for you, dear voters, to make your choice judiciously.

'Manifesto 2050 - Humans First', the book that has been released just now, is not a run-of-the-mill manifesto prepared by professional ideologues or Popats. It is the culmination of a month's efforts, living through it every day. From A to Z, it covers almost every aspect of our social, economic, cultural, and political life. Politics, like life, is a continuum. Old clichés like '*Roti, Kapda, aur Makan*' may have faded but we still need to look at them with the lenses of 2050. Oft-repeated issues like '*Bijli, Pani, Sadak*' and '*Naukari*' still have relevance, only their scope and context have changed. With the advent of Popats, AI, and the virtual world, we are faced with brand new challenges in 2050.

Without realizing it, technology is changing our lives irreversibly. Therefore, we need to constantly monitor the direction we take. While we enjoy the benefits of technology, we should exercise circumspection to ensure that our journey is not down the hill, that the machines do not overtake us, that we always put humans first, and that we create a better society for ourselves and for future generations.

Ladies and Gentlemen, I reiterate my commitment to the 'Humans First, Better Humans' policy and present my Manifesto for 2050. It is for you to choose between manifesto-2050 and Mindset-2020. Your choice will determine where we shall stand not only in 2050 but in 2070 as well.

Vote without fail, and do not fail to think before voting. Thank you.'

There was deafening applause to Y2K's spirited address. Jholus declared the rally a grand success and predicted that *Hawa* could turn slightly in favor of Y2K. Jhallus also had high intensity debates on the prospects of both the candidates. For a change, there was consensus amongst all the Lappus that it was going to be the closest contest in the history of Kautuk Mandal.

Mr. Mahan was the only person who was hundred percent confident that Y2K would win. To mark the big occasion, he had created a '*Manifesto-2050 Thali*' comprising twenty-six dishes from A to Z. However, the tension of waiting for the result was so palpable that Y2K could sample hardly a few of the dishes from the large *Thali*. To build up the suspense further, there were constant announcements delaying the declaration of results. The intentional delay heightened the tension and fueled speculation, much to the delight of Jhallus who continued to debate endlessly.

Finally, an official from the EC appeared in the breaking news. He also took his own sweet time in announcing the result. He first gave statistics, detailed the SOP, and thanked one and all for making the election a grand success. After having tested the patience of everyone, he came to the concluding part as he slowly spoke,

'Both the candidates have given a good account of themselves in the best tradition of democracy. It was an extremely close fight. As far as the result is concerned, I am happy to announce that there is no winner today. The vote margin between the two candidates is less than zero point one percent. Therefore, under the Representation of People Act, Amendment 23 of 2037, the 'Rule of Compulsory Voting' is being invoked. As per the rule, voting by all eligible voters is now declared mandatory. Those who have already voted need not vote but those who have not voted will be given one more opportunity to do so till tomorrow evening. No further campaigning will be allowed tomorrow. Eligible voters can vote from anywhere, anytime. Differently-abled and those who are immobilized will be assisted by EC Popateers. Anyone who fails to vote by the closing time tomorrow will invite civil penalties like a reduction in insurance benefits, state benefits, subsidies, etc. I, therefore, enjoin upon every citizen who has not voted to exercise his right before the deadline ends. The winner will be announced on a total vote count basis tomorrow night.'

The announcement of the EC official came as an anti-climax. There were no shouts of joy, no distribution of sweets, no lamenting on a missed opportunity, no discussion on what went right or wrong. Jholus and Jhallus were caught unaware and went back to their databases to ferret out tidbits. Y2K, the most affected party, finished his dinner quickly and braced himself for another day's grind. Mr. Mahan, the most ardent fan of Y2K, closed his shop early thinking of what to curate for the big day tomorrow.

Y2K was neither dejected nor overjoyed. He was just more tense. Besides the election, there was another task whose result he was more concerned with. He had planned to propose to Vartika after dinner, irrespective of the result. Unexpectedly, there was no result and Vartika seemed to be aloof and distant, immersed in her thoughts. She too was perhaps disappointed at the turn of events despite her hard work. Y2K reckoned that tonight was not the most appropriate time for the make-or-break decision. Tomorrow will be a full moon day. Tomorrow, under the bright moonlight with the clouds of uncertainty gone, his chances of winning Vartika's heart may be brighter. Y2K decided to wait until tomorrow.

Chapter XLVII

The Y2K gang didn't know whether to congratulate Y2K or rue the fact that they had missed the bus by a whisker. Naturally, the mode of election came under discussion as Kattu wondered aloud

'Isn't the compulsory voting rule a bit harsh? To vote or not to vote is the question that every individual should be free to decide.'

'I don't think so. In a democracy, the majority wins but that majority should be eked out from the full set of eligible voters. The current rule is finely calibrated and invoked only in rare situations. It helps in selecting the best candidate most democratically,' replied Mattu.

'Maybe, but I have a better idea. When the two candidates are evenly matched, the winner should be decided by a competitive exam designed to test their skills needed for the job,' suggested Lattu. Everyone laughed. For the first time, Lattu's suggestion was rejected without discussion. Since no campaigning was allowed, there was no discussion on strategy either. A defeat was not on their mind, so the discussion veered around the impending victory. A victory would necessitate meticulous planning for celebrations, media interaction, and much more. Unanimously, that was left to Vartika and D2Y2 to work out. Having thus discussed the last detail for the penultimate day, the Y2K gang dispersed.

While the gang was around, Y2K felt at ease. The moment they left, a tense feeling overtook him. It was the most important day of his life. With nothing to do and nothing to plan, Y2K kept brooding about what would happen tonight. The more he thought about it, the more tense he felt. So he turned to D2Y2.

'What do you think will happen tonight, D2Y2?' he asked.

'There can be only four outcomes tonight. In the best possible scenario, you will win both the election and Vartika's hand. In that case, you will be over the moon. There are equal chances that you get a 'Yes' from the voters but a 'No' from Vartika or a 'Yes' from Vartika but 'No' from the voters. In both cases, you will have to rationalize and accept the half-victory. In the worst scenario, you may lose both the election and Vartika. In that case, you will be shattered and I'll have a tough time handling you,' replied D2Y2 with a straight face. Y2K felt irritated at such a matter-of-fact analysis.

As the tension mounted, Y2K started pacing the room like a caged tiger.

'Why don't you go out and take a walk. Fresh air will do some good to your agitated mind,' suggested D2Y2 who had been observing Y2K with some concern. Y2K did not remember the last time he had gone out for a walk. He looked outside. It was a perfect day inviting anyone to take a stroll and soak the sun.

Y2K knew exactly where to go and find some peace.

The mild winter sun, the slightly chilly breeze, and the spring flower blooms in the garden made Y2K feel calm and content. After meandering aimlessly through the garden he sat down on a bench. It was the same bench where he and Vartika would often sit together during their post-dinner walks to gaze at the moon, converse, and spend a few romantic moments. Y2K wished Vartika was there. It was at that moment a pigeon landed right in his lap and startled him. Y2K noticed that the pigeon had a piece of paper in its beak and took the paper out. He was startled to see that it was a handwritten letter from Vartika. In 2050, no one wrote a letter by hand, let alone send it through a pigeon. The whole thing seemed to be straight out of an old Bollywood movie. Perplexed, Y2K read the letter slowly,

'Dear Y2K,

This mode of communication may take you by surprise. As you read along, there will be many more surprises. Some may hurt. Forgive me, if you can.

It will not come as a surprise to you if I confess that I love you. Somewhere in the middle of the campaign and after-dinner walks, I fell in love with you. It does not need any 'Thought Mining' to know that you are in the same boat. I know that you plan to propose as soon as the elections are out of the way. Under ordinary circumstances, I would have been overjoyed and overwhelmingly said 'Yes'. Alas, we live in extraordinary times in 2050. That makes the answer complicated, necessitating a few confessions and many explanations.

Let me start from the beginning. My joining your team was not a coincidence. It was a small part of my work on 'Project Pygmalion' for an ambitious startup called 'Futain', a name derived from

'Future Certain'. As the name suggests, Futain aims to make the future certain and offer it as a service. 'Project Pygmalion' is the pilot project of Futain to test its secret 'Predict and Edit Future As A Service' technology. It works on a simple principle of dividing the future into a number of discrete time-slices, then simulate scenarios in a controlled environment using predictive AI, use systems modeling to devise optimal intervention, and create a closed-loop feedback system to re-predict and re-simulate till the outcome is an edited future. The tricky part is the 'intervention' that requires a 'human', designated as an 'Intervenger' meaning 'Intervention-Manager' who serves as a link between the subject and the 'Architecture'.

Let me cut out the technical details and confess that you were one of the chosen 'subjects' and I was one of the 'Intervenger' in the 'Project Pygmalion'. End objective was to so edit the future that you as a chosen one would reach the final round of the elections.

I would have liked you to believe that reaching the final round was all due to your ability, perseverance, and teamwork. But I have to confess that a large part of it was scripted by the 'Project Pygmalion' in which I played the lead role. Initially, I viewed my part in 'Project Pygmalion' as re-enacting of 'My Fair Lady'. However, my infatuation for enacting 'My Fair Lady' like role didn't last long. As I came to understand you and fell in love with you, I realized how sinister the 'Project Pygmalion' could be.

I have to admit that everything we did or discussed was known to the 'Architecture'. Besides smart-snooping, Futain identifies, creates, and uses 'Assitors' who perform a specific task either voluntarily or involuntarily, advertently or inadvertently. Much of the script was facilitated by these 'Assistors'. The 'Architecture' predicted and directed every scene, as if it was preordained. Of course, the unpredictable can always happen, like your wife's divorce. Believe me, even for that contingency, it was the 'Architecture' that knew how to sort things out.

It was the 'Architecture' that controlled the events at every stage. You may scoff at this revelation and ask how 'Architecture' can control fate. For example, you could argue that winning the toss of a coin was pure luck that determined the outcome of the semi-final round. True, the toss was vital. But it was Futain's job to make it certain that fate favors whom Futain chooses, one hundred percent and not fifty percent. That was taken care of by a small device installed without your knowledge. Had you known, you would have called it fixing and rejected it as unethical. If Prada had access to it she would have gone ahead terming it as the last resort. It was the classical case of ethics vs. expediency. For me, it was a wake-up call.

It may also come as a surprise to you that Kappuswamy was the other candidate backed by Futain in 'Project Pygmalion'. Futain had a candidate least likely to win and another one most likely to win. The 'Architecture' scripted the battle in such a way that both reached the last round for a final showdown. I do not know who would win but Futain knows. Irrespective of who wins, 'Project Pygmalion' is already a winner. It has successfully edited the future by ensuring that only the chosen one wins, despite the odds.

Do you remember our small discussion on whether machines could rule us in the future? Now, imagine what happens if the 'Project Pygmalion' is scaled up. Futain may choose and edit the future to have control of the Mandals, of the country, and even of the continents. Futain also may decide to sell its proprietary 'future editing technology' to the highest bidder, whether worthy or not, scrupulous or not, and state-controlled or not. In all such cases, humans may not come first in the 'Edited Future'. I have, therefore, decided to resign from Futain and quit politics altogether. I shall devote my time and energy to pursuing causes that would help put 'Humans First'.

Coming back to our relationship, there is a confession but no explanation. The idea of living together after having betrayed you knowingly is not very comforting. The feeling of guilt and the feeling of love make a deadly mixture. Before they get mixed up, we need to deal with it. The feeling of love will endure but I need distance to forget and you need time to forgive. I am, therefore, leaving. I do not know what lies in store for us in the future. Maybe our paths will cross in the future. Maybe not. But whatever the future, I do not wish it to be an edited one.

Goodbye.

Vartika.'

To say that Y2K was shocked and devastated would be an understatement. He felt immobile and sat there for a long time staring at the letter. A passing thought of going back to his virtual world crossed his mind but was dismissed immediately. The virtual world would give him solace but not peace. Y2K looked at the gentle winter sun, the serene and green garden, and the flowers swaying under the cool air. It was a real world view without any editing. Y2K suddenly realized that all he wanted to do was to sleep. So he did what he had not done ever before. He slept on the bench in the garden under the open sky and shut out the whole world. In 2050, thoughts could be mined, even edited, but not the dreams. So no one would ever know what he dreamed.